THE SWING AROUND

Barbara Anderson is the author of six previous novels, *Girls High*, *Portrait of the Artist's Wife* (Winner of the 1992 Wattie Award), *All the Nice Girls*, *The House Guest*, *Proud Garments* and *Long Hot Summer*, and two collections of stories, *I think we should go into the jungle* and *Glorious Things*. She lives in New Zealand.

ALSO BY BARBARA ANDERSON

I think we should go into the jungle
Girls High
Portrait of the Artist's Wife
All the Nice Girls
The House Guest
Proud Garments
Glorious Things and Other Stories
Long Hot Summer

Barbara Anderson

THE SWING AROUND

V

VINTAGE

Published by Vintage 2003

2 4 6 8 10 9 7 5 3 1

First published in Great Britain in 2002 by
Jonathan Cape

Vintage
Random House, 20 Vauxhall Bridge Road,
London SW1V 2SA

The Random House Group Limited Reg. No. 954009
www.randomhouse.co.uk

A CIP catalogue record for this book
is available from the British Library

ISBN 0 099 43735 X

MIX
Paper | Supporting
responsible forestry
FSC® C018179

Printed and bound in Great Britain by Clays Ltd, St Ives PLC

To Neil

there remains the problem of goodness
—*Jorge-Luis Borges*

1

The party at the Embassy in the western suburbs was hotting up. His Excellency, Mr Carlos Luigi, was a generous host. Where his guests wined they dined and where they dined they boogied, they got down man, they sang. His greatest pleasure was for his guests, his friends, the whole world, to sing along with him. To dance and be happy.

Apart from the Guest of Honour, General Alsarvo d'Riva from the Ambassador's own country, and the presence of the Prime Minister, the guest list was much as usual; fellow members of the Diplomatic Corps, a few locals, a Cabinet Minister or two, a captain of industry with trade links, chiefs of staff, civil servants of high rank, Embassy staff and attendant spouses of all concerned were invited to cluster around the piano with General d'Riva and their host. Most did so, if not with alacrity, then with an edgy acceptance of the inevitable. Stragglers were rounded up, conversations interrupted so that all could participate in the Ambassador's singalong.

The Guest of Honour sat on the piano stool beside a dark-eyed young woman from the administrative section of the Ministry of Cultural Links and Trade who appeared to be trying to dissuade him from his choice of song. 'No, no, General,' she said, 'not that one. No.'

'I insist,' he said and moved closer.

Violet Redpath's head lifted as she edged along the stool, still attempting dissuasion to no effect.

Down in the cornfields, roared the General
Hear that mournful song
All the darkies are a'weeping
Massa's in the cold cold ground.

Freddy Manders (Foreign Affairs) gave a quick sideways chuck of his head towards a tall black man who stood silent and resplendent in a white embroidered djellabah and matching cap.

'Wildly insensitive,' said Manders to a passing youth. 'Stop them at once.'

'Would Frank mind?' said his assistant. 'In this day and age?'

'For God's sake, man!' Manders moved forward.

But the General had stopped himself. He now, with profuse apologies and single-minded intent, flung himself across Ms Redpath's lap to adjust her side of the piano stool.

Ms Redpath, pink and angry, tried to rise. The General held his ground, his burnished head hung across her lap, his large fingers busy with the controls of the adjustable seat.

'General!' she said.

Molly Carew, wife of Hamish Carew, the Minister of Cultural Links and Trade, moved forward to help. She plucked the songbook from its stand and waved another one in front of the Ambassador's now startled face.

'May we have this one, Ambassador? It's one of my favourites.'

She placed the new book on its stand, tugged her maroon crepe straight and prepared to sing.

General d'Riva righted himself with some difficulty, smoothed both hands over his hair and prepared to accompany her.

Ms Redpath put out a hand. 'Sssh.'

The room stilled. Ministers of the Crown, Ambassadors at large, wives and wide-eyed tray-holding young women, even the Papal Nuncio, lifted their heads to gaze as Molly sang. Her voice was deep and true and filled with longing.

Some enchanted evening
When you find your true love
When you hear her call you across a crowded room
Then fly to her side and make her your own
Or all through your life you may dream all alone
Once you have found her . . .

Molly lifted her hands, held them motionless for a moment like a gospel singer in glory, then flung them higher as she beseeched, insisted upon participation.

And got it. *'Never let her go,'* boomed the *basso profundo* of Frank Sato in the djellabah. '*Go*,' sang the Papal Nuncio and the General, fractionally late as they were not well versed in the song but knew vision when they saw it. '*Go*,' mouthed the wide-eyed waitresses. '*Go*,' roared the Ambassador who was happier than he had ever been in his present posting and hoping for an extension.

Molly smiled, bowed. The corners of her wide mouth lifted, she bowed again.

There was a cry from the back of the room as a rake-thin simultaneous translator remembered her grandfather's party piece. 'More,' she cried. 'Please.'

Molly shook her head. 'Another time,' she said, taking a glass of orange juice from a tray carried by one of the diminutive helpers.

The young woman put out a hand to touch her arm. 'Lovely, lady,' she whispered. 'Lovely.'

'Your lady wife,' said the Prime Minister to Hamish Carew in passing, 'has a strong voice.' He gave a quick authoritative movement of his shoulders, a regrouping before departure. 'Come along, Priscilla. Time we were going.'

'Thank you, Prime Minister,' said Hamish Carew, uneasily. 'Thank you. Good night. Good night, Priscilla. Good night, sir.'

Tossing an occasional stern nod of recognition to right or left the Prime Minister led the way, his wife scuttling in his wake.

The Minister of Transport stood alongside Hamish, calm in the knowledge that his wife would never make a fool of herself. That was one thing you could say about Trudy: she had never made of a fool of herself in her life and was unlikely to start now. He glanced across the room at a rangy, red-haired woman with something almost like affection. She was busy telling Molly Carew the whereabouts of the best place in Singapore to buy crocodile bags, belts, wallets, the lot. Molly couldn't miss it, she said, and anyway the girls at the High Commission would know. It was the one with the crocodile in a tank at the back. 'And tell them I sent you.'

Molly, who had stopped listening some time ago, came to. 'How big is the tank?'

Lean hands sketched an oblong.

'But that's no bigger than a cattle trough. Can it turn round?'

'I didn't notice.' Startled by the look on Molly's previously blank face, Trudy rallied. 'It looked quite happy,' she said, and turned to mingle.

'But why do they have it there at all?' Molly asked her back.

'Why indeed?' murmured Freddy Manders in passing.

The Minister's wife had a beautiful smile. It was sweet – a word Freddy disliked and never used, but he could think of no other to describe it. Molly Carew's smile was sweet, welcoming, and slightly moist.

Manders backed away slightly. His wife Bridget had left him six months ago. There was no one else involved, a fact which gave him little comfort. Some wild, uncontrollable, across-a-crowded-room passion for another man or woman would have been loathsome, scalding, but at least more understandable than Bridget's insistence that she must join a secular health organisation where she could train as a professional field officer.

She was very fond of him, she insisted. No, truly she was. Of course it wasn't sex. Ask yourself. It would be easier if there had been something wrong, much easier for both of them. The feeling was impossible to put it into words, just a conviction, a certain knowledge that she must find some way to help the helpless. Join some organisation that had the skills, the funds, the back-up to go into disaster areas.

'In caps presumably?' he said. 'Disaster Areas. DAs for short.'

She scarcely glanced at him.

It was different now, she told him. It doesn't have to be for God. There were several places where the young and healthy with language and administrative skills could train. The World Health Organisation, United Nations, Red Cross. There was a new place called Humanitaire she'd just heard about in Paris. Something like Médecins sans Frontières, but you don't have to be medically trained.

'But why *now*?' he begged.

'How could I have left New Zealand while Jane was still alive?'

13

'So you're free now. Free to take up your non cross?'

She took a step back. 'You know it's not like that.'

'All right. Then what is it like? *Why?*'

'Oh Freddy. How can you possibly understand? I can hardly understand myself. Of course it's unfair for you. Of course, of course.'

'Any moment soon,' he snarled, sweaty, bewildered and sick as a dog, 'you'll be saying this is bigger than both of us.'

'You've got it,' she said.

She had applied to Humanitaire in Paris, been accepted and would leave as soon as possible. She did her best, showed him how the new drying machine worked, left things organised. There was a note on the kitchen table when he got home from work. *Dearest Freddy and Jazz – Forgive me – Bridget.*

He got rid of the cat. Gave it to the child next door.

Now women made him wary, each and every one of them. Their mincing walks and strong strides, their yapping chatter and bleating coos. Their goddamn ubiquitous presence.

He cranked up a smile, bent towards Mrs Carew. 'What other type of music do you like, Mrs Carew?'

'Everything,' she beamed. 'I love it all. But especially country and western.'

What else. What else.

'Did you know that a contemporary writer described western cattle punchers as "poorly fed, underpaid, overworked, deprived of sleep, and prone to boredom and loneliness"?'

She smiled. 'Why are you telling me this, Mr Manders?'

He could feel the weight of his drooping eyelids. Because you're a silly old bat and I have to say something. 'Because it's true,' he said, 'and I thought you might be interested.'

Mrs Carew thought about this, gave it her attention. 'I agree. Truth is best, yes, as a general rule of thumb, so long as you don't tell someone what a disaster their nose is or something equally offensive. Whether unasked-for truths are always a good idea I'm not so sure. Think what it would be like if we could read each other's thoughts.'

He heard his laugh cackling around inside his skull. 'True. About the crocodile. Do you love all animals, Mrs Carew?'

'There's no point in liking only the pretty ones. I had a magnet on my refrigerator once – *Save the ugly animals too* – but it disappeared.' She looked around the assembled company for a moment, then gave up. 'Gecko green it was. I suppose it fell off. People don't look hard enough for beauty. Snakes, for example, snakes are truly beautiful. And crocodiles, I imagine.'

He wanted to confound her sentimental wobbliness, her faith in whatever it was that enabled her to love the whole world, to bless the bloody ship of life and all who sailed in her.

'Perhaps you might accompany the Minister to Singapore sometime,' he said. 'Then you could get a good look at the one in the back of the bag shop.'

She looked him in the eye, laid a gentle dissuading hand on his arm.

Sickened by goodwill, Freddy was not going to stop now. 'There was a seventeenth-century theologian who decided animals would go to heaven too. But even he had serious doubts concerning poisonous ants. How do you go on poisonous ants, Mrs Carew?'

'I don't know about heaven, Mr Manders.'

He stood silent and seething in front of her serenity. The wretched woman was making him behave badly. 'I don't know about heaven.' As though she were discussing the rules of real tennis or revealing that canvas work had lost its interest for her. As though all the attributes and mysteries of heaven could or would be revealed later, when she chose to study it, to take the course, to read the subject in depth.

She was without guile, let alone self-importance. Why then did she confuse and irritate him, make him feel both flatfooted and pompous?

'And how is your wife?' she continued. 'She was a tower of strength on our Handicap Committee. Someone so young, a busy professional woman like her giving up so much of her time. I thought it was wonderful, unexpected, if you know what I mean.'

Inquisitive too. It often lives with kindness.

'Her sister Jane was physically handicapped. Extremely so.'

'I'm sorry.'

'Not your fault.'

'No,' she said, even more gently.

Don't appease her, you fool. But how else to shut her up? 'Bridget was bored with Foreign Affairs. She's gone to Paris to train for a field job with Humanitaire, some sort of World Health outfit.'

Her face, her happy hands. 'How wonderful.'

'Did you know,' he continued, 'that in some poverty-stricken countries handicapped children are chained up all day, or hidden from sight.'

'Yes. But to be doing something. How proud you must be of her.'

'It had nothing to do with me.'

'But she's your wife?'

'Not at the moment.'

She stood silent with her hands still clasped, then nodded her head in dismissal and turned to talk to the Minister of Transport.

Manders dipped his head and blundered away with his heart thudding. She knew, this maroon-encased woman. She knew he was a mess, a fucked-up quaking bog of a mess. How dare she know.

The Minister of Transport greeted Molly Carew with little enthusiasm. She was a maverick, a one-off. You never knew what she was going to do next. He too was discomfited by her.

That song, the way she had sung that song, for example. She didn't even have the nous to sing a Maori song – *Po kare kare ana* or something less well known. She would undoubtedly know them all. He would put money on that.

———

16

Before Hamish Carew went into politics, his and Molly's feet had hit the floor boards at 4.30 each morning. In winter their feet groped about for work socks, their breath steamed in the cold air, and their gumboots splintered black ice or ploughed through ankle-deep mud to the milking sheds. In summer the mud turned to clay, then to baked clay and finally dust.

Each morning Hamish went straight to the sheds while Molly brought the herd up, singing. Her voice lifted to the dark rim of the hills, stopped short to cajole or calm a skittish beast or leap to avoid a splashing rush of dung.

Her range of songs was large but specialised; the sadder, the more haunting the lyric, the more she treasured it. She had rooms full of roses. Old dogs and children and watermelon wine were the only things you could trust. Sad movies made her cry.

The cows appeared to approve of her choice. They let down their milk and stood silent in the bails, their grassy breath sweet, their stump-tails idle. Even after Molly had removed the cups, had hand-stripped each teat and slapped each warm hide with the palm of her hand, some would linger. The scattiest of cows became content, all goblins stilled. The weekly yield increased and the butterfat soared.

Even after so long in Wellington Molly missed her captive audience. Hamish tended to rise to his feet when she sang and leave the room, smiling slightly to indicate he did not dislike the rich booming echoes of her songs but had business elsewhere.

He had had to ask her not to sing in the car. It put George, the driver, off, he had explained. She understood completely, would refrain. This evening she had forgotten, had burst into *Ruby, don't take your love to town* as the ministerial LTD slipped up the gorge, its lights swinging deep into the scrubby bush at the corners before sweeping the road once more. The silhouette of George's head was dark, the bristles of his haircut stiff against the moon.

George was reliable, Hamish told Molly. He was also, she suspected, a bully. Nevertheless he knew where the clean lavatories were throughout the land and was a nimble parker of the cigar car. He took pride, as did all the drivers, in getting the nearest park to the entrance at each official occasion or reception, so that his Minister and the wife could sail out and up and in without any undignified trailing around on the outskirts. The trouble being, of course, that Mrs Carew had never learned the art of sailing anywhere.

This evening had been no exception. On arrival at the Embassy she had muddled things once again by her concern for a hedgehog caught in the glare of the lights, had insisted that it be moved. She would be quite happy to move it if George would just back a little: there must be some sort of shovel in the boot, was there not? No? Oh well, she could manage.

'Molly,' said Hamish.

'But dear . . .'

'The Ambassador is waiting.'

'Oh. George, perhaps you could . . . ?'

George sucked his teeth. 'Leave it to me, ma'am,' he said having already worked out which would be the best angle from which to boot the creature into the shrubbery as soon as the front door closed.

'Thank you so much,' murmured Molly.

She had told Ambassador Luigi her problem as they shook hands. His English, though adequate, did not include hedgehogs. He gazed at his wife, whose command of the language was better than his, with the trusting faith of a man reaching for a lifebelt. Senora Luigi, however, weighed down with silver and turquoise, declined to assist. She gave an ample and graceful shrug and motioned Mrs Carew towards the nearby Ladies Room which she personally had decorated for Christmas.

Molly, concerned for hedgehogs and unable to catch the

senora's drift, found herself in a small room with yuletide greetings and festive follies from top to bottom, from bottom to top. All, all were there. Father Christmas and reindeer cutouts, plastic holly, looping tinsel, golden wreaths and scarlet bows. Robins sang and red-capped old men laughed on the roller towel. Molly counted them. Fourteen Father Christmases, counting the roller towel. She pulled it: *Jingle bells, jingle bells, jingle all the way* tinkled the mechanism.

She must get out of this place immediately. Must check on George and the hedgehog.

George and the car had disappeared. Molly knew why. The driver of a minister more senior in Cabinet than Hamish would have pulled rank and indicated that George should move his car to a less desirable position so that his minister and spouse could sweep with more ease. Hierarchy is all in ministerial parking.

There was no sign of the hedgehog. The senior minister's driver had seen neither hair nor hide. 'Hedgehog, was it, ma'am?' He would keep an eye out. He shut the door once more, turned on the ignition and moved the heater to full bore.

Molly thanked him and turned to go, her black cloak trailing in gravel, her mind far away.

Her only child Roberta had enjoyed hedgehogs. Milk had soured in saucers or disappeared overnight year after year. She and Molly had tracked them with torches, Bobby yelping with approval the first time she saw the creature's defence mechanism. The next week she had found it, or its friend, squashed flat near the garage. Molly had tried to hide the corpse but Hamish disagreed. Bobby had to learn.

And learn she did, quickly. Bobby could put the cups on the cows' teats at eight, was an expert milker by eleven and dagging sheep at fourteen. Hamish had a lot of time for his daughter. She was, as he said, a natural.

She had been Daddy's girl since earliest youth. Her first

smiles, her first lurching steps had all been directed towards Hamish while Molly applauded. The child was stricken when he went into Parliament.

'Why don't you stay home, Daddy?'

'Because, darling, I have to go.'

'Why?'

Why indeed.

Life, for his daughter, lurched from ecstatic weekends to doleful weekdays and back again. Weekends with puddings and Daddy and fun were followed by the slough of Mondays and Mum.

It had been difficult for a time, but fortunately Molly was so busy minding the child and supervising the sharemilker and running the house, to say nothing of the garden, that time passed quickly and Bobby calmed down. Quite soon in fact.

Molly came to suddenly, glanced at the small smiling man beside her.

'We dine soon, madam. Perhaps?'

'Yes, of course.' Molly breathed deeply. 'The air is so fresh tonight, is it not?'

'Yes, madam,' replied the Ambassador's emissary, smiling more firmly than ever.

Hamish Carew sat silent as the car purred home, his mind busy with the Cabinet committee meeting he was chairing tomorrow on Restructuring Policy. It would be a difficult meeting, very difficult. He would have to watch Saunders, a man who combined the attributes of a snake in the grass with well-developed nest-feathering instincts. He considered telling Molly, she liked little jokes of that kind, but she was asleep, her head on his shoulder, her breath whistling gently down the folds of her cloak.

Restructuring involves tearing down something you have and constructing another structure, preferably elsewhere, in which case you are said to have relocated by logistic redeployment. Restructured, Relocated, Resited. All useful words, words with meat on their bones to work for you. Every male or female on the committee had restructured his or her life in order to become a member of Parliament. They therefore knew about, had views on restructuring. The restructuring of the electoral processes of the New Zealand House of Representatives held no qualms for them.

Before entering Parliament Hamish had served for many years as a district councillor; had, as he said, cut his teeth on the locals. The members would pass with dispatch a motion before the council on road works involving many thousands of dollars, whereas a proposal to renew the council teacups could be bogged down for twice the time. Reactions would be heated. Everyone knew about teacups.

Hamish rearranged Molly's sleeping head against his shoulder and thought about her performance tonight. Hedgehogs and cowboys. Enough in all conscience for one ambassadorial reception. More than enough. He supposed he was lucky she hadn't launched into something worse in front of the PM. He heard her voice dipping, soaring to a crescendo: *I'll be loving you Always, tumpty tumpty tum, Always.*

Perhaps he could get Bobby to have a word with her. On second thoughts, no. Definitely not. Bobby, for all her virtues, was not subtle. He heard her voice: 'Dad wants you to stop being such a dope, Mum. Cool it a bit.'

Hamish shifted in his seat. He knew, they all knew, or should, that Molly had in fact been doing that this evening. Had been trying to cool it, had gone to the aid of a young woman caught in an awkward situation with an over-enthusiastic general.

He glanced in the rear-vision mirror to check that he was not within George's field of vision and took his sleeping wife's hand.

Her eyes opened. 'Do you think I should check with Mrs Luigi tomorrow about the hedgehog?'

'No. By the way there's a trade trip coming up.'

'Oh. Where?'

'A Swing Around, the PM called it. An American phrase he heard from the Commander in Chief Pacific when he was on a stopover in Hawaii recently. A large patch, the Pacific, as you can imagine. Periodically the CICP used to fly off on what he called a Swing Around the Pacific. The PM was rather taken by the phrase. Mine will be South-East Asia.'

'Oh.'

The car drew to a halt before the ministerial front door.

'Thank you, George.'

'Thank you, sir. Good night, sir.'

'Thank you, George,' said Molly, heaving and tugging yet again at her cloak.

George sucked his teeth and departed.

2

Shafts of light slid through the venetian blinds on to banana skins, coffee grounds and dark crusts of wholegrain.

Hamish stood banging one hand against his leg in his usual pre-departure gesture. Molly's eyes scanned him. You have to check. Last week a senior minister had had pumpkin down his front.

'And what does your day hold?' he asked.

Her immediate task each morning was to read the newspaper. How else could she keep up with the world and its astonishments, including those of the House of Representatives. Hamish, as he often said, never talked shop at home. A statement which irritated her, as though there might be some risk involved, that his home was not a safe house, which it was.

Nevertheless Molly knew about the state of the nation. The enormously decreased majority at the last election had come as no surprise to her. Her knowledge of the rise in inflation, the increase in interest rates and the threat of economic stagnation came from that suspect bunch of left-wing no-hopers, as Hamish called the media. It was the ignorant young reporters and their scurrilous seniors, the cocky bastard columnists and the pinkos in the press gallery, who kept her informed.

Hamish hated them all and with some reason. They seemed to Molly to circle him from a distance or pad alongside, intent and tireless as hyenas eyeing a lagging warthog.

They showed her the rest of the world as well. The papers set the scene of the major disasters: Pol Pot toppled and the homeless in Cambodia, the ongoing tragedy of the boat people, the floods in the Sudan. The television provided images of the stricken areas and stunned victims and an address to which donations could be sent. The radio was best for detail.

'I'm getting my hair cut for the trip, then I thought I'd have a go at the Scrub-a-Dub car wash. Our car needs a clean.'

'Do you think that's a good idea?' said Hamish, his lips brushing her cheek.

'Mmmn,' she said. 'Goodbye, dear.'

Molly slapped the pages flat and turned to Deaths.

George, boot-faced as ever, opened the offside front door. Ministers were known among the drivers as front-seat guys or back-seat guys. Front guys were preferred. Back guys were suspected of having tickets on themselves.

'George,' said Hamish, 'have you ever used one of those car-cleaning machines? Wash-and-Dry, Scrub-a-Dub, whatever?'

George's glance was startled. 'Me, sir? No, no, not me, sir.'

'Quite straightforward to use, I suppose?'

'As to that, sir, I couldn't say. None of the other guys use them – well, not to my knowledge.' George's tone indicated that it stood to reason. If a man was wanker enough to use one of those things he wasn't going to let on, was he. 'Why do you ask, sir?'

'Mrs Carew thought she might have a go.'

George breathed out. 'Aah,' he said, navigating past a wobbly little girl on a pink bike. 'Is that right?'

'Yes.'

'Aah.'

Arthur, his ears flat against his shaven head and his narrow face creased with pleasure, waved a blow drier in greeting. Mrs Carew was a pleasant woman and her needs were simple. Chop it off when it gets too long. Nothing fancy.

Sometimes when she was a little down, the House sitting later and later and her scraps of time with Hamish reduced to shreds, Molly wondered if there was anyone else in the world as pleased to see her as Arthur.

She settled herself in the chair with the small contented wriggle of one about to be pampered.

'Quite a bit off please, Arthur. I'm going overseas, so it'll be straight under the shower and out. And how is Lollipop?'

Lollipop was well. Photographs of Lollipop were produced. Lollipop, a Bichon Frise with a lovely nature, stood on her hind legs, begged on her hunkers and peeped from behind a velvet cushion. 'She is the joy of our lives,' said Arthur. 'And when are you off then?'

'Soon,' said Molly. 'However, I will see more of my husband.'

Admittedly only at night, at functions of varying formality, splendour or tedium, would they be together, would they stand side by side, meet and greet and smile and get to bed later and later with less and less chance of sleeping together. It had occurred to Molly long ago that there is no sensible phrase for the act itself, in the same way as some parts of the human body are ill served by words. One can only lurch between extremes, from overly basic to coy euphemism, from belly to tum tum, from bum to *derrière*.

But there would be helicopters and scenic wonders and interesting people and shared memories and connubial confidences. Hamish was different offshore. He told her things, confided, had time to answer her questions.

'How could you bear to kiss that terrifying woman?' she had asked once.

He had smiled, patted her behind. 'I regard it as part of the job.'

And people were so kind.

And the trip so important.

And the people so interesting.

And important.

Molly watched Arthur's quick hands snipping and checking for balance. Would the years be kind to Arthur? One could only hope. And there was always Lollipop.

The Scrub-a-Dub car wash was in the centre of the city.

'Can't go wrong,' said the young attendant. 'Just wait for the green.'

Molly drove across concrete and inserted her ticket in the machine. The car rolled forward and stopped. There was a moment's calm before the deluge, then sheets of water sprang from all sides. Green ropes of man-made fabric, previously spent and flaccid as beached bladderwrack, swung into action, lashing, slapping, flaying torrents of water in every direction. Something clicked. The green ropes changed direction, charged at the windscreen. 'Goodness me,' said Molly.

Water was now streaming in the top of the slightly open

offside window. Charlie Chaplin flashed into her mind, Auntie Vi who had machined her own finger on the Singer, that bug-eyed youth on TV. Clowns, dupes, victims of the world shared the car with her, sat alongside or peered over her shoulder at sheets of water, shuddering with the shared shame of the technologically impaired.

The apparatus stilled once more. Her efforts to close the open window failed. She must get out, seek help. She clambered out, at which moment the whole fandango began again. The machine rolled along its predestined tracks, water surged forth; drenching, roaring floods of water besieged her. The bruising washers lashed around her.

Gasping, her reason deafened and her eyes blinded by ropes of acrylic, Molly blundered her way out to dry concrete.

She stood still, gasping for breath. Thousands upon thousands of people must have died like this in real floods, pummelled by trees, rocks, drowned in swirling mud.

It was no help, this thought, either to the drowned or herself. She headed for assistance.

The young attendant slapped the winged horse logo on his red shirt and gaped at her.

'What on earth did you *do?*'

'Nothing. The water, everything, it all went mad, and then suddenly it stopped. Completely, or so I thought. I'd better get help, I thought, and then lo and behold it all began again.'

'It's meant to stop. Then the cycle begins again. It's pro-grammed.'

'Oh.'

He looked at her sourly. 'You're wet,' he said.

'Yes.'

'I can't leave the shop, it's school holidays.' He indicated row after row of shiny wrapped candy bars, see-through bags of Oddfellows, Crazy Dips, Moo Choos, Snifters, Black Knights. All these would disappear if he left his station. 'They'd clean this lot out in seconds, no sweat.'

They looked at each other, baffled. Water overflowed her shoes, ran on to the yellow and black vinyl and flowed in rivulets towards the door. She took off her glasses, realised she had nothing to dry them with and stood flapping them in one hand, smiling at the child to indicate that this was just a temporary hiccup. That these things happen, that there was no need to fuss.

'But what on earth did you *do*,' he said again.

'The wrong thing,' snapped Molly. 'Perhaps I could borrow a towel?'

'Pete,' he roared.

Small, dark and nimble, Pete appeared clutching a half-eaten meat pie.

'Hullo, Mrs Carew. What's the problem?'

'The lady got stuck in the Scrub-a-Dub.'

'The first thing the lady needs is a towel,' said Pete, handing her a doubtful-looking pink one.

They walked across the sunlit concrete with their heads close together. Molly stopped to empty her shoes.

'We'll just have to let her run out, finish her cycle,' said Pete, brushing his hand across an upended packing case. 'We'll wait here.'

The young man watched through his plate-glass window. They sat side by side like mates in a primary school playground. Pete was holding his pie towards the woman as though offering a bite.

'And how's Carole?' said Molly.

'She's given up basketwork, thank God. The place is knee deep already.' Pete wiped his hands on his bright overalls. 'She's into Russian at the moment.'

'Goodness.'

'Yeah. You've got to hand it to her. It's Spanish next.' He stood up. 'Right, she's finished now. Keys inside? OK. Meet me round the other side.'

He slipped out of the driver's seat within minutes. 'Keep

the towel for now, Mrs C. Drop it off sometime.' He grinned, dragged a hand through tough black curls.

'Thank you,' said Molly.

'You'd better get home, then.'

'No, I have to pick up something at my husband's office.'

'Whaat?'

She lifted a hand.

Startled glances followed her damp progress across the forecourt of the House of Representatives and up the long flight of steps to the official entrance. The last time Molly had seen them, the red carpet had flowed down in honour of the Governor-General's Official Opening of Parliament.

There had been some unpleasantness at the occasion. A group of demonstrators protesting at the rising cost of living had thrown eggs and tomatoes at the Governor-General and the official party on these same steps. Rumours had flashed inside, skidded around the seated guests waiting in the Legislative Chamber.

Schadenfreude flickered, excitement grew. Somebody had heard a tomato had made contact with His Excellency. Would there be evidence of *lèse-majesté*: a damp pip, a fragment of shell?

Molly had felt both guilty and hopeful.

Black Rod's entrance to the Legislative Chamber at the head of the procession had never been more welcome. People leapt to their feet, heads craned at impossible angles, but there was no sign of anything extraneous on any garment of the Vice-Regal party or their attendants.

This proved nothing to Molly. They could have cleaned up en route.

His Excellency summoned the members of the House of Representatives into the Chamber. They came with considerable noise, their demeanour ranging from solemn to chatty to almost loutish. Backs were slapped, were slapped back, sniggers half-suppressed and stern looks given.

The speech from the Throne began.

It was not until the company had reassembled in the Banqueting Hall for tea afterwards that the rumours were confirmed. A tomato had made contact with the Governor-General; several eggs had smashed against the steps.

Molly was as concerned as everyone else, but as usual she was hampered by seeing both sides of the question. After all, the discontent of the people was not His Excellency's fault. People had tried to vote the present party out and had almost succeeded. Previous demonstrations had failed. What were they do? But tomatoes? And worse, eggs? Such questions worried her and there was no one to discuss them with. Nevertheless she was sorry to have missed the sight. The reactions of human beings interested her; she would have liked to have seen the reaction of Her Majesty's Representative to hostile fire.

This morning her passage across the foyer and attendant corridors was uncomfortable but without incident. She was getting along quite nicely.

Now for the lift.

In past ascents Molly had travelled with go-getters on business bent, members of the House, under-secretaries, a clutch of personal assistants or PR personnel. Men and women in dark suits in control of themselves and their world. People whose confidence was palpable and laughter loud. The journeys Molly enjoyed most were those when she shared a lift with a minister of the Crown and his cohorts. The behaviour of these attendant men and women interested her; their particular blend of deference and camaraderie on the move became them. Their willing smiles and strong laughs, their air of having picked the right horse at the right time was complemented by the minister's graciousness. They were his stalwarts, his praetorian guard. There was a sense of ritualised respect, of power on the move.

This air of deference in motion was not, she had noticed,

so evident with female ministers and their attendant staff. She wondered why.

Today the only other occupant of the lift was a young man who was obviously neither public relations nor media. Molly felt tempted to tell him the name of the anti-acne cream she had found for Bobby and what a success it had been. To lay her hand on the safe area between his wrist and elbow and say it was quite all right, that she knew she was dripping wet and he needn't pretend not to notice. Her empathy flowed over him and frightened him rigid. The only thing to do, she realised, was to stare at the device indicating floor level and smile benignly.

Did the young man, she wondered, work for Hamish? Did he check appointments, work a shredder? Had he already put his small polished shoe on the first rung of the ladder? It seemed unlikely but you never knew.

They reached the appropriate floor. The door opened. Molly nodded and stepped out.

'Is this your floor?' she asked.

'Yes, I think so.'

'You will have to learn,' she said. 'Decision is all.'

She did not look back. The trousers of her suit were binding. Discomfort was increasing, the trickle into her shoes still obvious. Resisting her almost overwhelming impulse to tug wet olive-green gaberdine from her crotch, Molly sidled into Hamish's outer office.

The Minister's new typist, Mrs Webster, lifted her eyes. She was small and trim, her spun-sugar hair backcombed into a proud beehive. After a quick startled glance she turned away, admired her artificial peonies and looked again.

'Mrs Carew,' she cried. 'How nice to see you. How are you?'

'Wet,' said Molly. 'Please may I see my husband?'

'I am afraid the Minister is currently tied up in conference. Perhaps you might care to wait.'

'No. I don't want to wait. I want to see my husband. This is a matter of some importance. And I can't sit down,' said Molly, glancing at dove-blue Draylon chairs in the waiting area. 'I would wet your chair.'

'Normally there would be no problem,' explained Mrs Webster, indicating the unoccupied desk across the room. 'Owen Spencer is fully cleared. But unfortunately he's currently out of the office and my clearance is not through yet.'

'When will Mr Spencer be back?'

'That I couldn't say. It's something for the Minister. You chose a bad time.' Mrs Webster smiled. 'But do sit on his chair. I'm sure he wouldn't mind.'

'Thank you,' said Molly, and did so.

She picked up a snapshot from Mr Spencer's desk. Two wide-eyed bullet-headed toddlers were cleaning their teeth; one clutched a red toothbrush, one a blue. Their wide gaping mouths, their concentration, the effort required in learning the elements of oral hygiene depressed her. One day they would know all there was to know, including the judgement required not to sit on ministerial blue Draylon in wet suits. Would have been taught to look for a more suitable alternative if possible. It was only a matter of time. And effort.

People passed in the corridor outside, came and went through the outer office. Purposeful young men with moustaches checked briefcases, young women tripped by in short skirts and Cuban heeled shoes or boots which clunked. To a man, to a woman, they averted their eyes from the sodden grey-green heap perched on the edge of Owen Spencer's office chair.

Molly stood. 'This is ridiculous,' she said. 'I am going to find my husband.'

'But this is a Top Secret meeting, cleared eyes only,' cried Mrs Webster. 'I couldn't . . . They haven't even got the consultants in there yet. They come this afternoon. Even they're not sufficiently cleared for this session.'

'The who?'

'Experts. Consultants.'

'Highly paid?'

'Extremely.'

'In that case wouldn't it better to get rid of me first? Before they arrive.'

'But I . . .'

Violet Redpath entered the office. She seemed taller than ever in office clothes, her asymmetrical haircut more multi-directional. Black wisps of varying lengths framed her pale face. Her earrings did not match. One was a small carved cameo, the other a long trailing loop of something shiny.

'Mrs Carew,' she said, 'what on earth's happened? Shall I send the Minister's driver home for dry clothes?'

Molly was on her feet. 'That's the trouble, Ms Redpath.'

'Violet, please.'

'Violet. I had an aunt called Violet. She taught me how to braise celery.'

'Ah,' said Violet. 'You were saying?'

'Yes,' said Molly, 'it's the house key, you see. I find I've brought the wrong set. They normally hang on a little bronze thing shaped like a flat teapot with hooks on the bottom that I picked up in Singapore. '

Violet nodded. 'The Minister will have his.'

'Yes, but apparently' – Molly gave a quick movement of her head towards Mrs Webster poised at her typewriter – 'he's currently in conference and his secretary is out of the office at this moment in time. I gather I may well be still sitting here indefinitely.'

Ms Redpath grinned. 'Owen Spencer currently tied up too, is he?'

'Just out, I gather. And Mrs Webster is not fully cleared. It's cleared eyes only, you see.' Molly's top teeth held her lower lip. She stood silent before them: large, green and wet, and totally uncleared.

'Ah,' said Violet. 'Don't worry. I'll just bang on the door.'

Mrs Webster was on her feet. 'Are you fully cleared, Ms Redpath?'

'I'm Secret,' said Violet, looking with interest at Mrs Webster's anxious diamond-laden paws. 'But not Top Secret. I'll tell you what, Mrs Webster. I'll bang on the door and then when some fully cleared person, a more junior member of the conference no doubt, comes to the door, they will open it a crack and hiss at me that the Minister is currently in conference and can't be disturbed, and I will hiss back that Mrs Carew needs to get home as quickly as possible and please could the Minister hand the hisser the key to the ministerial home, so that he can hand it to me and I can relocate it with his wife.' Violet paused. 'I think that's it at the moment, don't you?'

'Yes,' said Molly.

Mrs Webster remained hopeful. 'What if he won't?'

'Then we will implement Plan B,' said Violet, marching through the outer office towards the Conference Room, heels clanking and tattered head high.

Molly stared at the carpet. Mrs Webster's small fingers moved faster than ever.

After some time Hamish Carew, followed by Ms Redpath, appeared dangling a bunch of keys from one finger. He put an arm around his wife's wet shoulder and burped.

'Pardon,' he said. 'Banana. Don't tell me. Let me guess. The Scrub-a-Dub?'

Molly put her palm to his cheek and turned to Ms Redpath. 'Thank you, Violet. Was it Plan A or B?'

'A,' murmured Ms Redpath.

'And what was B?'

Ms Redpath smiled. Her head moved from side to side in noncommittal silence.

3

'Succulent,' said Hamish, banging a napkin at his face and reaching for more wine. 'I've always liked succulence. A good hock, trotters, cheek. Remember when I killed a pig at the farm?'

'Yes,' said Molly. The squeals, the gut-wrenching, hideous squeals, her pathetic efforts to hide them from Roberta.

And the time Hamish drowned the kittens.

'Let's play in the other room, darling,' she'd cried, slamming the back door. 'Come on. Quick, now, quick.'

Wide-eyed and hesitant, Bobby dragged her heels. 'What's Daddy going to do with Smoky's kittens?'

'Look! Here we are. Let's play Ring a ring o' roses . . . Come on. Big voice. Now the other way. Knees up. Good *girl*. And again. And we all fall *down!*'

'I'm going to watch,' yelped Bobby, skidding to the door.

'You are not going to watch. We're going to *romp* and have fun.'

'I'm going.'

For the first time in her life Molly seized the struggling child and shook her. 'No.'

Bobby stamped her foot. 'I'll tell Daddy on you!'

Guilt-ridden and scarlet in the face, Molly tried again. 'Daddy can't see you now, darling. He's busy.'

'Don't be potty,' growled Bobby. 'Daddy loves me.'

Molly shivered, stared at the calm harbour, the late-night ferry slicing its way through black water edged with shuddering ribbons of orange, pink and purple light. On top of the ship's funnel sat an empty dining chair.

'Look!' she cried. 'One of our chairs is sitting on top of the ferry's funnel.'

Hamish glanced, chewed for a moment. 'Reflection,' he said.

'Of course it's a reflection.'

'Then why mention it?'

'Because it's unusual. Chairs on top of funnels. You don't expect that.'

Preliminaries over, Molly leaned forward. 'There's something I want to talk to you about, Hamish.'

'Hh?'

'The trip offshore. Do I have to come?'

'You mean you don't want to?'

'I want to be with you, of course . . .' she said carefully. 'It's just that sometimes I feel . . . I know it might sound silly to you, but it's not my sort of thing. I'm not any good at it.'

'Most women would give their eye teeth.'

'I'm never sure which ones they are.'

'What do you mean you're not good at it? What is there to be good at? Nothing but roses all the way for you girls. And you are good with people. Always have been.'

'Yes, but . . .'

'And what about the shopping?' he said.

'That's one of the worst things. I don't know how to shop, you know that. My mind turns to mush and I can't think and there's acres of stuff gleaming and the escort ladies are all so hopeful. They think I'll be so excited and love it and I stand there thinking, Please God, when can I stop doing this. I hate it – the feeling more than the shopping. I feel so awkward. I'm no good at it.'

'Then don't do it. No shopping,' said Hamish, tossing it away. 'I'll get them to put it on the programme. Tell me what you do want and I'll get Spencer to brief them at the respective posts. Kuala Lumpur and Hong Kong at the moment.'

'But the poor things will have to do something with me, won't they? I know from experience, you *want* your visitors to have a good time. Like that exquisite little woman, you know, that Asian wife when she found the carved kiwi with a paua clock in its middle. Such joy, it was lovely to see. You want it all to be like that. Everyone does. A success. A beautiful success. Flops are dreadful, like a dud New Year's Eve party, only worse. Remember that time we took those Australians jetboating and her hair got wet and she was livid? And those rock-hard avocados at the Hermitage. Couldn't get your spoon in, I didn't know where to look.

'I want to like shopping. I really do. That's why I try so hard and get it wrong, and they're all watching and waiting and I go on buying rubbish and talking and talking as though there's some demon inside me and I can't stop and the whole thing turns into a nightmare.'

She paused, clasped her hands. 'Do you really want me to come, Hamish?'

'Of course, dear.' There were always things to be attended to: laundry to organise, lists to be checked, thank-you notes.

'I know you like my being there, of course, but am I *necessary*?'

'The government has received invitations from Hong Kong and Malaysia for the Minister of Trade and Cultural Links and Mrs Carew to make an official visit to their shores. Official,' murmured Hamish, replenishing his glass and waving it at her. 'I think they would be deeply insulted if you said no. Unless there was a good reason. Bobby having a baby or something.'

'Why would Bobby suddenly have a baby?'

'To get you out of having to go on this trip to fascinating Asian countries as a hostess and representative of New Zealand womanhood.'

'But I'm not. That's the whole point,' cried Molly.

'They don't know that.'

'I'm bad at it. Like kissing. I get it wrong every time. I kiss the ones who don't want to be kissed and they rear back, and I don't notice the ones who do want to, all puckered up waiting, and then it's too late, and if I aim for the right they go to the left, and now people are beginning to do it both sides and I think that's awkward unless you're born to it. I know it's ridiculous but it worries me. And I never know what to do about lipstick marks either. Do you mop them? If so, how? Especially the men. You can scarcely use spit. Do you just ignore? There must be some way to get it right.'

'There is. Take your time. Don't rush into it.'

'Hamish, I do admire you,' said Molly. 'You're so balanced.'

'Besides, what would you do with yourself here while I was away?'

'Not much. I'm not like you. Having been so busy for so long I enjoy not doing much, just pottering, watching, looking at the harbour. I could go up and see Bobby perhaps, but ...' She shrugged. 'We'll see.'

Hamish looked at her, gave her his full attention. 'What

on earth have you done to your hair?' he said.

'Had it cut,' she said, flinging her hands upwards. 'What's wrong with it?'

Somebody, Education, Foreign Affairs, one of those arty types, had propped himself against the bar at Bellamy's the other day and recited a poem. Weird enough in all conscience, at that time and place. Hamish, as he said, was a practical man, a plain man and proud of it. What he didn't understand didn't interest him. But the words he could hear above the cheers and the jeers and the clatter at the bar had stayed in his mind.

He had met Violet Redpath striding along the corridor on his return to the office. Had she, he asked, ever heard a poem about someone 'who whistled, could sit still'?

She smiled. 'Yes. Shall I get you a copy?'

'Thank you. Yes.'

It was on his desk next day. The second verse was the one.

With all his honours, he sighed for one
Who, say astonished critics, lived at home;
Did little jobs about the house with skill
And nothing else; could whistle, would sit still
Or potter round the garden; answered some
Of his long marvellous letters but kept none.

The sense of surprise the words had caused returned. He had written Molly very few letters in his life. Those he had had been anything but marvellous, but she had kept them.

'Nothing's wrong,' he said. 'Nothing. I'm sorry you feel that this trip may not be much to your liking but I think you should come.' He put out his hand, patted hers. 'I'm not being pompous, am I?'

'Oh, do be quiet.'

He stared at the harbour. No help out there. 'No,' he said, 'I'm sure you'll enjoy yourself when you get there. You always do and you're a good ambassador. Understanding. Pleasant.'

'"Under All Circumstances,"' she snapped, 'like Brown Owl?'

Hamish, torn between sarcasm and concurrence, gave up. 'Quite,' he said and headed for the door. 'Toilet.'

Molly was in her La-Z-Boy chair when he returned. Her hands were folded on her lap, her eyes on the still harbour. She turned towards him as he climbed into his chair and worked the controls. His legs lifted, he lay at ease.

'All right,' she said, 'I'll come.'

'That's the girl.'

'On one condition.'

He looked at her kindly. 'And what's that?'

'That Ms Redpath comes too. As a member of your ministerial party. One of your handlers.'

'Why on earth?'

'Because I like her. And she's discreet.'

'Molly, for heaven's sake. I like her too, though I never thought of her as particularly discreet. She's competent, a little brusque perhaps, a little unexpected in some ways, but that is no conceivable reason for her to accompany me. Us. What would she do?'

'Your secretarial work.'

'Owen Spencer does that. And is useful in endless ways. He knows the scene, the background, the routine. Very sound, Spencer. That reminds me. Do we have such a thing as a Tooth Fairy Card?'

Molly yanked the lever of her chair. Its leg support folded, her stiff-backed anger swung upright. 'I don't ask much of you, Hamish, as regards your time. I realise you have giant responsibilities, endless concerns. The buck stops here and all that nonsense, though of course it doesn't.' She was on her feet, her face near his. 'I will not be detailed off to buy Tooth Fairy Cards.'

'But Spencer's eldest has lost his first tooth. The man was quite excited. They have them apparently, the cards. I just thought it would be a nice gesture.'

'It would be an obscene gesture, but make it if you wish.

Send him out to get one for you. Or ask that little thing with the rings. She would know exactly where to find them.'

'That's not like you, Molly.'

'Oh, yes it is.'

He sat silent, watching her back view as she marched from the room.

She came back bearing coffee, calm as usual as far as he could tell, except for an unusual aversion to eye contact.

He touched her hand as she placed his cup beside him. 'I'm sorry I upset you. But what would Ms Redpath . . . ?'

'Violet.'

'Violet. Do?'

'She would be my companion and your secretary's secretary. Normally there is more than one New Zealand wife on these visits, as you know. I refuse to go,' said Molly, high-rumped and firm, 'unaccompanied.'

'You won't be unaccompanied. The girls from the High Commissions will look after you.'

'"The girls from the High Commissions"!' The phrase shot out, expelled from her lips like a foreign body. 'Intelligent hard-working young women from Foreign Affairs on overseas postings, do you mean? Or the wives?'

'Both.'

'No, Hamish. No. I refuse to go.'

They sat silent and morose, their eyes on the sea. A plane homed into the airport, its starboard light blinking.

Hamish tried diversion.

'You say you hate shopping,' he said. 'What about clothes? Look at you. You look all right. You always look all right.'

'Bobby tells me. She knows about colours. Things that go and don't go. Accessories.' Molly made a noise somewhere between a giggle and a snort.

Hamish joined her. They sat side by side in their hydraulically assisted armchairs, snuffling and hooting in unison, enjoying the guilty pleasure of parental disloyalty.

—

41

Hamish worked on constituency business all weekend. There was little chat, but the silence was companionable.

He came home from the House late on Monday night. Very late and very angry. Spencer was not coming on the trip.

'Oh?'

'His wife is pregnant.'

'Ah.'

He glared at her gentle mouth, her round blue eyes.

'Pregnant.'

'You said.'

'Due quite soon apparently. She needs support.'

Hamish roamed around the living room, bouncing on the government-issue carpet which cushioned his feet both night and day, pausing at corners to glare at her once more.

'So Spencer can't come.'

'Can't?' asked Molly.

'Won't. He says his wife needs him.'

'Ah.'

'Of course I could make him. The thing's ridiculous. But my colleagues advised against it. There was a very tricky case last year. Picket lines, the lot. Someone had leaked something about a pregnant secretary being denied something. A chair or something. There was quite a kerfuffle.'

'Chair?'

'Some special thing. Back support. Something.'

'He'll be able to help his boys brush their teeth,' murmured Molly.

Hamish snorted but said nothing. His reactions to events of his world usually showed common sense and logic. He did his best. But changes in social attitudes and mores seemed to be catching up on him.

His father had felt the same about methods of transport. He had seen the first motor car in Taranaki when he was a child – 'a Darraq, lad, remember that, not many Darraqs around now' – and had lived to see the first astronaut bouncing about on the moon. What was the man's name? The first man ever? Hamish clenched his teeth to assist memory, walked towards the drinks cupboard and came away again. He would not pour a nightcap till he could remember the name. He owed the man that much. Armstrong? Shepherd? Armstrong. Thank God. He poured a whisky, looked at it happily and headed for the kitchen tap.

'Drink?'

'No thank you.'

He returned to tipped-back comfort and thought of change.

When he and Molly had driven off in the Buick after their wedding, with the tin cans clanging from the back bumper and a sign saying *Newly married*, Molly had worn a navy blue going-away suit which had been a dead-ringer for her mother's but smaller. Definitely smaller at the time. On her arrival at her new home she had cooked the same meals, the same hunks of meat and vegetables roasted in boiling fat as her mother and her grandmothers had done. Like them she had been trained for matrimony and achieved it.

And now Bobby had told him she had no intention of marrying. A mug's game if ever there was one. She would continue to live at the farm, breed prize Jerseys and to hell with the lot of them.

Owen Spencer's nervous face rose before him: 'My place, Minister, is with my wife.'

Molly marched in. 'You have eaten, I presume?'

'Yes. It'll will work out – be all right.'

'What?'

'Spencer's defection.'

'What will happen?'

'Fred Manders is about to be seconded to CLAT from Foreign Affairs. He'll come, and Ms Redpath.'

Molly dipped her head at a passing gull. 'Good.'

43

'And you and me.'

'Yes,' said Molly.

'No banana?' said Molly, aiming one at him.

'No, they repeat on me.'

Molly looked at the banana with interest. 'Oh, yes. You said.'

He waved a forgiving hand and reached for the toast. 'I was thinking. In the night. It might be an idea to ask Fred Manders and Miss Redpath up to the farm for a weekend.'

Molly continued licking the honey spoon. 'Why?'

'I have to go anyway to check on the new sharemilker. I thought we could regard it as a sort of shakedown cruise. Get to know each other.'

'Why?' she said, sucking harder.

The sight irritated him, her reaction more so.

'What do you think?' he said.

She put the spoon down.

'Would they want to?' said Molly.

4

Manders knew about the miseries of rejection but this was different. Rage engulfed him, seared his ego like a naked flame. His ego which, he was prepared to admit, was as big as the next man's if not bigger, as it had every right to be. Damn the incompetent shits, damn their eyes and blast their buttocks. And the worst of them was his immediate boss Squires, a crawler with knee pads whose main concern was to keep talent stewing. Precocious ability, let alone excellence in his juniors, terrified the man.

Squires had propped his arse against the window sill and, between the flick of the Bic and his first drag, had dropped his bombshell. Upstairs had turned down Manders' request for Paris. Not only that. He was to be seconded from Foreign Affairs to hold the hand of the Minister for Cultural Links and Trade. Seconded to CLAT. He of all people. Him. He. Manders, sound as a bell, brilliant track record, virtually bilingual and with judgement to burn, was to make the path straight for Hamish Carew, a man known as a hard worker and decent enough but no thruster. Not a man to hitch a rising star to. Not a Valley of the Bones type of boss but . . .

Why? The word churned and flapped in his mind. *Why?*

Cultural Links and Trade. Trade was OK. He could do Trade. Trade was essential. Nothing more important. Why hadn't they put the essential component first, Trade and Cultural Links. T A C L, as in Tackle. Or T A L C, a soothing blend of economic and cultural. When he had been in Thailand a few years ago holding some other minister's hand, the standard-issue medical kit had included something labelled Foot and Body Talc. The one-stop talc. He had it still. Excellent stuff. Killed anything.

Why the hell had he given up smoking.

And he could certainly do Culture. Like any self-respecting Young Turk in Foreign Affairs he collected New Zealand art. Or had. He read New Zealand literature, especially history, which was becoming more interesting by the minute as the revisionist stuff came out. He had always been interested in the customs and culture of the indigenous people, was well versed in Maoritanga.

And he loved the place. There was nothing wrong with the country. A fine and noble land. Beautiful. Beautiful.

Or its people.

Or was there? Surely not. It was more, he realised with an unwelcome stab of self-knowledge, that he had gone off them. Gone dog on them, as his father used to say, indicating his sister mooching in a corner. 'Watch it, Freddy, Madam la Zonga's gone dog on us.'

Manders leapt to his feet, stared out the window at two large water tanks on the flat grey roof, at air ducts and a pigeon drinking from a large rippling puddle. At buildings, more buildings and the bush-covered hills of the town belt beyond.

Did he like his fellow countrymen and women, was the thought which had stopped him in mid-snarl. Did he in fact like anyone? And this, this was the point. Did it show?

Manders was a reasonably honest man. If he didn't like the human race it bloody well should show. *Esse quam videre.* To be rather than to seem. A good motto, he had always thought. One that should be framed above the beds of leaders and force-fed to frauds.

The wind was getting stronger. A sparrow now stood in water, the pigeon had disappeared. The reflections of the surrounding high rises, cream, brown and smoky blue, shuddered in the dark puddle.

Manders pulled a yellow legal pad towards him and wrote:

APPRECIATION OF SITUATION

a) I have become a supercilious shit.
b) It shows.
c) Is this why I have been seconded to a job in Cultural Links and Trade?
d) Unlikely. Both C L & T need charm and bonhomie.
e) So does an overseas posting.
f) I want an overseas posting.
g) An overseas posting at this stage is essential for my career.
h) Bridget.

OPTIONS / ACTION

1) Do the CLAT job superbly and get sent back to FA as soon as possible for an Overseas Posting.
2) How else to achieve desired posting?
a. Get charming. You used to charm. Get charming.

b. What about EQV?
c. Bugger EQV.
d. Practise on someone.
e. Who?

Freddy snatched the page from the yellow pad and screwed it up. Then reconsidered and tore it to pieces. No point in advertising angst at this stage. He looked out the window. Not a bird in sight: the sparrow had shot through. Cold feet perhaps.

The telephone rang. Freddy snatched it to him. 'Manders,' he barked.

'Is that you, Mr Manders?'

'Yes.' Who else, chucky, who else.

'Mr Manders, it's Tania Webster, Mr Carew's personal assistant, speaking. Mr Carew wants to see you as soon as possible about arrangements for the ASEAN trip.'

'Trip. When?'

'After you join CLAT.'

Oh Christ. One of those balls-aching chatting and shopping ministerial trips dreaded by High Commissions, Embassies and handlers alike. And I'll be there to dance attendance, to be one of *them*; there to bear-lead Carew and piss on my colleagues.

Freddy drew a deep breath.

'Thank you, Ms Webster . . .'

'Mrs,' squeaked the telephone.

'I do apologise, Mrs. Shall I come over forthwith?' (A bit much, forthwith, but let her swing.)

'No, no, the Minister is completely tied up till Thursday.'

The old game. I'll show you my diary if you show me yours and mine will be bigger and fatter and packed full with meaty interest because my boss is the biggest fucker in the forest and you're ground cover.

'Thursday,' muttered Freddy, 'will be fine.'

48

He put down the receiver with exaggerated care and wrote *CLAT, 2.30* in his diary.

The future did not beckon.

He would go and see Steve Roper on the Asian desk. Steve might know something, some hidden and hopeful agenda, some gleam of light, some *sense* behind this grisly scenario, this seconding of brilliance.

Round-shouldered and intent, he loped along the corridor in search of comfort he knew he was unlikely to receive.

Friends, even good friends like Steve, get the confiding business wrong. They listen for a few moments, tell you where you went wrong, tell you what they would have done in similar circumstances, which is usually the exact opposite to what you have done, and then slide gently into their problems which are invariably serious, unlike your sweaty little quibbles against fate. Your bad fortune, they intimate, lies within yourself. Their troubles are the ones predestined by malevolent stars.

Steve, as expected, was useless, worse than useless. He said that you have to expect bum postings occasionally and that Freddy's trouble was he'd always been so bloody brilliant he thought the department owed him a living, which it didn't, and that Freddy should wait until he landed a really shitty job like Steve's, *and* a boss like Agent Orange, and then he would have something to moan about, and how about a game of squash sometime. Oh, and had Freddy seen the photos of the party at the Luigi's the other night?

'No.'

Steve produced an elaborate padded album with the word *Photographs* embossed in gold letters and a handwritten inscription inside. *With the compliments of Ambassador Constantine Luigi and Senora Luigi on the occasion of the visit of General Alsarvo d'Riva.*

From the evidence of the photographs the party had been an outstanding success. Most of the participants seemed to have spent the evening shrieking with joy, although there was one unfortunate shot of the Minister of Transport clutching his saffron-suited groin alongside a large floral arrangement of red kniphofias, birds of paradise and giant toi toi.

Freddy's eyes lingered on one of Molly Carew nose to nose with the guest of honour. She appeared to be adjusting his right epaulette while he screamed for help. Her dress had turned purple, his eyes scarlet.

The dancing before the singalong had not been ignored. The Ambassador boogied with a variety of women ranging from the ecstatic to the hysterical. Only Frank Sato from Nigeria and Ms Redpath from CLAT appeared to maintain their composure, he silent and impassive in his djellabah, she serene as she shimmied low with the Head of Security who was known to be both ruthless and competent. His mouth was open, his eyes fixed on the curve of her bottle-green neckline. It was a ludicrous image, but oddly touching. They were, in theory, having fun, letting go, getting down, yet the only things indicative of abandon were his mouth and her haircut.

Steve looked at the picture over his shoulder. 'Violet Redpath never sees me. Complete hairy eyeball, frozen mitt. No recognition at all, not a glance.'

'Why?'

'I asked her once how tall she was. Daphne and I had been having a bet on it at some ball. Daph was too chicken, so I did.'

'What did she say?'

'She drew herself up to her full height and asked me how much Daphne weighed.'

Freddy laughed. He laughed and laughed and laughed. He flung back his head and laughed till he wept. 'What,' he gasped finally, 'did Daphne say?'

'Oh, I didn't tell Daph,' huffed Steve. 'She would have been most upset. It wasn't too funny at the time, I can tell you.'

Manders pulled himself together. 'Why have you been honoured with this?' he asked, tapping the album.

'Every desk has one. Asian, French, US. The lot.'

'Very generous.'

'They are generous, the Luigis. Last time they dined with us they gave Daphne and me a set of coasters. Sort of mottled stone, brown and white like a cow. Rather attractive in a weird sort of way.'

'Brindled.'

'If you say so.'

'We got them too.'

'Well, you would, wouldn't you? Same seniority.'

'Sixty-six, wasn't it?

'Nnn. Sixty-six.'

'As long as that.'

'Amazing.'

They stared at each other bleakly.

'God knows where they are now,' said Manders.

Steve's head moved from side to side.

'Probably,' continued Freddy, 'Bridget took them with her.'

'God, you're a supercilious bastard,' exploded Steve. 'What would a woman like Bridget, an independent wonderful woman like that, want with four joint-matrimonial stone coasters in Paris?'

He had asked for it, he supposed. Asked for it and got it. Bared his breast for consolation and received insult. It is one thing to wonder in your secret soul whether you might conceivably be a bastard, but another to be told so . . . The man hadn't even smiled.

Manders grabbed his briefcase and headed outside. He would sit in the sun. He would indulge himself and have a nice time eating his sandwiches. He made his own lunch most mornings. It gave structure to the whole bloody business of getting up and getting out of the house and walking down the hill and buying a paper at the dairy and shooting up to the eighth floor and sitting down at his desk. Structure, focus, is the thing.

Merely a question of taking the day in small bites. Or large ones, ha, ha. Salmon and cream cheese today. He must have known something.

Now for fresh air, the therapeutic wind on the sodding heath.

There was wind, sneaky and capricious, and too much of it. Spring, he supposed. Equinoctial gales. Fucking spring again. He headed for shelter.

'Manders,' called a voice.

Violet Redpath, crouched on a rock wall beneath a Norfolk pine, sat eating a large, unwieldy filled roll. Her knees seemed to be above ear level.

'Why did you call me that?' he said.

'I used to work with Bridget. She called you that.'

'She was my wife.'

Violet nodded solemnly. Too solemnly. 'True,' she murmured.

He lowered himself beside her and sat in silence. There was little point in attempting conversation until the roll and contents had been disposed of.

'What did you want to ask me about?' he said finally.

She screwed up the empty bag and tossed it into a rubbish tin some distance away.

'You're going on this trip, aren't you?' she said. 'With the Minister to Asia?'

'Yes. For my sins.'

She looked at him through fly-away streaks of dark hair. 'You know,' she said, 'when people say that I always feel a bit sick. I don't mean I'm going to toss or anything . . .'

'Good.'

Her smile was changeable as the gusting wind: on, off, quick as a flicked switch. 'It's just that catch at the back of your nose somewhere, and you think, Dear God don't let him say it, though of course you already had.'

He nodded, quite understood. Why the hell had he said it.

'Do you have any other pass-the-sick-bags?' he asked.

'Yes. But I'm ashamed of them. Womb. Puberty. Straightforward sensible words. I fear it may be Freudian, and that's another conversation clunker. Like "Heigh ho". Not as in "Off to work we go". I can cope with that, Grumpy, Stumpy and whoever all Heigh ho-ing away. It's when people say things like, "Heigh ho, such is life".'

She turned to him, sat waiting for comment.

'Ned Kelly's last words were "Such is life".'

'Yes. Fantastic. But not "Heigh ho".'

'No,' he said, his fingers hunting for a sharp stone beneath his bum. 'Ah, that's better.'

'I wonder about that sort of thing quite a lot: which comes first?' she continued. 'Like discovering that someone you don't like doesn't like you. Not unexpected exactly but still a surprise. Is it the things people say or do that make you instinctively like or dislike them? Or is it just pheromones, chemical attraction or lack of it, so that the things which drive you insane in A are OK in B? B gets away with it because you like/love him/her.' She paused, thought about it. 'I suppose it's a variant of "love is blind". But that's not right because you see clearly both the warts and the non-warts and yet . . .'

Perhaps she was dumb, one of those bright dumb ones. The worst sort of all, sitting beside him on her stoneless rock, bleating muddle-headed scatter-shot metaphysics at him. He could feel another stone, a sharp one. He stood up.

'Why are you interested in the Minister's Asian visit?'

'Because I'm going on it.'

Just Molly and me, and Baby makes three. 'Oh,' he said.

She unfolded the sharp angles of her legs and stood smiling beside him. 'I thought you'd be pleased.'

'Why are you coming?'

'Because Mrs Spencer is having a baby and Owen's place is at his wife's side.'

'So you'll be the Minister's secretary!'

'You and me. We will share it. We will liaise.'

'Oh God,' said Freddy, and turned away across the sunny grass.

Gratuitous rudeness. Uncalled for and unwarranted. The only sort worth having.

He turned to lift a hand in some sort of apology but she had disappeared.

5

The first of the preliminary programme meetings was held in the Ministerial Office. Steven Roper came over from Foreign Affairs with the brief from the Asian Desk.

'I don't need to tell you, Minister,' he said sternly, 'how embarrassing it would be if any of these papers were mislaid . . . You know only too well. New Zealand Eyes Only. Top Security. Burn before reading type thing. Upstairs have stressed the security aspect at all times and this is pretty heady stuff. Personal assessments on all the people you're going to meet and some minor luminaries you may never even see. Standers in the wings, *eminences grises,* a woman or two suspected of undesirable influence, straws in the wind, that sort of thing. Background, historical perspective, ideological stance *vis à vis* each other and the rest of the world. Particularly as it concerns New Zealand, of course. Possible areas of change or tension. It all adds up. I'll say no more about that at the moment, Minister.' Steve glanced around the room, cleared his throat. 'Am I right in saying that not all of us are fully cleared at this point in time ... ?'

All eyes turned to meet Violet's cheerful gaze.

'Me,' she said.

'What clearance have you at the moment, Ms Redpath?' asked the Minister.

'Secret.'

'And when does your Top Secret come through?'

'On Friday.'

'But today's only Wednesday.'

'That's right.'

'As you say then, Roper, no more at the moment.' Hamish looked uneasy. 'Wouldn't it have been better to have had the meeting next week?'

'Time is of the essence, sir. There are many Secret topics to discuss and we can reconvene for Top Secret next week.'

Hamish dipped his head. 'Very good.'

'So this meeting,' continued Steve, 'is in the nature of a pre-preliminary brief if you like. Logistics, that sort of thing.'

'Yes,' said Hamish.

'And of course Trade in depth. Trade, trade and more trade.'

Steve picked up the bulging grey folder stamped NZEO in red, gave it a final pat and handed it to the Minister, who received it with care.

Manders found his head dipping in imitation.

Steve produced more papers. 'And of course the proposed programme.' He handed sheets around. 'Everyone got one?'

More nods.

'This is our first draft, of course,' said Steve. 'Just to get a feel for things, a general run-through at this stage. Route, Aims, Options, Opinions. Then we'll flash any changes or suggestions you might care to make off to our experts at the posts concerned. They, of course, may well come back to us with counter suggestions.'

All heads bent to read.

Thank God, thought Manders, First Class.

He glanced at Violet's yellow pad alongside him. She had written something under 'First Class'. He squinted at the word: 'Yippee.'

'You and Mrs Carew, Minister, will of course be travelling First Class. As to Mr Manders and Ms Redpath: obviously, Minister, you will want your secretary with you at all times. And because appearances are so important in that part of world, the logistics people have decided – subject to your approval, of course, sir – that Ms Redpath should also travel First Class to obviate the necessity of her having to move through from Economy each time the aircraft is due to land.'

The whole party nodded.

Years ago when Manders had been to Bangkok on some other ministerial trip he and Bridget had scratched and saved and saved again so she could fly Economy in the same aircraft. It had been a good time and worth the effort. Bridget had declined the Minister of Foreign Affairs' kind invitation to join them in First Class before landing. She had come down the Economy exit ladder smiling – rather ostentatiously, he had thought at the time. Little Cinders pulls through.

'As you all know, this ministerial visit, unlike most Asian tours, does not include Singapore,' Steve continued. 'Our two objectives, venues if you like, for discussion are Hong Kong and Kuala Lumpur. Singapore will be completely unofficial, just a one-night stopover. This of course is because of the successful' – he dipped his head at Hamish, who dipped back – 'recent visit of the Singaporean Minister of Trade to New

Zealand and the highly successful, quite outstandingly so if I may so, talks which took place between our Minister and Mr Yo.'

Hamish said nothing. The talks had gone well. The spin-offs in milk powder and hides had been particularly good. The Prime Minister had congratulated him in person.

The ministerial gifts of sheepskin car-seat covers had also been a success. Molly, however, had had a difficult time with Mrs Yo and her attendants at the Mountains of the Moon Thermal Park. The guests had disliked the sunshine intensely. Parasols had been requested. One of the younger New Zealand members of the party had sprinted to the office in the Reception Area, but there were none available. Molly hadn't thought for a minute there would be any, but Ms James had offered and at least it showed willing. Newspapers had been pressed into service instead.

No Singapore, thought Manders. Mrs Carew would be spared the sight of the unfortunate crocodile. Why on earth did they keep the damn thing anyhow. What did they hope to achieve. Good public relations. Consumer interest. Trade name integrity. We are all mad and some are madder than others.

He swallowed a yawn.

On the other hand, Mrs Carew would miss Monty the Air Force python. Manders had fond memories of Monty. He was as beautiful as Mrs Carew had suggested. Manders recalled the smooth silky feel of its iridescent scales on his skin as the animal had poured itself over him before swinging on to the shoulders of the VIP wife he had been escorting. Mrs Barker stood her ground, smiling and cooing gently. There had been just a moment of awkwardness when Monty seemed in danger of disappearing up her nervous companion's skirt but was hooked away instantly by his handler.

'First stop Hong Kong,' continued Steve. 'Trade, trade, trade and more trade. Of course, sir, you will have been well briefed in all aspects of trade by your own department and by our trade commissioners in each venue. However, both Treasury and Foreign Affairs have taken the opportunity to do some tinkering as to Larger Aims, Future Scenarios, things of that nature.'

Steve pulled out another folder. 'And here is the general in-depth analysis of each venue, including things such as cultural links, museums etc, if you're interested. This aspect will also be dealt with more extensively later but there's no reason why we shouldn't get a feel for things today.'

Manders picked up the minutes of the meeting in the room which had once been a spare room and was now his office. Two single beds had been shoved to one side behind filing cabinets. His desk overflowed with paper. He did a lot of work at night.

INTERNAL MEMORANDUM

Minutes of the Programme Meeting for Proposed Visit of the Hon. Hamish Carew to Hong Kong, Malaysia and Singapore.
Copies to: The Minister, Hon. H. Carew (CLAT)
            Fred Manders (CLAT)
            Violet Redpath (CLAT)
            Owen Spencer (Secretary)
            Steven Roper (Foreign Affairs)

Mr Roper opened with some general remarks and explained the proposed itinerary in brief: Hong Kong 4 days, Malaysia 4 days, Singapore one-night stopover only.

The Foreign Affairs New Zealand Eyes Only briefing papers were discussed and handed over to the Minister for Minister's Eyes Only until Monday 24th.

Mr Roper handed around the proposed itinerary and invited comments.

The Minister said which one was the New Mandarin?

Mr Roper said that the New Mandarin was the newest hotel in the Central Business District of Hong Kong. That it had a glass bubble lift going up and down in the foyer.

Ms Redpath said that those glass lifts reminded her of anti-influenza capsules. She added that they sway a bit sometimes.

Mr Manders asked Ms Redpath if she would prefer a quick kip at the Y.

The Minister said that if either Ms Redpath or Mr Manders had anything useful to add to the discussion they should speak more loudly, or else be silent.

Mr Spencer said that presumably Mr Manders would prefer to have that last comment deleted.

Mr Manders said he had no opinion either way.

Mr Spencer said Yes or No.

Mr Manders said No.

Mr Roper asked were there any more questions at this stage.

The Minister said he would study the itinerary alongside the NZEO paper that night and get back to Mr Roper as soon as possible with his comments as to times etc. He added that he thought it essential that when Ms Redpath's Top Secret clearance came through the briefing paper on personalities and the proposed programme of meetings should be studied in conjunction with the itinerary. Close study would be required.

Mr Roper agreed with the Minister and moved on to the rest of the itinerary. Wellington to Hong Kong / 4 days HK / overnight Singapore / 4 days KL / KL to Wellington. Eleven days in all. He said it could be described as a brief tour, but as everyone was aware, the importance of these visits could not be overestimated.

He inquired as to whether the Minister played golf.

The Minister said that he enjoyed a game of golf when he could fit it in, but that happened less and less these days.

Mr Roper asked Mr Manders whether he played golf.

Mr Manders replied that he did not play golf, as Mr Roper very well knew.

Mr Roper said that he had forgotten but that Mr Manders need not worry because one of the chaps from the various posts would always be happy to play. In Hong Kong the ring-in was usually Bob Berkley, who was Trade anyway. He added that it never ceased to surprise him how much good work was done on the links, that the golf game with visiting VIPs was always a very important part of the programme as far as the offshore members of ASEAN were concerned. That in those parts there was a lot of mana attached to the game. And money. He had heard recently that you can get a thousand-dollars-a-hole game in KL any day of the week. That both countries had superb links and facilities and that green fees were astronomical, though of course that would not be a problem in this case.

Ms Redpath asked the Minister if Mrs Carew played golf.

Mr Carew said No, that Mrs Carew did not play golf, although she was an outdoor girl at heart.

Mr Roper said that brought him to the next item on his agenda. Both the posts wanted to know what Mrs Carew's interests were so they could liaise with the two host countries to ensure that a suitable Ladies Programme could be arranged. Mrs Carew would, of course, be accompanied at all times by one of the female staff or perhaps a spouse from the various posts. He understood that Ms Redpath was to have some part in this aspect of the visit, and that perhaps Ms Redpath could explain her role because our people at the various posts would want to get things quite clear as regards assistance required, protocol etc.

Ms Redpath said that just for the record she did not play golf either, and that she understood she was to have two roles on this trip. That she was to assist Mrs Carew in any way she could and accompany her on her engagements. That was, when Mr Manders was able to spare her.

Mr Manders said that he did not envisage any problems in that regard. That he was sure he would be able to spare Ms Redpath at any moment she could be of any use whatsoever to Mrs Carew. He added that Ms Redpath could be said to be wearing two hats on this trip.

Ms Redpath asked the Minister whether she could open a window.

Mr Carew said Certainly.

Mr Roper said Could the Minister tell him what Mrs Carew's interests were.

Mr Carew said No shopping.

Mr Roper said None at all?

Mr Carew said Mrs Carew would prefer that shopping excursions be kept to a minimum. He said that Mrs Carew did not enjoy shopping.

Mr Roper said Not even in Hong Kong?

Mr Carew said that Mrs Carew realised that some shopping was inevitable but she would be grateful if it could be kept to a minimum.

Mr Roper said he would certainly alert the interested parties. He asked Mr Carew what Mrs Carew's other interests were.

Mr Carew said that Mrs Carew liked animals.

Mr Roper said that in that case she would enjoy the

Hong Kong Zoo. Hong Kong had one, from memory. He did not know of any zoo near KL or its environs but he would find out.

Mr Carew said No zoos. Mrs Carew liked animals but she did not like zoos.

Mr Roper made another note. He asked Mr Carew if Mrs Carew had any other interests.

Mr Carew said Mrs Carew had many interests. That she liked gardens.

Mr Roper said in that case Mrs Carew would enjoy the Hong Kong Central Zoological and Botanical Gardens at the top end of Garden Road. That they were among the most beautiful zoological gardens in the world and had a magnificent collection of orchids.

Mr Carew said Mrs Carew was not so keen on orchids but never mind. He said that Mrs Carew's main interest in life was people. Mrs Carew was a people person. That she was interested in all people from all walks of life both rich and poor, though she had perhaps a slight bias towards the latter. That Mrs Carew was interested in people and their customs, their cultures and their lives.

Mr Roper asked Mr Carew whether Mrs Carew liked museums.

Mr Carew said that Mrs Carew did enjoy museums as long as they were people oriented and not too big, but mainly she enjoyed meeting different people from different countries, talking to them, enjoying their company, their customs, their lives. Mr Carew said that nothing surprised Mrs Carew and that Mrs Carew was a wonderful ambassador for her country.

Mr Roper said Yes indeed. He added that he had thought of a local attraction he had seen in Hong Kong which might be right up Mrs Carew's street.

The Minister said Attraction?

Mr Roper replied that one day in Kowloon he had come across a place called the Good Wish Bird Garden which was in fact a bird market. That the Chinese are very fond of birds, that you sometimes see Chinese men taking their pets for an airing. Birds are considered to be good luck, which is why you often see them at the races. That the birds had seemed quite happy in their cages. Attendants had served them live crickets through the bars with chopsticks.

The Minister said that was enough and were there any other suggestions.

Mr Manders said could he offer a suggestion as to something Mrs Carew might enjoy. That he felt Mrs Carew might enjoy a visit to the Orang Asli, the aboriginal people of Malaysia. Or those who were left.

Mr Roper said Who?

Mr Manders said Orang Asli, and did not Mr Roper remember when he and Mr Manders had had a duty run to Campbell Island years ago and how fascinating it had been to meet the Orang Asli.

Mr Roper said Oh, them.

Mr Manders said Yes. Them.

Mr Roper make a note.

After more general discussion on specialised topics (see Appendices One, Two, and Three) the meeting adjourned at 4pm.

Owen Spencer, Secretary

Manders sighed, folded his arms on top of the minutes, laid his head down beneath the green shaded desk light Bridget had picked up in Georgetown on their first overseas posting, and slept.

6

Manders' newly allocated office at CLAT had few charms. It was smaller and darker than the one he had vacated at Foreign Affairs, had a view of drainpipes and the fire escape of the National Mutual Society next door, and little else.

He stood at the desk, banging the bottom of one of its drawers. Paper clips balled in dust, scraps and screws of waste paper, pieces of a torn photograph and one untwisted paper clip spilled on to his desk. He looked at the last with distaste. Deconstructed paper clips are evidence of terminal boredom, or worse: ear probing.

His first true love, Zoë, had had an office directly above

his on The Terrace. She had made a daisy chain from paper clips, long enough to reach from her window to his, to which she had attached a bogus-Victorian card inscribed *When this you see, remember me*. The card fell off the first day, but the remainder of the token had waved before his desk in breezes and lashed in gales long after Zoë had departed. It could well still be there.

He picked up the torn pieces of the photograph and reassembled them. A fair-haired child appeared, her face solemn above a body distorted with the effort of holding a reluctant cat towards the camera.

He and Bridget had decided to 'put off' having children for a while. It had sounded to him at the time as though they were already in existence, these mythical beings, these genetic off-cuts waiting in the wings for a whistle which had never blown.

Manders returned to the image. You would have to dislike a child, wouldn't you, to tear up its photograph. Probably a colleague's child then, a distant cousin. Even so, why tear it up. One biff would have binned it. He glanced up, dusted his hands as Violet Redpath appeared against the door jamb.

'Hullo,' he said. 'I was thinking of you earlier.'

She crossed her feet, stared at her remedial-looking black boots. 'Apology?'

'What? Oh that. No. I was thinking what a good shot that was of yours, the one into the rubbish bin. Nice wrist action.'

'Hh.' She lost interest in her boots, looked him in the eye. 'I don't see how he can possibly expect us to go, do you? Not in our free time.'

'Go where?'

'Haven't you heard? The Minister thinks it would be a good idea if you and I spent next weekend with them at their farm.'

'Shit. Why?'

'I gather it's some sort of ghastly getting to know us. Find each other's skills, work as a team. Trust, all that.'

'Jesus.'

'Yes. So all we have to do is to be firm, both of us, to say we won't.' She paused. 'Isn't it?'

'I don't know anything about it.'

She levered herself from the door jamb, smoothed her ridiculously short skirt. 'I just thought I'd give you a chance to act collegiately before I tell him I'm not going.'

'I don't see any necessity for that.'

She gave an unattractive wet smack of tongue against palate. 'I didn't believe them,' she said, 'not at first.'

He said nothing, tugged at the next drawer down.

'Stuck? Oh dear. Yes, everyone told me how difficult you were, but I said a woman like Bridget wouldn't have put up with that nonsense for a moment.'

'Will you please stop talking about my . . .' (My what? Estranged wife? Ex wife?)

She glanced at his desk. 'Why did you tear up Gemma Kinsella's photo?'

'I'm getting rid of the previous clown's muck.'

'Her parents were divorced,' she said. 'One of those messy ones. But why tear up poor little Gemma? The bits must have been sitting there for ages. Barney Kinsella shot through to Paris years ago. Trade. Second secretary, I think.'

The stuck drawer exploded, shot towards his crotch. He leapt back. 'I – am – not – interested – in – Gemma Kinsella.'

'Oh good, it's opened,' she murmured. 'I used to think Barney was quite a nice guy. Mind you, I didn't know him well. He was very security conscious, I remember, quite paranoid long before the rest of us. It seems unlike him to leave evidence of a previous relationship, let alone in pieces. If he'd forgotten it you could understand.'

Manders banged harder. 'Will you excuse me,' he said above the small swirl of dislodged dust. 'Thank you,' he said to her back.

He tried to open the window. Stuck. As he struggled with it a man and a woman appeared around the corner of the building, skirted the nearby rubble and moved beneath the zig-zag fire escape. They looked around, kissed each other long and hard, produced cigarettes, lit up and talked for as long as the pleasure lasted, then took a long farewell and picked their way through urban rubble till the next time. They reminded him of pye-dogs, creatures shunned by the pure in heart, sneaking their pleasure where they found it.

He could ask Mrs Carew about these unloved species. 'Pye-dogs, Mrs Carew, how do you go on pye-dogs?' There would be plenty of chances during the weekend if by any ghastly chance Violet was right, as she probably was. He should have listened to the woman. It would have made sense to approach Carew together, to nip his balls-aching scheme in the bud. Why had he not done so? Because the woman raises the hackles. Violet, what a name. One 'n' and she's Violent. Nevertheless she was right. Go to the Minister. Now. Manders rubbed a dilatory hand over his desk. Now. At once.

He went, was met with courtesy and complete lack of success. The weekend together with the Carews at their farm was on. The Minister would drive the official car, as there would be electoral business to attend to as well and he did not wish to interfere with his driver's free time.

Manders loped back to his office and rang Violet.

'It's on,' he said.

'I told you.'

'I've just been to plead.'

'Any luck?'

'No. You were right. We should have gone together. Not that it would have made any difference.'

'Oh well. I suppose we've had shitty weekends before. And in our own time.'

We have. We have indeed.

———

'Mail!' cried Mrs Carew, leaping from the car.

Manders, whose thought processes had been on hold throughout the journey, came to with a jolt. 'I'll get it,' he called to Molly's back as it headed through deep grass to the mail box at the gate.

Violet still slept beside him, as she had done for most of the journey. Sleeping people usually look either peaceful or stupid, childlike innocents or slack-jawed grotesques. Violet, her body twisted and legs jackknifed behind the front seat, looked exhausted and rather beautiful. It must be something to do with the angles.

'Great God, look at that!' yelled Hamish.

Violet's head hit the car roof. 'Whaaa!'

'Where? Sir?' said Freddy.

'My *head*.'

'Over there,' cried Hamish, pointing at the sharemilker's cottage. 'Look.'

Molly returned clutching mail. 'Oh dear,' she said. 'But we don't know, though. There may be some reason.'

'*Reason*. Look. Look at them, four, no *five* clapped-out cars. What the hell's a sharemilker doing with five broken-down wrecks? Sharemilking's a full-time job, or should be. No time to fiddle about restoring wrecks when I was in charge. What's Bobby doing hiring this shower? No, no. Don't tell me. It's my fault, I should've come down. The poor girl hasn't had the experience. Visual pollution, that's what it is! Visual pollution from their local member. The whole district'll be up in arms.'

Molly offered balm. 'She couldn't have known he'd do this.'

'No, she couldn't, but I would have.'

'Perhaps he's going to get rid of them soon.'

'You bet your sweet life he is.'

Hamish ignored Molly's comments about Bobby's lovely show of agapanthus on the dry bank which had always been such a problem. He was now muttering, the confused half-audible mumble shared by the pious outraged and the belligerent drunk. Molly heard the word 'temerity'. It's not a word you hear often.

Freddy and Violet exchanged glances as the car swept up the hill.

Bobby came leaping down the back steps. 'Hi,' she yelled.

The back-seat passengers smiled weakly as Molly embraced her daughter.

'You look lovely, Bobby,' said her mother. And so she did, even in shorts. Her legs had never been her best point, but health, vitality and good-hearted energy flowed from her. Her strong curly hair, no longer yellow, had darkened to a rich brown; her eyes were brighter than ever, her lashes darker. Mascara? Surely not. And her skin. The tanned pink cheeks positively glowed. My daughter, thought Molly, is a nutbrown maiden.

'I've got a shopping list as long as my arm for the trip, Dad,' she called.

'That new man,' said Hamish. 'Forster? Foster?'

'Foster.'

'What's he think he's doing running some sort of wrecker's yard down there? Did he bring the whole shooting box with him? If I'd been here he wouldn't have got past the gate. Eyesore. Bloody eyesore. Visual pollution gone mad. What sort of a man would do a thing like that?'

'Ask him,' laughed Bobby.

'I will. You bet I will. Where's my boots.'

Bobby turned to Manders. 'Hi. You're Fred, right?'

'Yes.' Freddy looked at Violet. His voice was firm. 'Fred Manders, for my sins. Hello.'

'Hi, I'm Violet. Violet Redpath.'

'You know something?' said Bobby. 'You might be taller than he is. Stand back to back. Go on.'

Manders and Violet sprang apart as though zapped by cattle prods.

Bobby, undeterred and smiling, began heaving suitcases about. Manders took one from her hand. Violet snatched it from him.

'That's mine.'

'I do beg your pardon.'

'Oh shut up,' she hissed. She turned to storm across the back yard and marched straight into the whirly-gig clothes line.

His lip twitched. 'Are you all right?'

'No. I am not all right. I am very far from . . .'

'Now,' said Molly, climbing the steps, 'tea all round?'

'Not till I've had a go at that little lot,' said Hamish, reappearing in farm gear. 'Fred, Violet, you come with me. Give you a glimpse of how I deal with this sort of embuggerance. Instant action is the thing. Proactive.'

'May I put on my boots first, Minister?' said Violet.

'Yes, yes. You can catch us up.'

'Don't be ridiculous, Hamish,' said Molly.

Hamish didn't answer. He re-tied his already tied boots, took the carved stick presented to him by the elders of the local marae and stood banging it about till Violet reappeared.

Flanked by staff, Hamish bounded down the hill and headed for the back yard of the cottage, his outrage stoked by both his renewed sight of manmade desecration and the casual response from his daughter and wife. Bobby had seemed, if anything, slightly amused. Molly thought he had been overreacting. 'Calm down,' she had suggested.

The house had the usual plan of sharemilkers' cottages built before the First World War. Four box-like rooms formed a square, a lean-to kitchen with a sloping roof lay at the back, the outside lavatory had been moved inside. The place offered shelter but little else. Dry hydrangea heads brushed the windows; a tangle of wisteria fallen from its support lay on the ground, its mauve panicles flattened by their own weight. The air was steeped with its nutmeg smell.

There was no one in sight, just the non-biodegradable bodies of an early Ford, an old Holden, a sharp-finned Chrysler and a pink fish-delivery van with cartoon fish blowing bubbles. A Datsun lay eviscerated, the dark guts of its internal mechanisms piled beside it half covered by a blue plastic sheet.

Hamish walked around inspecting the remains, poked his stick at rust, inspected oil-streaked windows and battered panelwork. Freddy, whose interest in cars was minimal but felt something was required, kicked a tyre or two. Violet inspected the wisteria and sniffed deeply.

There seemed no sense in any of the mess, no organisation, no plan. It was impossible to tell if anyone was working, or indeed had ever been working on any of these abandoned wrecks. Two were on blocks.

'Wait here and I'll see if he's in,' said Hamish, disappearing around the corner.

He glanced around the messy kitchen and thought of Rowena, the previous sharemilker's wife, who was small and shy and liked things to be nice.

The sitting room was empty except for a large brown three-piece suite with no arms, an enormous TV, a framed wedding photograph and a poster.

'Anyone home?' he called, and sat down to wait. The armless brown chair rocked beneath him. As he steadied himself his eyes met those of the man in the poster, a stern moustached character in chaps astride a rearing horse. *'Life,'* cried the caption in large letters, *'is like a bronco. Ride it rough and hard.'*

Hamish picked up the wedding photograph. The bride, her hair piled high, clung to her husband's arm in what looked like terror. He, taller, gaunter and with less hair, stared at the camera, dazed as a nocturnal animal blinded by lights. The two groomsmen's expressions were much the same. Only the two bridesmaids, coiffed and buoyant in bouffant green, seemed at ease. It was infinitely sad.

———

'How are we going to learn how his mind works, standing around here?' said Violet.

'You obviously haven't been on a ministerial swing around before.'

'No, and I can't think why I'm going on this one.'

Manders let it pass. 'The thing to remember is you're a menial, a well-informed, reasonably well-paid menial, preferably with good health and judgement. As expendable as the next man, until there's a balls-up, when it becomes your responsibility to get them out of the mess immediately. You're a faceless right hand, a squib in the middle, a stander around.'

She was dusting petals from her skirt. 'Bad as that, huh?'

'Worse. Those petals are violet.'

'Just what I'd thought.'

He looked away. 'As I say, a large part of the time is spent waiting, standing around until required. Rosencrantz and Guildenstern knew the drill. Captains and kings from Ethelred to Elvis have all had their attendant lords, their retinue, their hangers on. To say nothing of politicians. Edward VII once upended a glass of champagne over one of his courtiers in a moment of *joie de vivre*. The man didn't move a muscle. Just stood there as the champagne flowed down his waistcoat, murmuring, "As your Majesty pleases."'

'Pathetic.'

'Yes. But well disciplined.'

The meanest-looking dog in the world bounded around the side of the pink fish van. Each rib showed beneath the pelt, every bone was visible. Long silky brown ears hung like cap flaps either side of its yelping, demented-looking face.

'Shuddup,' roared a voice.

The dog turned and slunk shuddering to the man's side. A hand dropped to its head for a second.

'OK, Spike. OK. What are you two doing here?'

'Waiting,' said Violet.

The man ignored her, turned to Manders. 'So?'

'Mr Carew is inside waiting to see you,' he said. 'This is Violet Redpath. Fred Manders.'

'So what are you doing here?'

'As Violet said, waiting.'

'I'll just tie the dog up then. C'mon Spike.'

Violet lay down on the grass. 'Good, I can do without Spike.'

Freddy sat beside her. 'It's wet.'

'My Aunt Doff says all that's for the birds. You don't get chills from grass, piles from concrete, lockjaw from cuts at the base of the thumb, or colds from the guy you sleep with. She had this theory: there are round germs and square germs, nothing more nor less. She wouldn't accept that "You gave me your cold" stuff. She said it showed lack of enterprise. Why didn't you go out and get your own if you were hell bent on being sick? Her only exceptions were TB because of Keats, and leprosy because of Father Damien. Otherwise you were on your own. Sickness was a failure of nerve and not to be pandered to.'

'A Christian Scientist?'

'Not at all, but I knew that girls could do anything by the time I was three.'

'So Aunt Doff has never felt the need for extraterrestrial guidance?'

'She has nothing against it. In fact I think she has more faith in the extraterrestrial than the terrestrial. She says there's too much of the terrestrial sort about. Everything from misfortune to bloody bad luck to deepest tragedy, some expert can be wheeled in to provide counselling. Crash a train, fail matrimony, lose a job, face a death – "The survivors are receiving counselling."'

She leaned towards him, more earnest than he had seen her, more intent. 'Don't they understand, these people, the counsellors, the counselled. It's like houses. Do you own a house?'

'Yes.'

'I don't, but I can imagine. Say suddenly, somewhere in your house a leak develops. It gets worse, it won't go away. You consult experts, you ask friends, they sympathise and go away, experts come to get to the bottom of it. But all the time, you see, it's your leak. It's not their leak, no matter how much you pay them to fix it. They take their money and go away home to their own leak-free house and forget yours, and why not. It doesn't haunt them. It's not *theirs*.'

'That's one of the attractions of flatmates, family, lovers, whoever. They don't attempt to counsel. They don't have to. They know what it's like. And the same with grief, I reckon.'

'Dr Johnson said no man ever lost a night's sleep from concern for another man.'

'Mm. Unless you love them.'

Freddy picked a blade of grass, put it between his thumbs and blew a loud squelching squawk. 'Did your aunt live with you?'

'Mum and I lived with her. Dad was killed in a car crash with the occupation force in Japan. Yeah, bad luck, wasn't it, right at the end or rather after the end. Mum sort of gave up – well, she didn't because she had to work, she was a dentist's receptionist for a thousand years. She didn't have much fun. She was in love with the pink pig, I think now, but maybe I'm just making that up. You know how you do.' She grinned at him. 'You don't want to hear all this.'

Manders considered, was surprised to find that he did. Violet Redpath appeared to him not to have a worry in the world, let alone any psychological hang-ups. You can never know, she could be quaking like the rest of us, but it seemed unlikely. He looked at her: her bright eyes, her frankness, her cheerful acceptance of a compulsory weekend in the company of a man she had little reason to like, who had declined to act collegiately in her attempted sabotage of the thing. And yet this balance, this calm acceptance of rough and smooth, this goddamn sunniness had come from a fatherless childhood, a hard-pressed mother and little money.

'Tell me about Aunt Doff. What did she do?'

'She was much older than Mum, a chiropractor. "The oldest manipulator in the business," she said. No, she would take too long. I'll leave her for now.'

And what would she tell him, anyway? Doff, happy as a sandboy in old jeans and a purple polka-dot hat, fishing from Queen's Wharf with the regulars, her bait stinking and her absorption complete. Doff demonstrating to her nearly thirty years ago how to stand on her head, how to swing herself along the parallel bars in the playground: 'Like this. Hand tight and swing, tight and swing. And again, tight and swing. Well done.'

Such memories made her sound eccentric in the extreme, if not slightly nuts. Doff had to be experienced.

'Is she still with us?' he asked.

'Oh heavens yes. I wanted to give her a parachute jump for her eightieth birthday, one of those piggyback ones, but Mum vetoed that.'

Violet lay down and closed her eyes.

Manders watched her. She seemed to be good at dropping off.

7

The sharemilker was a tall spare man with disconcertingly blue eyes.

Hamish put out his hand. 'Hamish Carew.'

'Bronson Foster. Sit down, Mr Carew, sit down. Thanks for coming down.' He dropped on to the armless sofa opposite Hamish and stared at his employer in silence.

Hamish sat wondering how to start. Perhaps the first sentence might not be the moment to begin his diatribe about pollution. The moustachioed cowboy in the poster glared down at him. Hamish dropped his eyes, picked up the wedding photograph.

'Is this you?'

One side of the dour mouth lifted. 'Who else?' Foster took the photograph from Hamish and tossed it upside down on the sofa beside him. 'The only thing missing in that photo is the shotgun.'

'You're married then?'

Bronson thought about it. Finally he lifted a hand and rocked it from side to side without comment.

This was getting ridiculous.

'Well now, Bron, I've come down to . . .'

'Who called me Bron?'

'My daughter.'

Silence. Total silence. Finally the head lifted, the blue eyes stared. 'Anything in particular you want to see me about?'

Hamish cleared his throat. 'Yes, I'm not happy with the shambles in your back yard. Those cars.'

'What about them?'

'They're an eyesore. You've got a complete car wrecker's dump out there *and* it's visible from the road. I've come to tell you straight away, I won't allow it.'

'Who says they're an eyesore?'

'I do. This a very green area round here. Green and prosperous. Racing stables. Prime herds. Breeders galore. Look at the fuss they go to to achieve eye appeal from the road, especially the racing boys. Brick columns, names of famous sires, fancy gates. Appearances are important round here. These people are my constituents and all of them will object and rightly so. They won't stand it for a minute. Not from anyone they wouldn't, let alone their local member.'

'So you're just fussed about a few votes.'

'Of course I'm fussed about votes. MPs are paid to fuss about votes. But that's not the main point as far as I'm concerned.'

Hamish leaned forward, a large man in woollen working pants, a man to be reckoned with.

'I will *not* allow that pile of junk on my farm. All of it,' cried Hamish, 'will have to go.'

'I live here,' said Bronson.

'And I own the land.'

The man was on his feet. 'I'm a trained mechanic. It's a sideline, see? How else d'y'think I'm going to save enough to get my own herd before I'm half dead. I'm not going to be stuck here for ever, I'll tell you now, but I'll work my butt off while I am.'

He stopped suddenly.

'Forget it,' he said. 'Like to have a look round?'

'Yes,' said Hamish. 'Yes.'

Bronson Foster knew his stuff. He was knowledgeable about yield, butterfat content, health and hygiene in the shed. Marketing interested him. He showed Hamish his books in a shack out the back which he used as an office. Everything was meticulous, the desk tidy, the files to hand.

They moved in silence to the herringbone cowshed which was also in perfect condition. Hamish wondered how on earth the man managed without anyone to help. No wonder he looked exhausted.

As they made their way back to the cottage Bronson lifted a hand in the direction of the disembowelled cars.

'There's screens you can get now,' he said. 'Trellises and that, at garden shops. I could price them. Put them up.'

'And who pays?'

'You.'

'No,' said Hamish.

They turned the corner in silence. Fred Manders lay sprawled on his back across the front seat of the pink van, his legs hanging out the door and his mouth open. On his stomach lay a dirty fluffy-dice car mascot made from black and white sheepskin.

On the grass beside the Holden Violet slept with her head on her hands, a long diorama of innocence amongst the petals.

Bronson stopped short. 'Christ.'

'They're asleep,' said Hamish.

'Yeah. I can see that. Why?'

Difficult to answer. 'They're my personal assistants. Violet Redpath and Fred Manders.'

'I know their names. It's what they do for a crust gets me,' said Bronson. He dismissed the pair with a chuck of his head and turned to Hamish, his face stern, his eyes the same hectic blue as the plastic covers. 'I have to have the cars,' he said. 'If they go I go. Right?'

There was little chat as Hamish and his staff walked back to the house. A sense of unfinished business, a dereliction of unspecified duties hung in the bright air. None of them had done well.

'I'll give him a ring,' grunted Hamish as they turned in the gate. 'Tell him to come up after milking tomorrow morning. There are things to discuss. Not just the cars, I've dealt with that, but we must go through the books together, Bronson and Bobby and me. There are several things I must check on.'

'Presumably you won't require Violet and me then, Minister,' said Manders. 'Not for private business matters.'

'Well, that depends, Fred. Normally I would agree with you, but on the other hand, as I keep telling you, I want you to get a feel for the way I operate. This is why we're here together in an informal situation over the weekend. To meet on a more personal level, kick things around, get inside each other's heads and discover our particular strengths. If anything in the nature of private business crops up I'll ask you to leave.'

Manders and Violet nodded.

Molly was calm at the news of Bronson's visit, Bobby less so. She disappeared to her room straight after breakfast next morning and reappeared hours later, hair washed, face glowing, legs brown and smooth as a new-laid egg.

Impeded by Violet's assistance and hung about by pot plants,

Molly made muffins. Bobby was into pots and indoor plants. Mother-of-millions trailed from hanging pots at different levels. African violets sprang from the backs of ceramic pigs, hens and cows. Every corner of the kitchen held a container with a face either smiling or downcast. A pottery version of an old working boot sat on the top of the refrigerator half-hidden by the purple and green foliage of a well-grown coleus. Bobby worked on her pot plants. They were green, living things. They deserved her attention and got it.

Foster's progress up the track was watched by all.

The man looked like a stand-in for Henry Fonda in *The Grapes of Wrath*. Firm jawed, resolute, holding an unexpected briefcase, he strode up the hill to the house.

The sight of the gaunt figure breasting the rise irritated Hamish. This was a smiling land, a land literally flowing with milk and honey. The man had no right to look so defeated. He, Hamish, never had. Admittedly he had inherited the farm from his father, but even so.

Molly moved forward. 'Good morning,' she said, stepping on to the verandah with outstretched hand. 'How nice to meet you, Bronson. I'm Molly Carew.'

Foster stood at the bottom of the wooden steps, stared at her for some time, then put out a hand. 'Hi.'

Bobby, all bright eyes and coral lipstick, called from inside. 'Come in, come in. What're you all doing standing out there like spare lemons? Why don't you ask him in, Mum?'

Bronson came in, sat down on the sofa and stared at his large and beautiful hands.

Violet stared at him. She had wondered about him yesterday but his reappearance as man-from-nowhere-climbs-hill-to-homestead confirmed her first impression. Tall, lean and very possibly mean, the man was the sexiest thing she had seen in years. Those eyes, for God's sake, that limber strength. The man was dripping with it.

81

She pressed her lips together briefly to make sure they were not hanging open, sat on a straight-backed chair at some distance from the sharemilker and the Carews, and crossed her legs with care.

Seated in a nearby chair, Manders gave her a broad wink. Violet ignored him, recrossed her legs and stared harder. You don't often get the chance to see a sensational-looking male from an unobserved vantage point except at the local pool, and then most of them are more excited about their swimmer's build than you are. And the same at the beach.

A good unobserved perv at a fine specimen of a male or female never did anyone any harm. The surprising thing is how few good ones there are. She had noticed this at the women's changing rooms. Too short, too tall, too squat, too skinny, breasts which scarcely existed or sagged or seemed inflated to danger point. The list was endless. So many imperfections to be eked out by forgiving eyes.

She glanced at Freddy who was still grinning at her. Nice grin when he wasn't biting your head off.

Bobby, smiling radiantly, plonked herself beside the sharemilker. Her hands moved, clutched the rounded end of the sofa as though she were in imminent danger of being blown from the room.

'Tea everyone?' said Molly, and headed for the kitchen followed by Violet. She picked up the tray from alongside a mother-in-law's-tongue in a duck pot and sailed back.

Bronson, surrounded by files, sat between Bobby and Hamish. Freddy was attempting an intelligent interest in the long-range weather forecast being revealed by Bronson. Rain was predicted, he told them, and believe it or not they could do with it.

He moved on to graphs, run-downs of figures, averages, lows and highs. All were meticulously recorded.

Hamish was puzzled. 'You have your own electric typewriter, do you?'

'Me? No, but Bobby lets me use your one for yields and that, don't you Bob?'

'Yeah,' breathed Bobby.

Discussions continued. Audits were produced. Sheet after sheet explained, invoices cleared and graphs examined once again.

'My aim,' said Bronson, 'is to increase the yield of the herd by twenty percent in five years. And I can do it. I know I can do it.'

'He will too,' said Bobby.

'Apart from anything else,' continued Bron without a glance, 'I like cows and they know that.' He sat silent for a moment, considering his comment, then lifted his head. 'It's important, that. Very important.'

'I adore them,' said Bobby.

Molly glanced at her daughter but said nothing.

Freddy, who had been wondering who it was who had defined hell as endless boredom, came to. 'Mrs Carew likes all animals,' he offered.

Molly smiled. 'But especially cows.'

Bronson slapped a hand on his jeans. 'I knew it, I can always tell.' He turned to his previously invisible hostess. 'They've all got different personalities, haven't they?'

'They certainly have,' said Molly. 'And all their tricks: the kickers, the ones who won't let down their milk, the stubborn devils. But most cows, good cows that have been well treated, have lovely natures. They're no fools either. They know if you don't like them. Hamish had a woman in once to help when I was sick and the yield dropped overnight.'

'That's it exactly,' cried Bronson. 'Right on the button. There's a lot of research coming through now about music in the sheds, stuff you wouldn't believe. I could go on for hours about it. Bobby's good at listening. Aren't you, mate?'

Bobby gave a light laugh. 'That's enough business for now, Bron. Let's get on to my shopping list.'

Violet and Fred, straight backed and unblinking as seated Pharaohs, stared straight ahead.

'I've put a lot of time into it,' continued Bobby. 'It's idiotic how people hit those vast shopping centres without a clue or any sort of planning beforehand. It's not like here where you can suss the place out in half an hour. It's the sheer size of them. You've got to compare prices, be organised. Like you, Bron. The trick is to know what you want and go for it. In those places you could be lost for ever.'

Bobby gave details of her research. She had consulted *Consumer* for whiteware and hairdryers, and made notes. She had checked out the glossies and the travel brochures. 'And don't forget to bargain, Mum.'

'I don't bargain,' said Molly.

'But you must. They'll see you coming. And besides, they love it. It's a game with them. Everyone knows that.'

Violet stirred. 'Not in the larger stores, I understand,' she murmured.

'And your mother has asked for as little shopping time as possible,' said Hamish.

Bobby laughed. 'Well you'll just have to run like a rigger when you get the chance, won't you, Ma?'

'I don't mind shopping for other people,' said Molly. 'But I don't think this is the time to be discussing your shopping lists, Bobby. I mean ...' *Later*, she mouthed, with one of those idiotic head movements with which foolish mothers make doomed attempts to deflect crassness in adult offspring.

'What's wrong?' said Bobby.

Bronson began packing his briefcase, stowing each document with tidy despatch. 'I'll be getting along then, thanks Mrs Carew.'

Bobby jumped to her feet. 'I'll come with you. I'll pick up that casserole dish of mine you're still sitting on.'

Molly watched their departure, her hand gripping the French door jamb.

Violet turned to Freddy, gulped.

Action was required and quickly. 'Come for a walk, Violet,' Freddy cried.

She shook her head. 'Dishes.'

'Bugger the dishes. Exit staff. Now.'

They heard Molly's voice as they left.

'Hamish?'

'Yes?'

'Come on,' said Freddy, increasing their speed.

'Hamish, is that man married?'

Freddy shut the kitchen door.

Hamish yawned, stretched his arms high and dropped them. 'Why on earth?'

'Married? Is he?'

'Er, yes. More or less, I gathered.'

'Then he must go.'

'Nonsense. I've dealt with the car-wrecking business. Quite simple really. I just told him to put up a screen, and smartly.'

'Bobby is in love with him.'

'He's only been here a month!' Hamish laughed. He looked at his wife's stricken face. 'Wake up, Mol,' he said, patting her knee, 'times have changed. Besides, Bobby's a grown woman. Pushing thirty, isn't she?'

'Last birthday,' muttered Molly.

'Well, there you are. Thirty last birthday and she's got her head screwed on and always has had, you know that. Bobby won't get herself in a mess. Never has and never will. Forget it,' he advised, sinking back into his wide chair.

'The man is married,' cried Molly. She began slapping the remains of the tea party on to the tray, piling cups busily, recklessly and at precarious angles. 'He may well have children. Will you speak to her or shall I?'

'She's thirty, for God's sake. I'm certainly not going to. So what if the man had a wife. She probably threw him out.'

'Then I will.'

85

'Good.'

Decisions made. Hamish tried safer topics. 'I think the weekend's panning out very well, don't you? The shake-down cruise?'

'I am not interested in your shake-down cruise,' said Molly, stumping out of the kitchen with its excess of verdant life. There was silence followed by the crash of falling crockery.

Hamish rose from his chair with a sigh and went to help.

8

Hong Kong. Ah yes, Hong Kong. So far so good in Hong Kong. The Minister and his handlers were currently in conference at the New Zealand Consulate. Molly and Violet, on the other hand, were at leisure. Sunk in the comfort of gold plush, they waited in the lobby of the New Mandarin for Ms Cushla Leary from the office to escort them to the Lan Lan Good Luck Downtown Emporium to break the back of Bobby's shopping list.

Like everything in the New Mandarin, the lobby was large. Space was everywhere and in everything; in the acres of marble beneath their feet, the mile-high walls and the enormous central glass dome with its constellation of lights pouring down on to the largest arrangement of fresh white orchids ever seen.

Reception, Reception, Reception, murmured small signs along the sweep of polished teak counter staffed by smooth-faced men and women. There were few queues, no rush, and plenty of space for all. The wealthy and the celebrated, the pop stars and the drug dealers, the truly good and the sleaze with style could all be accommodated and made welcome at the New Mandarin.

'I suppose they have to keep up,' said Molly, 'but it's just like the old Mandarin only bigger. Yes. It seemed a good idea, or did last night, to get on to Bobby's list straight away. That will be something done.' She looked upwards. 'Would you call those things chandeliers?'

'More like frozen dandelions,' said Violet. 'The Alamein Fountain in lights, upside down and twice as large. It weighs three tonnes and cost three million HK dollars. It says so in the brochure.'

She watched the two-tone glass gondola of the lift. Like an anti-flu capsule in motion, it got on with its job, soothing and calming on descent, ascending to lift the spirit. Josie, a former flatmate, prone to colds and chesty with it, had sworn by Coldrex. When in doubt she took two.

And now she is pregnant and I must get a present for the baby.

Molly thought about Bobby.

She had reappeared at the house after some time on that terrible morning. Molly heard her first, belting out one of her favourite weepies.

> . . . and there runs Mary,
> Hair of gold and lips like cherries.
> It's good to touch
> The green, green grass of home.

Cradling the red casserole dish in her arms she swung up the rise as Molly watched, her mind churning.

Bobby had had lovers before. She had that easy, teasing opportunism that goes with a keen awareness of the pleasures of life. Molly had reacted the first time with nervous calm. Obviously sexual mores had been reinvented by the advent of the Pill. She had tried to discuss the question with her daughter.

'Get real, Mum,' Bobby had said, flinging back her head to laugh. 'It's the seventies, for God's sake.'

So they had come and gone, these male friends. Bobby could be said to have played the field and kept her head. She was, as she said, a free agent. Molly had been pleased by her return to the farm. Like her, Bobby was a country girl at heart, and it would be nice if she married a farmer eventually.

But this affair was different. Some seismic jolt seemed to have transformed her. Molly had sensed something as Bobby danced down the back steps to greet them. She had been illuminated from within.

And the man was married. This must be discussed.

'Hi,' called Bobby from the back door. 'What did you think of Bron? Isn't he something?'

'He's married, isn't he?'

Bobby's glowing face froze. She stood still for a moment, then exploded. 'God, you would pick on that. I might've known you'd get it all wrong, try and mess everything up. You've done it all my life, never been interested, never cared, never . . .'

'Bobby.'

'Dad's the one who loves me, wants me to be happy. Not you. Never you. Well get this. Bron and I adore each other, have from the moment we set eyes on each other, and I don't give a damn what you think. I love him.'

Molly moved towards her. 'Bobby dear, I . . .'

Bobby clutched the red casserole to her like a shield. 'Don't you dare come near me, you silly old . . .' She swung around and came face to face with Violet and Manders standing rigid behind her.

Bobby gave a gasping yelp, shoved the casserole into Violet's hands and ran.

'Bobby is a little upset,' said Molly, relieving her of the casserole. 'Did you have a nice walk?'

Cushla Leary arrived eventually, in raspberry linen and without apology, her gilt-framed dark glasses high in her hair and her speech difficult to understand. She made the sounds required, you could hear them coming, but then something seemed to munch the vowels. Molly and Violet gathered, once they had learned how to listen, that Cushla means 'pulse of my heart' in Irish, that Cushla was an ace shopper because she was decisive and knew the best places, and where did they want to go first?

Molly produced the list. Ms Leary sank on to gold to check it out.

BOBBY'S LIST

N.B. BUY LARGEST SIZE AVAILABLE IN EVERYTHING. XL is 14 at most, Linda says.

1. 3 pairs satin pyjamas. 1 blue, 1 pink, 1 oyster. Real satin, not that slimy yuck.
2. 3 satin camisoles. Oyster, black, navy. Must be embroidered. You can pick them up anywhere Linda says.
3. Bead-work embroidered Cashmere jerseys. Biggest in the shop remember, and not too much bead-work. Go for restraint. Linda has two beauts. I want powder blue and black (the high-necked jacket sort, just the black). Cheap as dirt in the market Linda says. Don't just get the first thing you see.
4. A microwave which browns.
5. Pearls. Hong Kong's best Linda says. The bigger the pearls the better the buy. Earrings to match – pierced ears.

After some time Ms Leary rose to her feet. 'And what do you want?' she asked Molly.

Molly stood. 'Nothing, thank you.'

Violet tightened her folded arms. Mrs Carew had made her point, had indicated with courtesy both her boredom and her displeasure. You could learn from this woman. Look how she had picked up the pieces after Bobby's outburst at the farm.

'I think we should go first to the Lan Lan Good Luck Downtown Emporium,' continued Cushla. 'That's one of the more upmarket of the big stores.'

'Yes,' said Molly. 'I see that on the programme, but my daughter said I would get the best value at the markets.'

'Oh. We can't go to the markets. The Consulate wouldn't allow it. Security for one thing. Protocol. The driver wouldn't have a bar of it.'

Molly looked at her thoughtfully, her face serene. 'Good,' she said. 'That suits me beautifully. Shall we go?'

Cushla led them at a fast clip across floor after floor of polished space, past legions of stands of competing Brand Names, past belt racks, handbags in excess and scarves by the yard. Violet picked up a brand-name gold-lidded pot labelled Nutrition Bio-Protein Moisture Complex.

'What does it do?' she asked the attendant.

'Do, madam?' The gleaming lips smiled. 'It is for the skin, it is restorative. Every day our skin is changing. Protein leaches out of the cells from the skin itself, and the cells of the skin begin to lose their elasticity, ma'am, and the face begins to sag. Wrinkle,' she said, peering at Violet. 'So soon and such a shame. Protein must be replaced by bio-proteins and thus a beautiful smooth skin is maintained and so easy.'

'And so expensive.'

'Ah, ma'am, but so important.' The chanting stopped, the young woman meant every word. 'Where would we be, ma'am, without our beauty.'

Cushla whipped the straggler into line. Sharp eyed as a shepherd eyeing culls, she herded them on to an escalator which rolled upwards at unexpected speed and flung them off at Lingerie.

Mrs Carew, as expected, was hopeless. She kept drifting away from the froth of pastel silks and satin briefs which the young saleswoman piled on to the counter. Occasionally she picked up a wisp of pale blue or ivory but dropped it quickly. 'They're so, so . . . feminine,' she murmured, edging towards a rack of reassuringly dowdy dressing gowns. 'Cosy,' she said, stroking them. 'So cosy. We have all the time we want, do we not, Ms Leary? Why don't you choose for Bobby and I'll have a look around.' She dropped on to a high-legged pink satin chair and looked at her right leg with mild interest. 'A ladder already. Oh well,' she said.

Ms Leary was up to the task in hand. She chose the garments with speed and ticked Bobby's list decisively. She finished her assignment in forty-five minutes and looked for her flock. Violet was inspecting thong knickers and interesting bras. Molly was deep in a rack of striped rayon pyjamas.

'Would you like to inspect my choice?' asked Cushla.

Molly, pleased by decision in a situation which would normally have reduced her to pulp, agreed to everything and was lavish with her praise.

'Now what?' she asked.

'Pearls,' said Cushla. 'I know a good man on the pearl counter.'

'Pearls,' said Molly, her vicarious sense of achievement melting at the thought. Even Cushla could scarcely choose pearls without her assistance.

Violet, who had decided that Cushla was a pain in the neck and where did she get her clothes, was silent. *Pearls*. Pearls would take for ever. The thought of Molly plus pearls plus choice appalled her.

Molly smiled at her. 'There's no necessity for you to come

with us, Violet. Unless you'd like to, of course.'

'Thank you, Mrs Carew,' said Violet. 'But I think I should stay with you. It's on the programme? Look: "accompanied by Ms Redpath and Ms Leary".'

'I think, Violet, that I shall be quite safe with Ms Leary,' said Molly.

This was so transparently obvious there seemed little point in begging for permission to remain. 'Thank you,' Violet said, 'I do have a few things to catch up on. Let's check the rest of the programme, shall we. "Dinner at the Consulate tonight; seven thirty for eight" – so there's plenty of time. I'll see you back at the hotel. Thank you again.' She resisted the temptation to prance, dance or hop on one leg to the nearest escalator.

First she would find a gift for Josie's unborn child. Something soft and soothing. Nothing that banged or rattled or whizzed. A bear probably. Bears are always welcome.

The Toy Department in the basement had opted for quantity rather than quality. Gone was the wide spacious grandeur of the upper floors, the huge urns filled with barrowloads of orchids, the shimmering glass counters and the scented air. The drama and enticements of multiplying mirrors were not needed here. No neatly dressed personnel roamed attentive and anxious to assist. Glum-looking men and women waited at their checkouts. Slam, bang, who's next. Soft toys sell themselves; no charm was required, or offered.

Violet chose a brown bear. She inspected its expression, checked for safe eyes, buried her face in its false fur and lifted her head to see Freddy Manders standing with a white one under his arm. A mean cross-eyed sharp-nosed thing with short acrylic fur and a red ribbon.

'Yours is too prickly,' she said, holding out her choice. 'Try this one.'

'I see what you mean.'

'And its eyes are lethal. It depends who it's for, of course. Is it for comfort or for show?'

'It's for Owen Spencer's new one.'

'Those eyes will be swallowed in a flash. You have to check.' She upended the dud and pointed at the label: *Not safe for children under four.*

'How insane. Who else would want one?'

'The whole world, haven't you noticed. Penguins too, though the beaks are not so good. Apparently it's easier to raise money for penguins than people. And guide dogs rather than the blind.'

'Mrs Carew thinks we should save the ugly animals as well,' he said. 'Who's yours for?'

'My ex-flatmate's pregnant.'

Something lightened, lifted his heart. 'Good,' he said.

'Why?'

'I thought it might be for you. Some people collect them.'

'Do you *mind*.'

'Bridget did.'

'Oh,' said Violet nervously. 'Oh well.'

'Find me a safe bear and I'll shout you lunch at a weird Chinese place I know.'

'OK.' She inspected a few bears and handed him a fawn one.

'Thanks.'

'You've got a Mickey Mouse watch,' she said.

'Yes,' he said. 'Do you like it?'

Hard to say. She looked at the frenetic figure waggling and jigging on Manders' wrist. He seemed an unlikely buyer of cute kitsch.

'Its unexpected,' she said, 'on you.'

'I'm just giving it an airing. It's for my nephew but I want to make sure it doesn't go phut within days.'

'He's a case in point,' she said, pointing at Mickey's flattened face, 'of what I was saying. When Disney first drew him he had a long snout and small ears and eyes. However, research showed snub noses and big eyes and ears are more appealing.

Like babies, puppies, all helpless young. Even penguin chicks have cute little beaks. Cunning, isn't it?'

There she goes, he thought, wondering again if she had an informed intelligence or a scrapbag of useless information behind those dark eyes. Both probably. They are not necessarily contra-indicative.

'Why are you not working?' she said.

'Golf. And you?'

'Pearls. Cushla Leary's in charge.'

'Ah, Cushla the Pushla.'

Violet grinned. There is something warming about derogatory nicknames for colleagues you don't like.

'It's chemistry,' she explained. 'Like I said the other day. Also she's an ace shopper and that's a problem. We'd like to think we're not interested in all that getting and spending and laying waste our days stuff, but deep down we know we're no good at it. Haven't the required skills, wouldn't pass the physical. That's depressing for a start, let alone missing out on all that *fun*. I did see something nice this morning, though,' she said thoughtfully. 'A bra with holes for nipples. Have you ever seen one?'

At his suggestion he and Bridget had hunted Paris for one, on the condition that he asked for the thing. Weak kneed with laughter, they had found one eventually, but she had refused to wear it.

'Yes,' he said.

Surprised by his flat tone, she dipped her head.

The nape of her neck was white and vulnerable as a geisha's.

They sat side by side as the cable car ascended the near-vertical slope. The seat was too small for them, their knees jackknifed, their buttocks were pressed tight. There was no escape except by standing, which neither attempted. They would soon be sweating cheek to cheek, which would be interesting. He stared at her profile as she concentrated on the city below, above and all around them, at huts and car ports and houses cantilevered out from the hill, burrowed into the rock or suspended God knows how. There was not a yard between buildings, and little sign of life. He felt suddenly euphoric, pleased with the journey and the shape of her face.

Wary as a voyeur, he stared at her. A bright woman lacking in judgement, or a capable friendly one? Probably both, once more. Besides, look at that nose, that perfect little nose. He liked her nose.

'What on earth's sticking into me,' she said suddenly.

'What? Oh, sorry. It's my brick.'

He gave what he hoped was a sophisticated chuckle and, with difficulty, inserted a hand into his trouser pocket.

She stiffened, high-rumped. 'Your what?'

He was still groping against her. He tried to stand but gave up. The thought of the possible squelching on release put him off. Violet, now red faced and angry, slipped into the aisle at the same moment as he produced his walkie-talkie.

'My brick,' he said, waving it for verification.

'Why on earth do you call it that?'

'The Yanks started it. They're a bind and a drag, walkie-talkies, *but they give status*. They made that clear to me, even a guy who was mulching his vegetable garden in Hawaii when it rang. Carew can now get me at any hour of the twenty-four. I am brickworthy, necessary, one of the big shits. Temporarily, of course, ASEAN duties only.'

'Good God.'

He took a strand of her hair between his fingers and looked at it. 'Yes,' he said.

Two men carrying ladders appeared, ran up eight floors of zig-zag fire escape on a nearby building, leaned their ladders against the wall and lay down.

'If they had had a brick,' said Violet, 'they might not have been able to have a rest.'

'Exactly.'

The man clipped their tickets at the station and bowed. 'This way,' said Manders, heading off towards a shed-like building labelled *First Boston Chinese* in red Gothic script. The views, if you had a head for heights, were superb. If not, the only solution would be to crouch beside the large tank of edible fish at the entrance and crawl to your table on hands and knees.

Small white-covered tables overlaid with transparent plastic huddled close together, strong clips at each side ensuring the arrangement remained in place. On each table sat a small brass vase containing three stalks of artificial lily of the valley. Above their heads yards of white nylon looped and ruched and festooned around the ceiling, adorned at regular intervals with large red velvet bows. Each corner had two extra-large bows with trailing silk ribbons.

'This is when I tell you how the Peking duck is worth the trip,' said Freddy, 'but I just like the place.'

Wisps of hair lifted in the breeze. 'Why fuss? You like it, you ask me, I come. My decision. Besides, if you really had been fussed you wouldn't have asked me and I would have missed this fantastic place,' she said, looking at the gallant attempts to create glamour, style and grace in a tin shed clinging to a ledge half way up a mountain in Hong Kong.

She leaned towards him, her hands circling the brass vase. 'That's typical of us, isn't it. We talk such crap. Like parents saying they don't want to be a nuisance to their children when they are old. Who else are they going to be a nuisance to if not their children?'

He was getting used to her jump-cuts. 'I don't agree. They don't want to be a nuisance to anyone. They want to snuff it tidily, in bed, sliding from the stool in a pub, dropping dead while the egg boils. That seems a perfectly valid hope to me.'

'Does it? I find it rather a let-down, not being a nuisance to anyone. Not ever.'

She took a piece of lily of the valley from the vase and blew dust from it.

'Did you wear a wedding ring,' she said, 'when Bridget was with you?'

He flung himself back against the rickety little chair. Christ Almighty. The woman was not even house-trained.

'No,' he said.

She handed him the spray of green-covered wire with greyish white bells, stared at one as it fell off.

'I'm sorry,' she said, 'I've hurt your feelings.'

'Hurt my feelings! You sound like my sister. How on earth could you hurt my feelings?'

'I really am sorry, Manders.'

'Fred.'

'It's just that when I want to know, I ask.'

Which was obvious. There was no point in mentioning privacy, decency or even common sense. The woman was beyond redemption.

'You should go far in the Diplomatic Corps,' he said, picking up the tattered menu and putting it down quickly as he noticed the tremble in his hand. Her suggestion, her thought that he could be sitting up on the Peak wallowing in 'feelings', appalled him. What about the place, the view, the millions sweating beneath the view? What were they? Background, that was all, nothing but background for Fred Manders and his fucked-up feelings. The insides of his eyelids pricked with rage.

'What would you like to eat?' he asked bleakly.

She looked wretched.

Good.

She gave her order to the ancient waiter and sat silent.

On the flat roof of the apartment building below two men were dismantling corrugated iron tanks. He could see the sparks shooting off one man's skill-saw. The other man's wouldn't work. The searing heat on the roof, the rage and frustration of the small wiry figure in the black bandana were palpable even at this distance. The man put the thing down and kicked it long and hard.

Manders straightened himself.

Must stop. Will stop. Now.

He touched her hand. 'Read any good books lately?'

She smiled, not her normal quick flicker, a slower version as she nodded at a nearby table where a fragile-looking young Chinese woman in pale silk sat with a bearded older man. Scandinavian? German? Hard to tell. He was a large man, filling up so much more space, possessed of so much more authority, clout and size than his companion that Manders found himself thinking of giant wheels and white butterflies. White ones always seemed more fragile than others. No colour to buoy them up. The survivors on the raft of the Medusa told their rescuers they had seen clouds of fluttering white butterflies as they lay dying of thirst. He could tell Violet that useless gem, he thought sourly.

The man and woman sat smiling at each other. Hers was shy, his firm, a strong chomping smile. Between them sat a small machine like a tape recorder. The man spoke into the device and moved it to her. She touched the button, which presumably translated his message into Chinese. Her smile widened, she giggled, put up a hand to hide such indecorous mirth, pressed another button and typed her answer. Infinitely shy once more, she moved their conversational aid back to him. Again the button, again the burst of mirth and the giggling. His explosive roar filled the room, hung from red bows, sank into nylon.

The man seized both her hands and nodded vigorously. They could see his stomach shake, heave with laughter as he gazed at his little friend who had such delightful news to impart to him and the technical means whereby she could convey it.

'We need one of those,' said Violet.

'I can't see how it would help,' said Manders, 'unless we had something to say.'

99

She flinched, opened her mouth.

The brick rang. He jumped to his feet, held it to his ear. 'Manders.'

'Where the hell are you?' roared the voice. 'Get back here immediately. My wife has disappeared.'

'Sir?'

'You heard. Now.'

9

The lift swayed slightly as Manders and Violet swept up to the Plum Blossom Duplex. Manders' gut had been left flapping floors below.

Disappeared? How could she have disappeared? He could understand if she had been confused for a few moments in the maze of the Lan Lan Good Luck Emporium. Easy enough to do; in fact quite difficult to avoid unless you had a sharp eye and a well-honed sense of direction.

He saw Molly alone, sweating among multitudes, saw her blundering past ropes of pearls and hanks of golden chains, through ranks of costume jewellery and swathes of silk and shelves of plastic bonzai.

But Cushla had been in charge. Cushla of the steel-trap mind and twenty-twenty vision would have allowed a very short rein on anyone, let alone a Minister's wife. Ministers' wives do not get lost.

'I should have stayed, why didn't I stay?' said Violet, who had been virtually silent since they fled the restaurant.

'She'll be perfectly safe,' he snapped. 'There are guards everywhere. All she had to do was to make herself known, chat one up . . .'

'Yes, as long she didn't get outside. She's so hopelessly kind. She stopped to give money to a woman with a potbellied baby until the cops swept them out of the way.'

'Did she have her passport with her?'

'Oh, my God,' she said.

'Eighteen,' breathed a disembodied voice as the lift hissed to a stop. They fell out, tripping over each other as they ran. The guard at the door recognised Manders; Violet flashed her pass as they burst into the pastel luxury and tense atmosphere of the Duplex.

Hamish, Cushla and the New Zealand Consul General stood close together in what Molly had christened the Conversation Area – a zone of neutral ground between the bedrooms at either end, a place of pale green sofas and chairs, of glass tables and cane chairs with squabs and framed prints of plum trees flowering on mountains wreathed in mist. The serenity and calm of the decor hit you like the cool air conditioning. Only the people looked a mess.

Hamish's normal high colour had disappeared; his face had the pallor and texture of putty. Cushla looked like a waterlogged carpet. Gone were her organisational gifts, her shopping credentials, her attention to detail. If you poked a finger at her she would have squelched.

The New Zealand Consul General, Brian Nelligan, was telling the Minister about a rather nasty kidnap of an English woman which had occurred last month. Horrible thing, horrible.

The manager of the New Mandarin and a high-ranking official from the Lan Lan Emporium stood at a respectful distance. The manager bit a hangnail with a quick snap of his front teeth as they entered. Hong Kong could be confusing for strangers. He was aware of that.

'Where the hell've you been?' snapped Hamish.

'At the First Boston Chinese up the Peak,' said Manders. 'You did say, Minister, that I wouldn't be needed.'

'I know I did, but that didn't mean you could disappear up some bloody mountain. You should be on call, nearby. Both of you, both of you.' He turned to Violet. 'Why did you leave Mrs Carew like that? She trusted you, she wanted you to be part of the team. That's why you're here, to be at her side at all times.'

'She told me I could go and I went,' said Violet quietly.

'Yes. But you shouldn't have. She would have been thinking of you. How you might be bored or something. You know how her mind works. Frankly, I'm. Frankly I'm . . .' said Hamish, now striding about over silver-grey carpet. 'I'm disappointed. Very.'

Manders watched the man stoking his indignation at each step. Typical of the breed. Typical.

'Perhaps, Minister, if you could tell us what steps have already been taken . . .'

'I've got a headache,' mumbled Cushla.

'Headaches, headaches, we've all got headaches,' cried the Minister staring at Cushla as though he had momentarily forgotten who she was or what she was doing there. He had probably grilled the wretched child silly. 'Tell them,' he said.

Cushla did so. How they had been in pearls. How Mrs Carew seemed to fancy the little freshwater ones herself but her daughter wanted big ones and the man was getting out tray after tray after tray you know how they do to confuse you and Mrs Carew had just asked the price of a string and the calculator was clicking and she, Cushla, had just moved about two feet away to the black ones which she rather liked.

'And suddenly I heard the man cry out "Lady!", and I swung round and Mrs Carew had disappeared and I ran quick as a flash but she'd vanished, completely vanished, and the pearl man wouldn't help because of his trays, but he must have pressed an alarm. Masses of guards appeared and I rang the Residence immediately and then the police appeared.'

'Two feet,' she moaned, 'that's all. I thought she'd be there for hours. The man said he'd never seen anything like it. One minute she was peering and comparing prices and size and all that and the next minute she gave a cry and ran out of the boutique calling someone's name. The man didn't know the name. He really didn't, you could tell.'

Hamish Carew made a gigantic effort. 'Thank you, Ms Leary. Ms Redpath, please ring for a taxi back to the Consulate for Ms Leary.'

'I want to go home,' said Ms Leary.

'I suggest that you report to the Consulate before you do so,' said the Consul General.

Ms Leary departed.

Brian Nelligan and Mr Chan from the Lan Lan Emporium began speaking at once, bowed slightly and made conciliatory gestures. The Consul General carried on.

The Hong Kong Police had been informed instantly; the area around the Lan Lan had been thoroughly searched and was still being guarded. Last sightings were mentioned, new reports from witnesses. All the guards had been alerted, particularly those in the area of the pearl boutique. 'Nothing so far but it's early days – day, I should say,' said Brian Nelligan.

He turned to Mr Chan and asked him to put them in the picture once more for the benefit of the newcomers regarding managerial procedures in cases of this kind. 'Mrs Carew can't have been the only one . . .' His voice trailed off, he tugged the cuff of his linen jacket.

Mr Chan bowed once more and spoke cheerfully and at some length. He relayed anecdotes about previous middle-aged ladies who had been found stuck in lifts, locked in toilets, hidden beneath duvets. Anywhere. Everywhere. There was no knowing, he cried, his quick fingers scrabbling, springing apart in discoveries. One lady, from Iceland he believed, yes Iceland, had been found after closing time asleep on a Posturepedic Queen Size behind a Japanese screen. 'Always, they turn up. Always.'

He would spare them, he said, his smile fading, the story of the lady who had tampered with the mechanism of a Put-You-Up settee recently. 'That one was a horse of a very different colour.'

There was a knock on the door, movement, raised voices in the lobby. The security guard appeared, followed by a senior officer from the Hong Kong Police who strode in accompanied by three armed and uniformed young men who sprang to attention, then relaxed. But not entirely.

'Where've you been?' cried Hamish, grabbing the officer's hand as it descended from its snapping salute. 'It's hours since my wife disappeared. Hours.'

'We have been looking for your wife, sir,' said the officer. 'There are procedures to be put in place. We have put things in train. Now I am able to report in person.'

'Yes. Yes.'

'The Chief of Police sends his respects.'

'Thank you,' said Hamish, sweating with the effort of control, 'and mine, and mine. What is the *news*, man?'

The Senior Officer drew himself up to his full height. 'There is no news. No news at all, but everything is in train. Crime does not succeed in our country. We are the envy of the world in this and many other respects, as I'm sure you know, Minister.'

Hamish, on the verge of tears, nodded. Manders' and Violet's eyes met. She also looked agitated. Manders gave the smallest movement of his head. She turned away, ignored the attempted semaphore for calm.

The Senior Officer was still talking. 'We have a saying in our country Minister, "No news is good news." I have a joke. What did the reprieved man say to the warden?' He giggled slightly at the taut faces before him, snapped his heels together for the punchline. 'No noose is good noose,' he crowed.

From such small moments do disenchantments grow. Hamish and his team were appalled, all empathy and would-be gratitude blown away. They hated the man.

Nobody said anything. The Senior Officer was still chuckling.

A fire engine yahooed its way eighteen floors below. The uneaten sandwiches ordered an hour ago had sprung apart at the edges in the dry air. The manager of the New Mandarin ordered fresh ones.

'Eat them, eat them,' he begged the Minister on their arrival. 'And coffee, sir. Coffee.'

'Coffee?' said Hamish.

'See. It is already here,' said the manager.

'No, no, wait a minute, there's a bar. Does anyone want a drink?' Hamish leapt to his feet, squatted on his heels before the minuscule fridge. 'Brandy? Gin? No, no, I thought not. Still, there's fruit juice, fizzy stuff. Anyone want a . . . a . . . one of these things. Superintendent? Your men?'

The young policemen jumped backwards in fright, the Superintendent also declined, but the Minister, still on his heels, began snatching bright-coloured cans of juice and fizzy drinks from his store and throwing them about like a baby tossing toys from a pram.

Violet went to Hamish's aid, restacked the fridge, sat him down and gave him a glass of iced water.

Manders watched them without enthusiasm. How in the name of heaven do some men achieve it. Early in life they find their protector, someone to watch over them, to smooth the gritty surface of days while their partner got on with the tough stuff. They were the finders of lost objects these people, the buyers of underwear, the comforters.

These cherished men do not have to be brilliant though some have been. As a rule, however, they seem to be good-natured and reasonably pleasant about the home, devoted family men like Darwin, say, or Thomas Huxley. It might have seemed a fair trade-off for Victorian women. Or even Edwardian. Stephen Spender's wife, on their return from the honeymoon, picked up the coat he had thrown on the floor as usual, stowed it in its place without a word, and they lived happily ever after.

This again could be understood. It's the fact that such astonishments can still exist that is so weird.

Take Steve Roper's Daph, for example, who kept the children well and happy and out of his hair and the house reasonable and who worked part time for Statistics and still ran into town in her lunch hour to snap up balloon-seated shorts from the Kirkcaldies sale even though it was only a stone's throw from Steve's office.

Even if you paid for it, were in a position of authority, a big straw boss like Carew, you didn't always get this concern, this ministering. Yet look at Violet, an independent-minded woman if ever there was one. Any moment soon, he thought sourly, she will drop her hand on the man's shoulder, offer a little squeeze of comfort.

Manders swung away and joined Mr Chan and the members of the Hong Kong Police Force who were now eating newly made avocado and chicken sandwiches in preparation for what was beginning to look like a long haul. No help there.

He returned to the Minister and Violet. The Minister, recently fed and watered, looked faintly better.

'Sit down, Manders. Sit down.'

Manders dropped on to the green sofa beside them. The Minister and Violet clutched their coffee cups in silence.

Obviously something was expected. Freddy tried, though his offering was slight. 'The evidence of the manager of the pearl boutique was reassuring I felt, Minister.'

'In what way?'

'His evidence, as repeated by Ms Leary, "Mrs Carew glanced up, gave a sharp cry and ran, calling someone's name." This must mean that she recognised someone, dropped the pearls and ran after her or him. A friend, surely. Someone she was anxious to see.'

'Who?'

'I don't know but the fact that she was greeting someone ...'

The Senior Officer appeared with his radio telephone.

'What news?' cried Hamish.

'No news. No news is what I have to say. None.'

The Consul General appeared at the Minister's side. He and Manders shook hands and eyed each other warily. Freddy noticed with a flick of pleasure that Brian Nelligan, only six years senior to him and at one time considered a man to watch, now wore the slight perpetual frown of someone competent enough but in need of stiffening. The man was a fusser, known to his staff as Shy Nellie.

'Am I interrupting?' he asked.

No answer.

'An important meeting, rather tricky one with the ...' The Consul General leaned to whisper in the Minister's ear. 'Obviously can't be put off.' The man was becoming pinker, more fervent in his apologies by the minute.

Hamish sat staring straight ahead. Suddenly his hand flapped. 'Go, go, go!'

Nelligan went. Silence resumed.

It was broken eventually by the reappearance of the excited security guard, his smile pumpkin wide as he ushered in the wife of the Minister of Culture and Trade.

'Good afternoon,' cried Molly, making wide-armed gestures around the room. 'I'm Molly Carew.'

Reactions varied. Violet ran to embrace her, the manager of the New Mandarin and Mr Chan from the Lan Lan gave little whoops of satisfaction and pleasure. The members of the Hong Kong Police Force looked surprised.

Only the Minister remained seated.

'Where in God's name have you been? The whole place, the police, the Consul, all these these . . .' Words failed him. He stood and held out his arms.

Molly walked into them. 'I do hope you haven't been worried.'

'Where *were* you!'

'Not now, dear, not now.'

He peered at her. 'Your hair's a mess.'

She touched her head. 'Is it?' she said, putting out the other hand to Violet in an unconscious gesture which quickened Manders' heart. He couldn't take his eyes off Mrs Carew's dishevelled dignity. Her presence.

'I do apologise, gentlemen, for wasting so much of your time,' she said. 'Thank you all so much. Perhaps you might like to go now?' She turned to Hamish, still smiling. 'We have time to relax before our next engagement, don't we?'

He turned to her as the door shut. 'Don't ever do that again,' he said. 'Ever.'

'Very well,' said Molly, her voice muffled by the dress she was pulling off over her head. She looked at the crumpled thing with disgust. 'They told me this stuff *breathed*.'

'Why didn't you ring the Consulate?' he said.

'I meant to but it was all so moving I forgot.'

'You can't just *forget*.'

'I did.'

Hamish took off his tie, his tight shoes and hot jacket, and lay on the bed beside her, watching beneath lowered lids. He would never tell her the real reason for his alarm at her absence. That would be unkind. The fact that she was hopeless and completely inept without him would remain unsaid.

'I'll tell you about it later,' she said.

Hamish's eyes closed. 'Gooth,' he breathed. 'Gooth.'

'Violet,' said Molly next morning as the lift sighed downwards. 'What happened to the shopping?'

'Cushla gave it to me. I should have brought it to your room.'

'No, no. There's still the pearls though. Quite a lot more things I suppose. Did she give you the list?'

'Yes.'

'What a pity,' said Molly. She looked unwell. Her usually clear eyes were puffy, her lips tight.

'Did you sleep well, Mrs Carew?' asked Violet.

'No,' said Molly.

The silence lasted till the lift doors opened, and continued until they sat sipping fresh orange in the Harbour Bar Cafe for Speedy Service.

Molly stared at the display of fresh fruit on the serving table, at the exuberance of shapes and colours, the limpid green and coral melons, the cool sliced pineapples, golden pawpaws and pink citrus, and something dark, crinkled, and unknown.

'So many decisions,' she said.

Violet untangled herself from the cane legs of her chair. 'Let's just have a go, shall we? Try the lot.'

'Yes,' said Molly, not moving. 'Violet, I wonder if you would mind if I told you something. Something rather odd. I don't want to burden you with anything of course.'

'Burden?'

'Not burden exactly. There's probably a better word. In confidence, I mean. May I speak to you in confidence?'

Bobby and the hunk, thought Violet. Oh hell.

'Of course,' she said, 'now or later?'

'Now.'

'Tell me.'

10

'So different when freshly squeezed,' said Molly, downing the last of her juice. She smoothed her napkin and looked up.

'How well do you know Freddy Manders?' she asked.

Somewhere inside something clenched. Gut, groin, somewhere. 'Not well at all,' said Violet. 'Why do you ask?'

'You know he's married?'

'Separated,' said Violet. What on earth was the woman on about?

'Did you know Bridget?'

'Yes. I've worked with her.'

'Oh good,' said Molly. 'That will make things a lot easier. She's a wonderful person, isn't she?'

A strange easing descended on Violet, slackened her shoulders and slipped down her back. There was no more tension, just concentration as she thought of her reply. Was Bridget Manders a wonderful person, that was the question. A few weeks ago Violet herself had described her more or less in those terms. To Freddy of all people. She saw Bridget at her desk: pleasant, competent, helpful with the returns. And now this good woman had departed to fulfil her destiny and help those in need, had left a man who loved her and an agreeable life to do so. Had left Freddy flat in order to help strangers elsewhere. Which is goodness indeed, is it not? Disinterested altruism must come high on any scale of virtue.

The only problem being that her departure had left her husband a mess. What Doff would call a cot-case. And a bad tempered one at that, snapping away at would-be friendly advances like some endangered species of giant turtle.

But why should Freddy be such a mess? Men have been dumped before, many from a great height, and survived. They have been abandoned for other men or women, for more money, more power, more passion, but not often for altruism. Was this the needle, the small sharp bodkin which had deflated Freddy's ego. Was this why he was behaving like an enraged toddler whose ice cream has been tossed into the gutter not by another of his own fighting weight but by something beyond human control. Gravity perhaps, or earthquake.

Like the old story of the man who fled from Damascus because he heard Death was waiting for him, only to meet him when he arrived in Aleppo. 'Well met,' said Death, 'I had thought to meet you tomorrow in Damascus.'

That sort of grinding inevitability, of being an opponent of unassailable fate, must be hard to bear on occasion, even if you were a Muslim, and a great deal harder if you were not. F. Manders versus the inscrutable workings of a soul determined to love and serve humanity. Up against what Borges called the 'problem of goodness'. Nothing visible or invisible to fight against, to hate, to stick pins into wax models of. Nothing, even, to forgive.

Tough going.

'How do you know Bridget, Mrs Carew?' she asked.

'Oh, she was marvellous on our committee. Absolutely wonderful. So hardworking and inventive, such a talented, busy young professional. She did wonders. We were all heartbroken when she left.'

'So was Freddy.'

Molly gave her a quick glance and carried on. 'I *know*, and that's why I have to talk to you. It's so extraordinary. I don't want to be intrusive but it does seem so incredible, such a wonderful opportunity for them to get together again on neutral ground, as it were.'

Violet heard her voice, flat as a board and as noncommittal, 'Neutral ground,' she said.

'She's here, don't you see? Bridget is *here*.'

Shit.

'Oh,' said Violet. 'Why?'

'That's why I disappeared in that terrible place. I saw her from the pearl bar and ran after her. We had the most wonderful time. It was absolutely instinctive – I just dropped the pearls and ran. Goodness knows what the poor pearl man must have thought. She's tall, Bridget, not as tall as you, of course, but tall. And that wonderful hair – there was no mistaking her. We fell into each other's arms we were talking so hard, all about the training she has been doing in Paris and how lucky she was to have been picked for this brief Asian trip, not alone of course, more as a bag carrier to the senior officers, she said. On a fact-finding commission from Humanitaire, she said, but it was an amazing experience, appalling of course, some of the things they had seen, and I said, "But at least you're *doing* something," and she looked at me with those beautiful eyes and sort of breathed, "I know."

'I'll never forget it. Never.

'I suppose we'd been swept along by the crowd or something, because by the time we'd calmed down I couldn't see Cushla or the pearls or anything, so I said, "I must go back, they'll be wondering where I've got to," which of course they were, and I do feel badly about that, but on the other hand it was all so wonderful and astonishing. So after we'd been hunting and asking everybody for the pearl boutique and people kept on bowing and smiling and sending us in different directions – well, that's what it felt like to me, but I've never had much sense of direction. Hamish can't understand it. Finally Bridget looked at her watch and said she was sorry but she'd have to go because she was going to meet the rest of the team at a newly established sheltered workshop training place, I gathered, though she didn't call it that. For physically handicapped young women from the mainland. And I said, "Oh, I would love to come," and she said, "Why not? We'll ring the Consulate as soon as we arrive at the centre." And then she laughed and said, "Get Freddy on to it. How is he?"'

Violet's courtesy came out as a snarl. 'And may I ask what you said?'

'I'll tell you later. So off we went by cab, quite a long way out, past Aberdeen and the floating restaurants and all that area, and then we met the rest of the team. Amazing people, absolutely amazing, and they were quite happy for me to tag along. I think my visit was one of the most wonderful experiences of my life.'

'Why?'

'Because of the strength, the courage, the goodness. You could feel it, in those tiny concrete rooms you see in the tropics if you get to the real parts where people live. The rooms are little more than empty cells. They never seem to have windows. Perhaps it's because they aren't closed, but they look just like square holes ... And the heat, the sultry sweltering heat.

114

'And all so pragmatic, so calm, so . . . ordinary. There was one young woman with a growth the size of an egg on the bridge of her nose. It must have hindered her vision, it must have. Think of it. She was working alongside a young woman, a girl really, with no legs, chatting and giggling at two of those narrow looms they have.' Molly paused, looked into Violet's eyes. '*Why* are they so brave?'

'I don't know,' said Violet. 'I don't know.'

'No,' said Molly, 'no.' She sat silent, staring straight ahead. 'What's the name of that brown prickly fruit? It has a terrible smell, I believe.'

'Durian.'

'Yes?' Molly paused. 'What I wanted to discuss with you is something more simple. I think I must tell Freddy she's here, don't you?'

Violet sat still, and careful.

'Did you mention this to Bridget?' she said.

'Oh yes, we had quite a talk about it in the cab going out. Bridget wanted to know all about him, how he's getting on. I said I didn't think he was very happy.'

You don't, huh. 'And what did Bridget say about meeting the man she's deserted?' she asked.

Mrs Carew looked at her with her head on one side. 'She said she would like to see him, that she is very fond of him, but that it's up to Freddy.'

'Mrs Carew, it's nothing to do with me, but do you know if Bridget has any intention of returning to him?'

'Oh surely, yes. But perhaps not for some time. She is totally committed to her commitment.'

'Then,' said Violet, sitting upright and bright with decision, 'I can't think of any reason to tell him. The man's not some useless wreck. He's an intelligent man in good health with particularly good judgement. If he wants to talk to Bridget he can do so. Telephone, cable, a letter with a stamp in the corner. Go to Paris himself. There are plenty of ways.'

'Yes,' said Molly. 'But she's *here*. And we leave tomorrow for Kuala Lumpur.'

'Yes,' said Violet. 'Can I get you some more fruit?'

'Going down?' said Manders as she entered the lift.

She nodded. 'Mrs Carew and I are lunching with Mrs Nelligan at some enchanting little restaurant tucked away on the Peak. Aren't you meant to be somewhere?'

'Yes, the last trade session,' he said, patting a bulging folder, 'but the old man left half the bumph behind. Sent me back with the key. Nothing New Zealand Eyes Only, thank God, so no damage done, but it's still alarming. It could just as well have been Classified. CLAT is not doing well. Security lapse, wife gone walkabout.' His smile widened, beamed into her eyes. 'Wives, in fact. Bridget rang. Can you believe it? She's here.'

'Oh.'

'*Ground*,' sighed the opening lift.

'Yes, I'm going to see her tonight.'

'What about the Minister's Farewell Dinner?'

'Before. After. Somehow. Extraordinary, isn't it? And she's going to be in KL while we're there. Quite extraordinary. You'll be able to see her too. Bye.'

The Chinese driver from the Consulate swung the car around the curves of the Peak road with the same panache as George on the night of the Luigis' party, but for a much longer time. The car left Victoria, swung past the Jockey Club, through the Wanki Chong Gap, and continued upwards.

Periodically the driver stretched his long neck and dipped his head, straightened and repeated the performance. Remedial neck exercises presumably, and why not, thought Molly, except that the road seemed a bad place to practise. She glanced at Violet who obviously had noticed nothing.

There were few houses to be seen on this side, only infinite vistas of sea and sky interrupted by a few offshore islands, distant junks and the smaller dots of sampans.

'Wonderful view,' Molly assured Cathy Nelligan. 'Awe inspiring.'

'You haven't seen anything yet,' said Cathy. 'Wait till you see the houses at the top of the Peak.'

Mansions of varying size appeared behind high walls with elaborate wrought-iron gates.

'I suppose they are very expensive,' said Molly.

'Expensive is not the word!' cried Cathy.

Still doing his neck exercises, the driver drove along street after street and past mansion after mansion. Each set of gates seemed grander than the last.

'Wonderful. Wonderful,' Molly murmured.

'I always bring visitors up the Peak,' said Cathy. 'You see the best of both worlds up here. By the way, we're not having Chinese today. I never thought I'd get tired of Chinese but you know one can. Mind you, it's very different from Chinese as we know it at home. Much more, well, Chinese. Ethnic, if you like. You have to know what you're eating. I'll never forget the day Brian discovered the soup was snake.'

'Snake,' said Molly.

'In the New Territories. The open markets there are unbelievably grisly. All different sorts of flesh hanging about in rows. You'd never dare to ask what's what. And as for the ducks, it would put you off completely.'

'Do you get much golf here, Mrs Nelligan?' asked Violet quickly.

'Not much, no.'

'Tell me about the ducks,' said Molly.

'Oh, they're so pretty. Indian runners, or a local version. Those white ones with the long necks and bright yellow legs. I always think they look so Chinese somehow. Every tiny holding seems to have its own flock waddling along in front of a man with a stick, or bobbing up and down in some dirty

117

little pool. Then, fifty-five days to the day after hatching, the entire flock have their necks wrung, and off they go again, just like a sausage machine. So as I say, sometimes it's nice to have a change, and I thought we'd try French today. Monica Otherley says it's lovely and so's the food. Ah, here we are. Oh, it does look pretty, doesn't it? Thank you, Joe. Mind the step, Mrs Carew. What fun.'

Molly Carew stood in front of the mirror in the Plum Blossom Duplex, staring at her image as she had done as a child, searching beyond that face for the girl called Molly.

She had much to think about. The Centre for the Physically Disabled had been wonderful, inspirational; she had not given enough money, she must send more. There had been an awkward moment when the director, a genial man and unexpectedly tall for a Chinese, having gathered who she was from Bridget, had asked her whether her contribution was an official gift from the New Zealand Government, but Bridget had explained the situation with her usual ease and charm.

However much she sent would not be enough. The blind, for instance, get four months training and then they have to leave. A young woman from the New Territories had arrived that morning.

And another thing. Should she have told Violet about Bridget, who was nothing to do with Violet and everything to do with Freddy? Possibly not. She must tell him as soon as possible tonight at Mr Lui's Farewell Dinner. She saw herself: 'Freddy, I have something to tell you to your advantage.'

She sat, tugged slightly scuffed shoes on to her swollen feet.

'Hamish,' she called through the open bathroom door, 'I'm going to ring Bobby.'

'Whaaa? Thooo day.'

'I know it's only two days. Don't worry. I'll make it collect.'

The ringing tone was long and clear and unanswered.

118

Hamish appeared in a white bath sheet with his hair on end. 'I told you she wouldn't be there,' he said.

She could be in the garden, thought Molly, or inspecting her pedigree calves. Or helping Bronson. He would have finished milking. Molly could hear the moos of the herd filing up from the paddock, see them standing placid in the yard, the cajoling and nudging into place, the cleaning of teats, the fingers tugging to start the flow before slipping on the cups. Bobby could do it all standing on her head. She knew the routine down to the final hosing of the splattered concrete. Possibly at this moment she and Bron would be walking back to the cottage, brewing tea, yarning. Anything. The slow rhythm of Molly's memories of the cowshed were disturbed, fractured. My daughter is having an affair with a married man who might well have children.

She could scarcely ring Bronson collect, let alone ask to speak to her daughter.

Molly put down the receiver. Hamish could be right. Bronson's wife could have left him – deserted him, as Violet described Bridget as having done. And probably there were no children. And they had parted by mutual consent. She was making an unnecessary fuss and must stop immediately.

'Did you get her?' said Hamish, tackling his black tie with his usual mix of concentration and rage.

'No'

'So what are you doing now?'

'Thinking,' said Molly.

Violet Redpath stood staring at her reflection one floor down. She had had some difficulty steaming out the hand prints General d'Riva had left on the dark green velvet, but what the hell. She looked at herself: the depth of the curved neckline and the whiteness of her skin, her hair which pleased her and the heavily made-up eyes she was not sure about. She took a step backwards and pursed her pink lips.

It's always more infuriating, when the tentative snail horns of a new relationship meet quicklime and fizzle, if you are the one who has made the play however slight, the one who has stuck his or her neck out and come a gutser however mild. She preferred to be in charge, and despite her tendency to say what she thought, usually had been.

And no one could say she hadn't known that Manders was a loving husband. Nor had she been unaware that he had become 'difficult' after his wife had done a runner. Everyone knew that. Everyone. She grimaced, blew a raspberry at the dumb bum in the glass. So what did you think you were doing? Making the poor guy into some sort of dim challenge. Forget it, right? Fling yourself at the most attractive man at dinner, OK? Sure. Sure. She pulled a tissue from the box nearby. *Life*, she read, *is a teardrop waiting to fall*. Keats. She blotted her lips and reached for *Blood and Fire*.

Regrettably and unexpectedly, the best looking man at the private function in the Chrysanthemum Room of the New Mandarin was Shy Nellie Nelligan. Irritated but undeterred, Violet looked further afield. At good heads of hair and bald, at smooth-faced Asians and pink Europeans, at American teeth and Antipodean slouches. Their dinner jackets and black ties had turned them all into a universal brotherhood of the respected and the respectful. Decision-makers and power brokers, giants of industry, clout wielders and late starters milled about. Were serious, laughed strongly, were serious again. Men of substance shook hands, bowed, introduced their cohorts and bowed again.

Such serving of becks, such jutting out of bums.

There would be no unbuttoning at this feast. Bugger. She would have to try harder.

Violet's glance fell on an attractive-looking Malaysian about half her height who was standing alone and at ease. As she turned in his direction she saw Mrs Carew looking miserable beside a woman in a mink jacket. She changed tack. Duty replaced effort. Bit of a relief really. What was she trying to prove.

'Isn't it very hot?' Molly was asking.

'Hot?' cried the woman. 'Honey, it's heaven in this air conditioning. And it's so light.' She flapped a front panel at Molly. 'Feel it.'

Molly gave a tentative poke.

'Go on,' said the woman, still flapping. 'It won't bite.'

'Can I?' said Violet, and gave the front panel a slight yank. 'Goodness me, that is light.'

Mrs Leadbetter nodded. She was married to a multimillionaire on the Peak, she told them. She had a thing about mink. This was one of several.

'Oh look,' cried Molly, 'there's Freddy. Will you excuse me? I have something to tell him,' she murmured, heading towards the ice sculpture of Rodin's *The Kiss* at the entrance to the Chrysanthemum Room.

Violet glanced at her watch. Manders was late and looked distracted; even his spectacles were lopsided. Presumably he had already seen Bridget. They had been locked together, he had torn himself away, flung himself into a cab ... Oh *shut up*.

And now Mrs Carew is going tell him his wife's here, which he already knows. So why did she confide in me if she was going to tell Freddy anyway? Because people do. They never stop, they see me coming. They think I'm a nice girl. Fat chance.

'My favourite,' continued Mrs Leadbetter, 'is the creamy suede with the mink lining. I just love being subtle, don't you, Miss Redgrave?'

'No,' said Violet. 'And it's "path", not "grave".'

'Freddy,' cried Molly, 'I have something wonderful to tell you.'

Manders was standing stock still by the sculpture. 'What an obscene-looking thing.' He turned slowly to Molly, stared at her. 'Yes I know, thank you,' he said. 'I've just been seeing her.'

'Oh.'

'Look, the water's dripping from the man's big toe.'

'Oh. Yes. So it is.'

'Can I get you a drink, Mrs Carew?'

'I have one, thank you.'

'Ah yes, so you have. Lucky old you.'

Molly drew herself upright. 'What did you say?'

'I said, "Lucky old you." Shouldn't have done so. Do forgive me.'

He attempted a laugh, thought better of it. 'I didn't of course mean to be rude or ageist, as I'm sure you realise. Good heavens no. I could just as well have said, "Lucky you." Just a badly timed sort of quip. Mini quip. Yes. Ah, there's the man. Whisky is it? Thank you.' He lifted his glass to Molly. 'Here's to you, Mrs Carew,' he said, and drank, gave a grateful sigh. 'Ah,' he said again. 'Do you happen to know the ballad about Mad Carew?'

'Your shirt is very wet, Fred,' said Molly.

'But you'd love it,' he cried. 'Great stuff, Edwardian. J. Milton Hayes.' Manders dragged himself upright and declaimed:

There's a one-eyed yellow idol to the north of Khatmandu,
There's a little marble cross below the town,
There's a brokenhearted woman tends the grave of Mad Carew,
And the Yellow God forever gazes down.

He was known as 'Mad Carew' by the subs of Khatmandu,
He was hotter than they felt inclined to tell,
But for all his foolish pranks, he was worshipped in the ranks,
And the Colonel's daughter smiled on him as well.

Molly lifted a hand, was disregarded as Freddy thundered on:

He had loved her all along, with a passion of the strong,
The fact that she loved him was plain to all,
She was nearly twenty-one and arrangements had begun . . .

'Will you be *quiet*,' said Molly. 'I do like it, of course I do. But this is not the moment for you to be idiotic.'

'No,' said Manders. 'You're quite right. I apologise. Please forgive me.'

Molly looked up to his face. 'Yes,' she said. 'But don't do it again.'

'No,' said Freddy. 'No, I won't.'

11

When Manders was a child, a friend of his father's called Mr Hour and he had been left for some time in each other's company with not another soul in sight. There must have been some reason for his father's disappearance but all Manders can remember is staring at Mr Hour and Mr Hour staring back at him.

Mr Hour ('Call me Happy') picked up the current issue of *Time* and stabbed a forefinger at the cover.

'Know who this is, lad?'

'President Truman,' said Freddy.

'Good one, boy. This is the man,' said Mr Hour, still stabbing, 'who sacked General McArthur!'

'Oh.'

'You wouldn't pick it, would you? Not from that face.'

Freddy took a punt at it. 'No.'

Mr Hour put down the magazine, walked to the window and inspected the rain. 'Hosing,' he said. 'Absolutely hosing. You know, son, sometimes of an evening all the signs look like rain and it never comes, then you wake up in the morning and she's hosing down.'

Freddy, who had been about to make a break for it and dash to his room, said nothing.

Mr Hour swung round, clapped his hands together, 'Well now, Freddy. And what do you want to do when you grow up?'

'I want to be an electronic engineer.'

'Ah,' said Mr Hour. 'And why do you want to be that?'

'I like the sound of it.'

'Like the sound of what?' said his father from the door.

'You've got a bright lad here, Harry,' said Mr Hour. 'What age is he? Seven is it? Only seven and he's determined to be an electronic engineer.'

'Is that right,' said his father doubtfully. 'Sorry to leave you on your own, Happy. What about a beer?'

'You've never told us about this electronic engineer lark, Freddy,' he said later when Happy had finally squelched down the drive to his Morris. 'When did you decide on this career move?'

'I haven't,' said Freddy. 'I just wanted to shut him up.'

His father had laughed and applauded his good sense. His mother, a gentle woman prone to intermittent bursts of worry, had not been so pleased. Was there not perhaps something . . . No, not exactly deceitful, she didn't mean that, and she certainly didn't believe, not for a moment, that Freddy had lied deliberately to poor old Happy. Freddy was a particularly truthful child, she had noticed this in the past, but even so was there not some lack but some lack of . . . openness? Frankness even? After all, he was seven. Why had he not chatted away to Happy like Susie would have done. She hoped Freddy was not going to be one of those silent introverted sort of people. She had always felt people like that had such sad lives.

Freddy, who was now sitting in the kitchen with the evening paper spread on the table for a first go at the *Phantom* before Susan mucked it up, was interested by the overheard conversation but uninformed. He asked Mrs Trench, his teacher at school, what the word 'introverted' meant. She had looked at him carefully and told him to ask his mother. So obviously introverted was one of those words.

Manders had been born after his father went overseas in 1943 and was thus technically not a baby boomer, a fact which pleased him in a mild sort of way. He had never been much of a joiner.

His mother had driven herself to the hospital for her confinement. She hadn't wanted to be a nuisance to her mother-in-law who was playing afternoon bridge at the Club. Her mother-in-law, disgusted with such ridiculous behaviour, which as well as being so odd had made her look a fool in front of the other girls, had complained when she discovered what had happened. She had of course gone straight up to Maternity and helped Mary all evening, but everyone had assured her nothing would happen till next morning, so she had gone home to try and snatch some sleep and would you believe Mary hadn't bothered to ring her till eight next morning, by which time Frederick Henry was already four hours old. Mrs Manders, not fooled for a moment by Mary's explanation that she had decided not to wake her at 4 a.m., was outraged. She had missed those first precious moments of her grandson's existence. How could she describe them to poor Harry sitting over there in Italy worrying himself to death.

Freddy can remember little of his infancy except that letters were important and that everything would be wonderful when Daddy came home from the war. Until then his mother spent every moment either placating her mother-in-law or trying to make sure that Freddy did not come to any harm. What a tragedy if owing to her carelessness Harry never saw this wonder they had produced, this joy which caused her so much anxiety. Water, roads, heights, depths: all, all were dangerous.

And then Daddy came home and again there is little memory of his arrival. Just of people shouting and bands playing and his mother and Grandma both wanting to be the one to hold him up to a man who smelled of tobacco and hot wool that prickled.

And eventually the realisation had dawned that Daddy was not going to go away ever again.

That realisation was repeated two years later when Susan was born. Freddy approved of this new thing. He held it smiling for photographs and pointed out how small its fingers were. He poked its stomach politely, laughed when it smiled and poked it again.

One day he came to his mother with a suggestion. 'Why don't we take Susie to the airport and show her the planes landing?'

'Isn't that lovely,' cried his mother. 'He loves the planes so much he wants his baby sister to see them too.'

'Yes,' said Freddy. 'And then we come home and leave her there.'

Harry Manders laughed and laughed and laughed. 'You'll do me, Fred,' he said.

Freddy adjusted his headphones, shut his eyes and accepted the fact. He was still doing a Happy Hour. Still attempting to deflect friendly or disinterested inquiries about his life and well-being from fellow travellers. From Happy Hour to Susan, from Molly to Violet, honest straightforward Manders was prepared to lie like a rug to shut them up. Or better still stop them from starting their questions in the first place. He had no intention of listening to music or watching the film, but the earphones would protect him, at least during the flight to KL.

A particularly loud burst from the sound system opened his eyes to a trailer for an inflight movie. He glanced at the screen, and, suddenly alert, fumbled with the sound switch. Emile de Bec, the French planter, reduced to manikin size, was entertaining Nellie Forbush to lunch on his estate high above the sea on an island in the South Pacific. Emile wore casual gear, a short-sleeved check shirt and oatmeal-coloured trousers. Nellie was trim as a pin in a well-fitting Navy nurse's uniform. They had finished coffee and held brandy goblets. Emile was explaining to Nellie that in the summer planters' wives often go to Australia to escape the heat. Nellie assured him that it often got hot in Little Rock, Arkansas. Emile moved towards Nellie; she came to him. Backed by yellow skies they sang into each other's eyes, Nellie's voice all youth and yearning, Emile's soaring male passion.

Once you have found him, she sang, *Never let him go.*
Once you have found her, he replied, *NEV-er -let – her GO.*

'Look at Mrs Carew,' he whispered.

They glanced across the aisle. Molly, earphones in place and face transcended, was singing along with both voices. Her voice was drowned by the roar of the engines but they could see her mouth, wide and round for Emile's last long and plangent O.

'Isn't she wonderful?' whispered Violet.

Freddy nodded. She was, she certainly was, the inquisitive old bat.

He turned off his headphones and pretended to sleep.

Violet studied his face. No sideburns, thank God, and she liked men who wore glasses. Apart from anything else it is interesting to see how they look without them. Vacant? Vulnerable? Vague?

Blow this. She collected her belongings and moved to an empty seat nearer the flight deck.

Freddy watched her go. She had good legs, he had always

thought so, and she knew how to use them. Such a waste if they don't. He shut his eyes.

He had walked to Bridget's hotel last night. As she had said, it was no distance. First left at the monsoon drain, then keep on till you get here. He couldn't miss the sign.

He walked fast in the steaming heat, was tempted to run because there would be so little time to talk. He should not have changed first. If you sweat in a starched shirt you're a mess. Sodden front. Sweat round the neck. Catch your death.

What was he going to say? Come back, come back my love. You stupid bitch, come back.

The fact that she had rung him was a positive, more than positive sign. She had probably realised already that she was not suited for such a vocation, if you could call it that. And what else could you call it?

Why had she had insisted on going? That was what he had never been able to pin down, let alone understand. They could have worked something out. Of course they could. He had skills, plenty of skills, though whether he wanted to exercise them in tropical rainforest or drought-stricken hinterlands was food for thought, but she had never given him the option. Never even contemplated the fact that his presence was not necessarily inimical to a life devoted to helping others in uncomfortable places. Such an assumption was inexcusable. Unwarranted. He would tell her so. They would discuss the matter in depth. If he could understand the reason, he could argue, talk things through, explain. As it was, he was fighting cotton wool. All he had to do was find the reason.

But not tonight, better not even to start on it tonight: there would be plenty of time in KL. He saw the quiet pool at the High Commission, saw them talking in the reclining chairs, at ease, relaxed. There had never been any time at home; it was ridiculous how hard they had worked. Coming. Going. Both of them getting busier and busier as they scrambled up the heap.

'Have you got the meat?'

'No, you said you'd get it.'

'That was last week.'

'Oh, Christ. Why didn't you remind me.'

With the smell from a nearby drain getting worse by the minute and the humidity at eighty-nine percent Manders felt almost elated. In KL he would find out why she had this incomprehensible, indecipherable passion to serve. To help the sick, the destitute, the hungry, the mentally or physically handicapped. He had been tempted to ask her before she left whether she intended to specialise, but they were beyond cheap cracks by that stage.

It would be more understandable if she had had strong religious convictions. *What so ever thou doest for the least of thy brethren in my name*, or words to that effect, could make some sort of sense if you believed in it. The thought that there could be another life, a world where the help given to the 'least' would be rewarded, had repelled them both as they watched Jane's unremitting battle through this one. Here or nowhere is where it happens. Where you do it or don't do it. No prizes.

From the moment Jane died Bridget had begun planning towards leaving Wellington.

A giant sign winked and flashed before him. Bridget had been right about one thing. You could not miss the sign for the Plaza Royale.

What were the Humanitaire contingent doing staying at the Plaza Royale anyway? Why not some modest establishment around another corner, a place more in keeping with their calling. Manders dismissed the unattractive thought. He and Violet had been granted First Class flights so that they as well as the Minister and Mrs Carew, could arrive fresh. Could hit the tarmac running. The Humanitaire contingent also needed rest. Let us wallow while we can.

Bridget was sitting on the edge of a pink chair in the foyer. She sprang up and came towards him.

'Freddy. I'm not sure if this is a good idea.'

Manders took her in his arms. The same height, the same good fit, the same scent.

'Bridget,' he said, 'Bridget,' and kissed her.

She relaxed for a second, then dragged her mouth away.

'How could you do that?' he said. 'You . . . you . . .'

She seemed unable to take her eyes off him. 'Bitch?' she whispered. 'But I didn't think for a second that you'd imagine anything had changed. Nothing's changed. How could it change? I just wanted to see how you're getting on. You have to believe me. And Mrs Carew was so excited . . .'

'Bugger Mrs Carew,' roared Manders. People stared; Asians, Caucasians and races unknown glanced away or watched with frank and guileless interest.

'Come up to my room,' said Bridget.

'How can I come up to your fucking room if you won't even kiss me?'

'Please.'

'If I come up to your room I'll probably kill you.'

'I'll risk it.'

She slipped her hand into his in the lift. It was soft and firm, boneless and trusting as an infant's at kerb drill. He shook it off and flung himself against the mirrored wall.

He sat across the opulent room at some distance from her, refused a drink and answered her questions. Of course he was all right. Why the hell wouldn't he be all right? What did she think would have happened? Some sort of wilting decline? No word for six months and now suddenly she wants to find out 'how he's getting on'.

She murmured something about food. Housework.

He could cook, he had always been able to cook, as she very well knew. It would be more to the point if he asked her how she was getting on if cooking was an issue. And stuff housework.

'How's Jazz?'

'I gave him to Brendon next door.'

Her hands flew together. There were photographs of her like that, photos of surprise, excitement, delight. This time it looked something like shock.

'I thought he might be company.'

'Brendon seems quite satisfied.'

She seemed to be having trouble with the words. 'I mean for you.'

'Would you want my cat?'

'Yes, of course.' Her head moved from side to side. 'I love cats.'

He gave up. 'Tell me about Paris,' he said. 'Humanitaire.'

She did so. It was wonderful, everything about it was wonderful. Better than she could have hoped. The training, the people, the attitude of the whole place. Completely secular and non-judgemental; she would like to say non-political but nothing can ever be entirely that. As he knew, you didn't have to have a medical degree. Many did, and there were trained nurses and ancillary medics of all types. The training was totally professional, nothing woolly or sentimental about it. Exactly what she'd been looking for.

'Nothing do-gooder about it then?' said Manders.

'That's typical of you, Freddy.'

'Your smile is wry. Did you know? "She gave her ditched ex a wry smile."'

'Forget it. I know exactly what you're doing and I won't bite. Of course the Institute does good. Untold good.'

'So I would bloody well hope, from the name.'

'You have to swear at the sound of it, don't you?'

'Not at all. I've nothing against helping those in need. In fact I'm all for it. I just don't see why you should be so prickly about the possibility of being described as one who does good.'

'You're hopeless, absolutely hopeless,' laughed Bridget, and continued her saga of the wonders of Humanitaire.

He stopped listening. Sat staring at the carpet wondering

why he'd been such a clown as to give her the chance to bang on about the place. He loathed Humanitaire. Its completely secular mission statements and its excellent audit system, its honourable directors and their courageous never-ending fight for funds made him toss.

She unwrapped her bare legs from beneath her, stroked one. There was one thing he had to know. 'Are you seeing anyone?'

'What do you mean "seeing"?'

'Just what I say. Socialising, eating lunch, talking, having a drink, that sort of thing. What do you think I mean?'

'Male or female?'

'Male,' he snapped.

'Of course I see people. Lots of people, male people and female people. I like people.' She dropped her eyes. 'As you very well know.'

He nodded grimly. The conversation reminded him of that idiotic time with Violet in the grounds of the House of Representatives. The same verbal fencing, the same repressed rage. Except that there it hadn't mattered a damn, and it hadn't been rage, just irritation heightened by stones digging into his bum and not hers.

'I hope you're seeing people, Freddy,' said Bridget. 'Getting out. Not just sitting there . . .'

'Nursing a broken heart? That's what you'd like, isn't it?'

Her hand went to her mouth. 'Oh, Freddy,' she cried. 'What have I done to you?'

'Jesus wept!' he yelled, and lurched for the door.

She was on her feet. 'Please, I got it all *wrong*. Sit down. Please.'

'No.'

'All right. I'll tell you anyway. I should have told you before but I couldn't think how to say it. I still can't. But I do realise that I'm the one who left, not you. That you're a free agent and I don't expect . . . I mean you're an attractive man and . . .'

133

She stood shuddering in front of him. 'Oh Freddy, Freddy,' she wailed.

He took a step backwards. 'You're giving me a licence to screw, is that it?'

'Yes. No! Oh, get out.'

'Thank you,' he said. 'Thank you very much.' He walked to the door and opened it. 'I'll send you a photo. An action one.'

'Get out!' screamed Bridget.

Breathing deeply and sweating like a pig, Manders shut the door. The front of his shirt was sodden, his glasses misted. He took them off, swore, and groped his way to the nearby men's room, filled the marble basin, plunged his face in cold water, then ran the cold tap on his wrists. His mother, his pale gentle mother, had told him that when you are hot and bothered there is nothing more helpful than running cold water on your wrists. Poor old Mum had been in awe of Bridget: 'She has lovely hair, dear. And beautiful teeth.'

He cleaned his glasses and put them on. The large grey blur at the end of the far end of the room sharpened into a twelve-foot-high rock wall with a culvert running along its base.

Manders moved towards it. As he neared the wall, a curtain of water fell down its entire width. The thing was a urinal, a Plaza Royale speciality. A talking point. He must have broken the light beam.

He took a few steps back. The waterfall stopped. A few steps forward and the flow began again. He tried to pinpoint the exact position of the beam: step, step, sidestep. Nothing. He found himself teasing the thing, sneaking up on it and backing away.

The door swung open behind him. A Chinese man, well dressed and sleek as seals, stared at the capering figure for a moment and backed out hastily.

Manders, caught between sob and giggle, attempted a mop at his shirt front, wet his face again and marched out.

12

Molly watched the diminutive stewardesses dipping and bobbing as they checked their charges for fastened seatbelts, upright seat backs and unacceptable stowage of any kind. Their glossy lips pouted; they were kind but firm. Safety is our only concern, their quick hands indicated, we just happen to look like this. 'Quite exquisite, aren't they?' murmured Molly.

Hamish grunted. He was having a final check of the programme to confirm the sequence of events and the names and functions of the members of the Official Welcoming Committee waiting below.

Arrival, 11.00. *(Spot on.)*
Inspect Military Guard of Honour. *(Name of Commander?*
   Yes.)
Give Press Conference. *(Yes.)*
Police escort to Hotel Kuala Lumpur Hilton. *(Ah.)*

He glanced out the window for any activity. The red carpet usually showed up first, but there was no sign from this altitude. He licked two fingers, smoothed his eyebrows and turned to Molly.

'What?'

'The stewardesses.'

'What about them?'

'They're so tiny, so quick, so *nimble*. They must drop to their heels a thousand times per trip.' She looked at Hamish thoughtfully. 'Are you giving a press conference?'

'Yes.'

She patted his knee. 'Don't worry. They'll be very polite here. None of that awful business of bailing you up and asking impossible questions.'

'Are you organised?' he huffed. 'Ready to land?'

'As much I ever will be,' said Molly, her eyes still on the darting precision of the stewardesses. No wonder men fell for them. And look at all the children. School holidays presumably.

'The one to remember,' continued Hamish, 'is the Minister. Dato Ahmad Kamarul Ridza is his full title, Dato Ahmad for short. You have met him before but not his wife, Datin Ahmad. The rest are just more or less routine handlers.'

'Is Dato Ahmad the one who reminds me of Clark Gable?'

Hamish looked at her. 'He has a moustache if that's what you mean.'

'Yes, nice man.'

The aircraft settled its fuselage on the tarmac with the slight sideways dip of a resettling albatross. Hamish nodded in appreciation. He always acknowledged good landings.

Agile young men flung open doors to red carpet, martial music and the line of official welcomers. The Guard of Honour and their Commanding Officer sprang to attention.

Hamish descended the steps into the blast of humid heat with dignity and benign good will, followed by Molly, equally benign but less at ease. Formal ceremonial occasions confused her. There was so much one had to get right. So many things to remember, names to catch and attempt to retain, the functions of different functionaries and the faces which went with them. Even the mechanics of the arrival process were not simple. The business of ignoring the handrail (who needs it) while watching her step and smiling straight ahead required aplomb. She descended slowly, smiling radiantly in every direction except that assigned to the photographers.

Hamish and the Malaysian Minister of Trade Relations and Agriculture greeted each other warmly. They had met several times and had worked together with mutual if wary respect. They both realised they had had far more difficult representatives from far more intransigent trading nations to deal with in the past, and would no doubt have them again in the future. There was an element almost of relief in the prolonged exuberance of their handshake and the width of their smiles as they turned their heads to face the photographers and their clasped hands continued to pump.

Dato Ahmad turned to Molly. He bowed. He was enchanted. He was also puzzled. His wife, he explained, seemed to have disappeared. It was inexplicable. In the meantime, he laughed, indicating a serene young woman at his side, Miss Raya would attend to his honoured guest's every wish.

Molly, always relaxed in any unforeseen occurrence for which she was not responsible, laughed merrily and continued to do so down the receiving line. She recognised the New Zealand High Commissioner, Penn McPhee, which surprised them both and lifted her spirits.

Manders and Violet Redpath stood behind the VIPs,

Manders clutching the briefcase with the classified papers, Violet with her eyes on Miss Raya who was wearing traditional Malayan batiks of exceptional beauty. No one, including presumably the young woman herself, knew what role she was so unexpectedly required to fill, but it seemed likely that some leadership qualities would be required.

Violet, since the unpleasantness at the Lan Lan Good Luck Downtown Emporium, had become more aware of such things as responsibility and taking charge. Miss Raya had the fragile grace of a bird of paradise and would probably be about as much use. Violet now knew that Mrs Carew, kind, good Mrs Carew, must be watched constantly. Nobody could call her a loose cannon – that sounded both destructive and dangerous – but there was sometimes a waywardness about her, the inconsequential wilfulness of the true innocent, which was liable to affect her responses to the unexpected.

The Army band stopped playing, followed by an indecipherable roar from the Commander of the Guard. The Malaysian Guard leapt as one man; nailed boots crashed the tarmac; rifles clattered as they performed the ancient military ritual of Presenting Arms to a distinguished visitor. The Flunk, Flunk, Jump, Slam required to get a body of men from the Slope to Present went smoothly; the shally humps and shally hoops were seamless.

The Commander gave his men a final glare and strode across to Hamish, saluted with the traditional swirls of his naked sword, and invited him to inspect his Guard. Hamish bowed his head in return. The band resumed playing but the tune was no longer martial. The lilting strains of 'Raindrops Keep Falling on my Head' accompanied Hamish and his escort as they walked slowly past the rigid unity of the soldiers. Hamish stopped occasionally to speak with one or other of the men, who invariably answered with motionless and unblinking attention before Hamish nodded and moved on.

Hamish bowed his head one final time to the Commander

in acknowledgement and dismissal, and returned to the reception party with his usual air of authority. There are some things you know you do well. And it had been a good guard.

The Ministers and their respective staffs swept onwards to the press conference with the firm tread of substance on the move. No one was actually swept aside as they passed through the crowded airport, but then no one got in the way. Their path to the conference had been swept clear and was well guarded.

Half a dozen Malaysian journalists and several photographers sprang to their feet as they entered the room, followed, after a pause, by the New Zealand Press Association man and the man from Reuters.

The two Ministers, their secretaries and the New Zealand High Commissioner took their seats under large coloured photographs of the Malaysian King and Queen, solemn, bejewelled and in full regalia. Flashlights snapped as Hamish rose to his feet. He gave them their due, then began to speak in firm sonorous tones.

'It gives me great pleasure to be in your beautiful country once again,' he said, 'and as always I look forward to constructive trade discussions with my good friend, your Minister of Trade and Agriculture, Dato Ahmad Kamarul Ridza.'

Hamish nodded sternly at Dato Ahmad, who nodded back at his guest for several seconds.

'As you all know,' continued Hamish, 'relationships between our two countries have always been close. New Zealand troops have fought alongside your own gallant forces in your long struggle for Independence. My government continues to undertake joint training exercises (by invitation) in South-East Asia as a demonstration of New Zealand's continuing interest in the stability and security of the region. We also continue to respond to requests from ASEAN countries for military training (albeit limited) in New Zealand.

Surrounded as you are on all sides by conflicting ideological influences, you have become justly known as one of the bulwarks of Democracy in South-East Asia. It will come as no surprise to you to hear that your beautiful country is an example to us all in the racial harmony which exists between the different ethnic and cultural groups who make up the people of the Federation of Malaysia.'

'Huh,' said the Reuters man.

'Party line, party line,' murmured the New Zealander. 'Why doesn't he keep to trade?'

Freddy, who had been thinking the same thing, listened as Hamish moved on to give his audience facts of which they were already aware and told them of achievements they had already made.

'Even before the Federation of Malaysia was born in 1963,' he cried, 'you were already rebuilding your nation.

'In 1957 your Gross National Product was 4,948 million dollars. By 1966 it had risen to 8,058 million dollars and has continued to leap ahead each year. You are now the world's greatest producer of rubber, your tin production has multiplied, your palm oil industry has increased fourfold in a decade. New industries such as steel mills, tyre factories and oil refineries have sprung up.

'And throughout all these years,' his stabbing forefinger reminded them, 'New Zealand has been your friend.'

He paused, changed tack. 'As you know,' he said, 'New Zealand's overseas proportion of Gross National Product is among the highest in the world. My government is proud of its growing trade in meat and dairy produce with South-East Asia. In the five years between 1974 and 1978 New Zealand export markets to ASEAN countries have increased from 73 million New Zealand dollars to 150 million New Zealand dollars, and further substantial gains are foreseen as your beautiful country develops. As always our trading emphasis is based on bilateral relations. In 1978 New Zealand exports to

Malaysia totalled 39,187,000 dollars. In the same year our imports from Malaysia totalled 26,130,000 dollars.

'As I said, for some time there has been a growing trade in meat and dairy produce from my country to yours.' Hamish gave a quick honest laugh. 'I have to tell you that our butter export figures to Malaysia dropped slightly last year, but we plan to change that.'

'Tricky,' muttered the Reuters man. 'This place is on a boom.'

'We continue with our commitment to Official Development Assistance with our input of New Zealand expertise in the form of advisers on your capital resources such as fisheries and forestry. Colombo Plan students are made welcome in our universities and, as I said, a mutually beneficial programme of military training exchange exists, albeit to a limited degree.

'While I am here I hope to visit a milk powder reconstituting plant constructed with the help of my government's contribution to ODA.

'Finally I can assure you that your Minister and my discussions will be extensive, detailed and fruitful, to the mutual benefit of both our beautiful countries.

'Any questions?'

There was a respectful silence. Manders stared at the large photograph of the King and Queen. The King was middle aged, his Queen younger. Her diamond necklace and tiara were impressive, but the most eye-catching jewel was that worn by the King: a diamond star and crescent brooch the size of a fist pinned on the front of his traditional batik headdress. A headdress which would be, as his mother used to say, hard to wear. You wouldn't get any help from it, would have to be feeling up to it. His mother had many small maxims of this kind. Another was that there was no need, ever, to be bored. If you were bored, you were not trying hard enough. And besides you could always think of something else. Manders transposed the Queen's pleasant face with Bridget's. No good, useless. He tried again with Violet's. Ah, that was better. The tiara winking about her dark wisps of hair which was meant to look like that, the quick smile, the breast beneath the Sash of Honour.

He came to at the sound of a New Zealand voice. The man from the NZPA, a tall shambling character with a shock of prematurely white hair and a Kentucky Fried moustache, was on his feet.

'Minister, when is your government going to withdraw the New Zealand armed forces from Singapore?' he drawled.

The Malaysian reporters turned to look at the man. Hamish eyed him with distaste.

'My answer to that question is twofold: (a) I am not the Minister for Defence, and (b) this is not Singapore.'

A smile or two flickered around the room. The New Zealander chomped his moustache and drawled again.

'My answer to that, sir, is that it's a matter of great interest in this area. People here feel it's high time we heard something about what's going on.' He looked at Hamish intently. 'You must have heard something. Surely?'

'That question is out of order,' said Hamish. 'Any more questions?'

Mrs Carew and Violet were escorted by the silent Miss Raya into a small pink room at the rear of the airport building. The orchids also were pink. Molly attempted body language to express her appreciation of their beauty. She waved her arms, flung her hands together and apart.

'Beautiful,' she mouthed. The young woman bowed and smiled.

Molly touched the pattern of her batik skirt and prepared to start again when the young woman leapt to her feet as though stung. Molly's hand, startled at the unexpected reaction, flew to her chest. The young woman bowed low, touched her closed palms to her forehead and bowed again to a majestic-looking woman who swept into the room in a torrent of Malay. The young woman murmured something to the new arrival, who replied sharply and brushed her aside. Her exotic, almost barbaric presence filled the little room. Molly looked at her with appreciative interest. Violet found it difficult not to gape.

She had never seen such a beautiful garment before, not actually *on* someone. It must be a couturier's. French? Italian? The frock sang its credentials in languages unknown. Golden silk slashed with black slunk down her curves; her diamonds throbbed in the pink light as she stood proud as a Sumatran tigress, one who believed that the best defence is attack.

She put out a long-fingered hand at full stretch to Molly and said, 'Good afternoon, Mrs Carew. I am Datin Ahmad and I make you welcome on behalf of our beautiful country.

'Your aircraft was early,' she continued, 'and I was not informed. Also you are waiting in the wrong area. How could your people be so careless? Where,' she cried, glancing around the pink box, 'are the New Zealanders?'

'I suppose you mean apart from us,' said Molly. 'Perhaps the New Zealand High Commissioner's wife and her escorts are in another area.'

'Excuse me, Mrs Carew,' said Violet. 'You will remember that Mrs McPhee is on leave in New Zealand.'

'Oh,' said Molly. 'Ah. And the Commissioner is with my husband at his press conference. Perhaps there aren't any more.'

'Of course there must be some more. They have mislaid themselves!'

Molly stood straight. 'If you will allow me to say so, Datin Ahmad, that is extremely unlikely.'

Footsteps clattered on polished stone as the Malaysian Minister, Hamish, the New Zealand High Commissioner and their respective staffs entered.

The Malaysian Minister gave a quick cross glance in his wife's direction and bowed to Molly. He appeared to be even more delighted to welcome the charming wife of his honoured guest than he had been on the tarmac. He glanced at his wife again before swinging back to laugh at the hilarity of finding the wife of his honoured guest ensconced in the wrong room. She should have been in a quite different room: a large spacious room, a beautiful room, not in this room at all. He must apologise once again, he said, slinging a quick snarl at his wife, who snarled back, on behalf of each and every one of those responsible.

'Not at all,' said Molly, 'we have been having a delightful time, haven't we Violet?'

'Yes,' said Violet, wishing she was not in Manders' direct line of sight.

Molly looked from the resplendent Datin to her husband and back again. Dato Ahmad, as she had remembered, was a handsome man. On the tarmac he had looked even more like Clark Gable, with a touch of the bright-eyed insouciance of the born player. Now he could scarcely contain his rage.

They must have had a row, thought Molly, a real flamer earlier in the day. A dispute they would continue as soon as they had deposited their guests at the hotel and were alone and could resume the engagement in private. Molly knew the signs: the lack of eye contact, the rigid forward-staring eyes, the seething barely contained displeasure as they prepared to go through the motions of meeting and greeting strangers they had no wish to meet, greet or see. Or not at the moment.

Molly had seen the same thing at a reception at Government House in honour of the Queen and Duke of Edinburgh on the occasion of their recent state visit to New Zealand. The row must have taken place before they left their private apartments. Molly knew this as surely as if the Queen had confided or the Duke revealed. She saw it in the way they stood, heard it in the waves of distance rocketing between them. The Duke's face and form were wooden as a totem pole decked out in the full dress uniform of an Admiral of the

Fleet. The Queen also was in full fig, hung about with diamonds and doing her best as usual. Her diamond necklace must have been of such antiquity that the stones preceded modern cutting techniques. They looked like glass pebbles, each one surrounded by a rim of metal reminiscent of that used by dentists to isolate a tooth under repair. The interesting thing for Molly, the thought which pleased her throughout the evening, was that despite their vast size and lack of brilliance the diamonds must have been real. Queens don't do costume.

There had been a problem, explained Her Majesty to her audience, with the positioning of the TV cameras at the Official Parliamentary Luncheon to welcome their Royal Highnesses at the Beehive earlier in the day. The cameras, had they noticed, had been positioned in a small gallery above the swinging doors which led to the kitchens.

'I did, ma'am,' said Hamish. 'I thought at the time.'

Courtesy, continued Her Majesty, had required her to address her present audience gathered in the Banqueting Chamber, but if she had done so throughout the whole length of her speech, her nationwide television audience would have seen nothing but the top of her hat.

'What,' she asked, demonstrating the problem to Molly and Hamish with exasperated lifts and dips of her tiara, 'was one expected to do?'

Molly had made small conciliatory mews of distress appropriate to the occasion. Hamish and the Duke said nothing.

Nor did Hamish or the Minister of Trade and Agriculture, or the beautiful Miss Raya. Molly found herself nodding, smiling idiotically, even making vague whimpers of concern once more. Why me, she thought. I am in no way responsible for this rift, this domestic gulch between our hosts. I have a rift of my own, a rift with my well-loved daughter. Like everyone else in this room, with the probable exception of the still unblinking Miss Raya and some of the more easy-going members like Violet, I wish to be alone.

———

'What hotel is Bridget staying at, Freddy?' she asked as they waded through the sticky heat to the line of chauffeur-driven cars.

'I have no idea, Mrs Carew,' said Freddy, steering her towards the High Commissioner's one.

'How kind of you to put the air conditioning on in advance,' said Molly to the driver. 'What is your name?'

'Kamil, ma'am. No problem.'

The three-car cavalcade of visitors set off for the Hotel Hilton in order of seniority and line astern, accompanied by a six-man police escort on motor bicycles with sirens screaming. Traffic pulled over, stopped short; citizens leapt for cover.

'How silly,' said Molly.

'Not in this traffic,' replied Hamish.

'Hell's fangs,' said Violet in the car behind, 'do they always do this?'

'I don't know,' said Freddy, 'but it's good for the ministerial ego.'

Violet glanced at him sitting beside her in the car in which the air conditioning had not been turned on. So, she thought. You have no idea where Bridget is staying. Good. I am glad to hear it. Now let's have a bit of sense around here.

She looked at the hands splayed on his knees. They reminded her of Bronson Foster's – long fingers, strong, a good pair of hands.

'Did you play footy at school?' she asked.

He shook his head. 'Men seldom make passes at boys who wear glasses.'

'Who said that?'

'Dorothy Sayers didn't.'

He turned to her. You could trust that face; the eyes, the curve of the mouth, even the arch of the eyebrows were trustworthy. He heard his voice, the unexpected words as they fell.

'Do you ever go off people, Violet?'

146

She examined the query, required more. 'What form does it take?'

'Just that. Get sick of people. Go off them.'

'Everybody?'

He put his damp hand over hers. 'Not entirely,' he said.

'Yuck,' she said, dragging her hand out and turning to the window and the roadworks, shopping complexes, factories with British names, the bicycles and cars scattering before their sirens.

How could he have attempted to hold her hand in this heat. Mad.

'This was such a pretty place once,' he said, attempting casual conversation.

'No, I don't,' said Violet as though he had not spoken. 'But if I did, it wouldn't be me. There's no point in hating yourself. If you have to, make it someone else. Look, there's a banana palm.'

He was taken back, shocked into further idiocy. 'I don't hate me.'

She smiled, gave his cheek a friendly peck. 'Dear Freddy,' she said.

The Kuala Lumpur Hilton was larger, grander and even more elaborately ornate than the New Mandarin. It was also more security conscious. Two armed guards at the end of their corridor were to maintain twenty-four-hour surveillance, a fact of great interest to Molly.

'Are you licensed to kill?' she asked the young soldier who sprang to alarmed attention and said nothing.

'Excuse me, Minister,' said Manders as they walked from the lift to their rooms, 'may I have a word with you?'

They moved away. Manders put the secure communications briefcase between his feet and clamped a leg either side. 'Guards or no guards, sir, I will be taking this' – he gave the case an extra nudge with his calves – 'to the High

147

Commission Chancery each evening to put it in their safe.'

'Why didn't you do that at Hong Kong?'

'Because I had a safe in my room. I told Steve Roper that would be essential.'

'Why not in my room?'

'They're not usual in suites, sir. Not secure ones.' Manders sketched big ugly intrusive safes with his hands, shook his head, frowned slightly.

Hamish thought of something. 'Then why didn't you insist on a safe in your room here?'

'Because there aren't any.'

Hamish, relieved that he was not missing out on something desirable to which he was entitled, glanced around at the ladies. They were both present and correct, standing at a suitable distance from Fred and himself, their feet sinking into bright green carpet. Molly and Violet looked back. Hamish felt a faint flush of pride. Being the leader of a team never did anyone any harm, and he had found the drive from the airport exhilarating. Also it was nice to have the PM off his back for a while. He straightened, felt an easing, a sense of expansion.

'The High Commissioner gave me a run down on the cables from home' he said.

'Anything special?' said Manders.

'Not at the moment, no.'

'So,' said Hamish, moving back to his team. 'Lunch at the Smorgasbord Swiss Buttery in half an hour? You've all have the programme at your fingertips, I assume?'

The team nodded.

'They've obviously decided to get the sightseeing over this afternoon and get down to business tomorrow,' said Hamish. 'We'll be going at a fair lick to get them all in. First stop the New Parliament Building. They're not sitting at the moment. Then the Memorial to those who died in the Insurgency, then the National Mosque. And tonight there's the dinner at the

High Commission. You'll be able to leave the classified stuff at the residence then, Fred.'

Manders, who had no intention of carting a briefcase of classified papers around the sights of Kuala Lumpur in this heat, demurred.

'I think, Minister, it would be safer to get hold of a driver and slip along to the Chancery now.'

'What about lunch?' said Hamish.

'Oh, don't bother about me,' said Manders, who saw himself clutching a cold beer and a prawn and avocado sandwich beside the High Commission's swimming pool. Penn McPhee was a good friend and was reputed to have a good cook. Prawn and avocado would do.

He had an unwelcome flick of memory. There had been another plan, had there not, a plan of long resolving conversations by the pool with Bridget, of discussions as meaningful as those anticipated between the two Ministers. He put his hand to his cheek.

'What are you grinning about?' said Hamish.

'Was I, sir? Sorry. I would feel a lot happier, Minister, if I could get this safely stowed immediately.'

He pulled the programme from an inside pocket and checked it with his watch: *ETA 15.15 Main front entrance of New Parliament.*

'I'll be waiting at the Parliament Building at 15.00. Would that suit you, Minister?'

'It seems rather irregular,' said Hamish.

'If I may so, sir, it would be more irregular if the classified stuff went missing at the mosque.'

'Why would anyone pick on the mosque?'

'A visit to the mosque will be more, how shall I say, informal,' said Freddy smoothly. 'The public obviously can't be banned from being there and there will be taking off of shoes, putting on of long-sleeved garments for the ladies, all rather casual situations as regards security. If I have your permission in principle,' he continued, 'I'll get on to Penn McPhee as regards transport, etc. My aim is to leave the classified documents in the Chancery safe and bring back anything of interest to you from the High Commission bag.'

'Yes, yes, in principle,' said Hamish. 'Get on to McPhee and give me a ring.' He looked around. 'Where's Molly?'

'Violet has escorted her to the suite, sir.'

'Oh. Good.'

13

'Good,' roared Penn down the phone. 'It'll be a chance for us to talk things over. There are one or two things going on here you should be privy to. And you can give me the guts on the new job. Yes, well, we all think that from time to time.

'I don't normally go home for lunch but Amanda and the kids aren't here as you know, and it's rather peaceful by the pool with a sandwich and a beer. What you had in mind? Well there you go ... great minds, all that crap. I'll get Kamil to pick you up first. Twelve thirty too early? Right. See you then. We'll put the stuff in the safe and shove off. Have you time for a swim? No? Tough.'

The New Zealand Chancery was housed in what had been an old colonial-style home on the corner of two roads. A pleasant two-storeyed building with wide verandahs, it stood at the top of a slight rise, screened on all sides by large trees.

Penn McPhee came to meet him. He had the rough curly hair and ruddy face of a man who, if he had been born a few generations back, had been a foot slogger in the First World War, say, or an air gunner in the Second or a swagger in between, would have been called Curly. Even his stance was resolute as he stood, head forward, feet apart, guarding his safe.

'I can't give you the combination, of course, and I'd prefer to secure and release the stuff myself rather than any of the staff. OK?'

'Sure. It'll take a bit of liaising in the evenings but I quite understand,' said Manders, who was not sure that he did, but if the man wanted to be coy about his combination you could hardly query it. The ultimate responsibly was still Penn's, however gung-ho his behaviour. 'I'll turn my back now.'

'Arse,' said Penn cheerfully. 'I'll tell you why later.' He opened the safe and stowed the confidential papers. 'Do you want the briefcase?'

'Yes. Any letters for the Minister or Mrs Carew in the bag?'

'Two,' said Penn, handing them over.

'You've met Kamil, haven't you?' he said at the car.

'Yes, several times,' said Freddy. 'I was asking him on the way over how many years he's been with us. Seventeen isn't it, Kamil?'

'Yes, sir,' said Kamil, jumping behind the wheel as the two climbed in. 'Seventeen it is, sir.'

'Good to see you again, you old bastard,' said Penn stretching his legs.

'Yeah,' said Freddy. 'How's life?'

'Good. And you?'

'Mustn't grumble.'

'I don't see why not. How's Bridget?'

'She's gone to Paris.'

'Yes, I heard. Bit weird.'

'Yes.'

'Yes, well. How's your so-called Swing Around going? Everything OK?'

'So far.'

'Good, good.'

The car swung out on to the road. 'You don't have a guard at the gate?' said Freddy.

'Good God no. We're always pleased to see anyone.' Penn nodded at the back of Kamil's head. 'We'll keep El Supremo for the poolside.'

'Definitely,' said Freddy.

'And the lady? Some of them are the pits. We've had some shockers through here. Ask Amanda.'

'Not Mrs Carew. She's different. For one thing she'd tie herself in knots to avoid being a nuisance. Definitely different.'

'A complex character?'

'I would have thought so. However, she managed to go walkabout in Hong Kong.'

'Jeez.'

'Yeah, it was.'

'And who's this Violet woman?'

Manders thought. 'She's tall. I like her.'

'Good. But what's she doing on this trip?'

Manders was silent, remembering his same thought and his more forcible expression of it.

It occurred to him now, bowling along in air-conditioned comfort beside a good friend in a chauffeur-driven Holden, that he could not visualise the Swing Around without Violet. It was impossible. She was there, supportive, tolerant yet crisp, with an eye for absurdities and an ear for gossip. Attractive and getting more so. Some women do in the tropics; others just melt. He saw her across the rickety table at the Boston

New Chinese where he had bitten her head off. Completely justified of course, but . . .

'She's in CLAT,' he said. 'Administration. Here to help with the work if I get bogged down. But I guess the main reason is for her to support Mrs Carew. There's usually more than one woman on these trips and you're on your own at the moment.'

'True. Does Mrs Carew need support?'

'I don't think it does her any harm.'

'Hmm. And have you got "bogged down"?'

Manders gave him a quick glance. 'No, I haven't.'

They left the commercial centre with its air of buoyant chaos, that tearing down of buildings and replacing with bigger ones which indicates economic growth in developing countries. The place was throbbing, undoubtedly on the way up. Roads seemed to disappear overnight to be flung up the next day by half-naked men in safety helmets driving large machines or pushing barrows at the trot.

'Booming,' Freddy muttered.

'Yes,' said Penn. 'The Vietnam War didn't do your country any harm, did it, Kamil?'

Kamil glanced in the rear vision mirror. 'No sir,' he said.

Freddy took the hint. Silent, polite servants have the art of disappearing from view while still present. Anecdotal shop is best.

'So who's going to get Rome next?' said Penn.

'The smart money's on Barratt, with Cockburn as an outside chance.'

'You don't mean Cockup Cockburn?'

'Of course I do. How many do you want?'

'Christ. They wouldn't dare. Not Cockup. Not *Rome*. Whatever happened to Lockie? He was the frontrunner when we left and that's not two years ago.'

Manders smiled the slow satisfied smile of a man who finds himself with an attentive audience and an untold story.

'Don't tell me you haven't heard about the balls-up in Brussels?'

'Tell me.'

'It's a long story,' said Freddy.

In fact the story, despite one or two embellishments, was not long. It was a story which has been retold for ever, the one about the cuckolded husband and the young bride, her fiery young lover and the husband's revenge. A story of lust and betrayal and discovery and farce, of slamming doors and skidding feet, of ups and downs and naked bodies and moans in strange places.

'You don't mean *literally* under the desk,' roared Penn.

'So they tell me,' said Freddy as Kamil turned into the gates of the residence. 'Nice, isn't it.'

'Poor old Lockie. I don't know whether to laugh or cry,' laughed Penn.

The High Commissioner's residence was Manders' favourite among tropical posts. Like most of the houses in the area it was backed by giant trees twenty metres or more in height. The rooms, with their high ceilings and stone floors, were large and pleasant, with cross-draughts and overhead fans dating from pre-air conditioning days.

Penn's predecessor, a keen art collector, had brought some of his favourite pictures with him to enhance the government issue already there. There were still some rather obvious gaps on the walls where the man had, as Penn put it, 'marched off with the lot'.

Amanda McPhee, like every Head of Mission's wife Freddy had ever met, had got rid of as much as possible of the crud chosen by the previous spouse; had replaced the wobbly rattan tables with Korean chests, swapped the chintzes for blue and white cottons, and ditched the artificial flower arrangements. It now possessed, thought Freddy, the fundamental requirements for comfort in the tropics: cool floors, cool colours, and plenty of light and air. It also possessed that essential ingredient for official houses abroad: enough space not only to entertain in but to impress.

He wondered if the cane furniture by the swimming pool still had holes in the arms for the cool glass. His mother would have approved of those. It was the small things, what she called 'the little touches', that count. She must be about to have a birthday soon. Bridget dealt with birthdays, but Bridget was no longer in residence and never would be. She had left him, had shot through for ever and ever and ever.

Penn and the Chinese amah who had greeted them departed for a word with the cook. Get him to rustle up something.

Manders wandered out to the swimming pool and lowered himself into the cane chair under the vine-covered shelter. He noted with pleasure that the holes for glasses were still there, put his feet up and gazed beyond the glinting water to the tropical exuberance of the garden. Above the ubiquitous hibiscus, one giant tree flamed with red flowers, another with yellow. Maintaining a garden in the midst of such lush growth must be largely a matter of unremitting hacking and slashing and avoidance of snakes.

He felt drowsy, yawned. Even the strutting mynas seemed subdued. Freddy lowered the straw hat Penn had lent him over his eyes and thought about Bridget. He relived the scene in the Plaza Royale, saw her white-lipped passionate conviction. She would never change. This commitment was not one of those little touches, and never had been. He realised, accepted, knew that now. It had taken him long enough.

'Are you deep in thought or half asleep?' said Penn.

'Both.'

Penn swung his legs on to his recliner. 'Anything interesting? You look as though you've seen a great light.'

'Yes. I was thinking,' said Freddy. 'It's not the end of the world, is it?'

'Not as far as I know.' Penn adjusted his hat, rubbed his

hands. 'Now tell me about Carew. Fill me in. Can he be trusted?'

'Of course he can be trusted. He's honourable, decent, had a good war.'

Penn raised a hand as the amah shuffled forward with their beer. 'Thanks, Ah Sue. Carry on,' he said as she disappeared.

'No wonder you waited till we were out of the car,' huffed Manders.

'Yes, it's never fair to talk in front of them. Not that it would have mattered with Kamil. You could trust him anywhere. Wonderful man. Loyal as they come. Did I ever tell you his story about the cobra in the compound?'

'No.'

'Remind me sometime. What I really want to know is, can Carew be trusted in a crisis? Does he tend to panic, anticipate the worst if there's an emergency. When his wife disappeared, for example. How did he react?'

Freddy blinked, saw the slumped figure on the lime green sofa, Violet bending over it. 'He certainly anticipated the worst,' he said with care. 'I merely thought he was showing connubial concern.' He thought a moment, corrected himself. 'No that's not quite right. He did panic a bit. But why ask?'

Penn leaned forward. 'What do you know about "Lightning Storm"?'

Freddy yawned. 'Not a sausage.'

'Smartarse. Have you heard of them?'

'No.'

'Well, you should have.'

'Tell me.'

'Ah Sue will be back in a minute with the sandwiches. I'll tell you about Kamil and the cobra.'

'If you insist.'

'Just to give you an idea of the type of man he is. Amanda and the children were home for a mid-year break and I found I was a bit lonely. Well, not lonely exactly, and Amanda deserved the break, she'd been half killing herself fighting the

Ministry to come across with the refurbishing money and then she'd had to oversee every move the locals made on the job. You know what it's like.'

'No.'

'But I did miss them, especially the twins. They'd just turned six, cute kids. You'll notice all the small things in this house come in twos.' Penn waved an arm at two pink tricycles beside a couple of identical-sized dolls' prams. 'Twice the evidence of absence wherever you look. Extraordinary.

'And you know what,' he said, flinging his palms upwards, 'Kamil took me under his wing.'

'What?'

'Yes. I didn't say anything of course,' said Penn quickly. 'He must've just sensed it. He took to telling me stories on the way home each night.'

Freddy glanced at him warily.

'Normally we don't talk much but I liked his stories. Like most Malays he's got a nice sense of humour, and of drama. No hand gestures of course, but the voice going up and down, booming and cooing and rising to the climax. Stories about his youth up north where his father and his grandfather were both armed civilians against the communists for years. Kamil was toting a rifle when he was twelve. But my favourite story is the one about the cobra.'

'Forget the bloody cobra,' said Freddy, 'tell me about things here.'

'It's an interesting time to be here, as you can imagine,' said Penn, unperturbed. 'Economy booming as you see.'

'All set fair in racial relationships now?'

'Yes, though I wondered where Carew got his platitudes. Still, it's ten years now since the real troubles. There are a few isolated incidents, but racial harmony is the national song. They're doing well by and large, considering the number of ethnic groups involved and the nationalisation programme. A certain amount of "pork eaters, yah", "beef eaters, yah", perhaps. I imagine that still goes on. Kamil doesn't live here. The cook and the amahs, all the inside staff, are Chinese. And of course there's the problem of the boat people. I heard the other day there's a million Chinese going to be expelled from Vietnam next. What the hell's going to happen to the poor buggers? Sure it's a worldwide problem, but places round here are the obvious ports of call.'

Penn sat up straight. 'Thanks, Ah Sue, that looks good.'

The two cane trays were as identical as the dolls' prams but more engaging. Plates of avocado and prawn sandwiches lay beside bright napkins. Tomatoes had been fashioned into lotus flowers, radishes into roses, celery formed into slender hoops encircling salmon-pink hibiscus flowers.

'They eat with their eyes, don't they,' said Freddy.

'Not only that. For the well-heeled everything must be beautiful to look at, to hold, to wear, to eat. Amazing place, used to be quite Byzantine, I gather.' Penn glanced at his watch. 'Kamil's cobra's missed its flip again. But back to Lightning Storm.' He hitched his behind closer, leaned forward to confide. 'Has it occurred to you that terrorism has been re-invented recently?'

Freddy inspected a radish. 'It's never needed to be re-invented.'

'No, but think of the way they operate now. Small, completely dedicated cells of highly trained men prepared to die for the cause, to operate thousands of miles from their headquarters if necessary. Think of Black September at Munich. That's the sort of outfit I'm talking about: the murder of the Italian Prime Minister, the general proliferation of kidnapping, hijacking, the deliberate targeting of civilians in bomb attacks. Baader Meinhoff, Weathermen. All in the seventies, the lot of them.'

'You'd better get a guard on the gate,' said Manders.

Penn gave him a long look. 'You really are up yourself, aren't you?'

'OK. OK. Tell me about Lightning Storm.'

'After that build-up I have to admit they're not in the same league. We don't know much about them except that they specialise in kidnaps and hefty ransoms. They're thought to be a Chinese outfit, or were originally, but the experts, in particular Beaucott our defence attaché and the local Special Branch, seem to think they've left their home ground and infiltrated other parts of Asia.'

'Communist then?'

'Not necessarily, apparently. I gather they don't seem to be ideologically inspired. More a particularly nasty pack of thugs.'

'But what's this got to do with Carew?'

'Ah, thank you,' said Penn, springing to his feet and handing the old woman his tray. 'Finished with your tray, Freddy? Yes? Thank you. And the beer.' He watched the black-trousered figure depart again. 'This is getting ridiculous,' he said. 'Have you met Beaucott?'

'Briefly.'

'What did you think of him?'

'His shoes were well polished.'

Penn sucked his teeth. 'Yes, that sounds like him. He'll have to brief the Minister about all this, it's his part of the ship, but he's rather . . . well, not jittery exactly, but frankly I can't think why Security ever sent him. So if Carew and he get excited together they might blow the thing out of all proportion. Go off at half cock before we've got enough on them. Singapore and Bangkok have both been in touch with me, and I've been sending cables home about it every few days. No one seems interested. I've been wondering about advising the PM direct.'

'Upstairs would hate that,' said Freddy serenely.

'Yeah, I'll have a quiet word with the Minister tonight after dinner. Soothing atmosphere, man to man, that sort of thing. And you can get alongside Beaucott, see what you make of him. Barney'll keep the girls in play.'

'Barney who?'

'Kinsella. Trade. Haven't you met him? Bit of a shit, but he has his uses. Damn, we'll have to go. Must have another word with the cook, make sure tonight's dinner is under control. Extraordinary the things I get landed with when Amanda is away.

'Come on,' he said, patting the hood of a toy pram in passing.

Manders was waiting at the main front entrance of the Parliament Buildings when the party and their escorts appeared at 15.15. Violet gave him a discreet wink which touched his heart. His grandmother had had a brooch in the form of a minuscule golden hand on which lay a plump red enamel heart. She had had some difficulty explaining its significance to him.

'But why is the gentleman's heart in the lady's hand, Granny?'

Granny had plumped for the soft option. 'You'll understand one day, dear.'

Hamish was speaking to him. 'Yes Minister,' he said, 'the classified things are in the safe. Penn McPhee put them in himself.'

'Was there any mail for me in the bag, Freddy?' asked Molly.

'Yes, Mrs Carew,' said Freddy, banging his briefcase with his hand in confirmation. 'Would you like it now?'

'Did you happen to notice the post mark?'

He looked into her pale eyes. 'As a matter of fact I did. It looked like Hamilton.'

'Hamilton,' she said softly. 'No thank you, Freddy. I'll wait till we get back to the hotel. I was just saying to Datin Ahmad how beautiful the Parliament Buildings are. I'm sorry you missed them.'

———

It had been a very interesting afternoon. The Parliament Buildings had indeed been impressive, the bronze sculptured War Memorial, both beautiful and heartbreaking and the National Mosque unforgettable. A peaceful place, different and unknown. Sometimes it doesn't matter if one knows nothing and understands less; just to stand, draped in long-sleeved black gauze and surrounded by space and silence. To look.

Molly swung her stockinged feet on to the pale satin and tore open her letter. It was cheating, especially after the mosque, but the words formed in her mind. Please don't let her hate me.

The letter had several pages.

Home. Tuesday.

Dear Mum and Dad,

I know you won't arrive in KL for days but I'm sending this via the bag like you said Dad, so's it will be waiting when you arrive.

I hope you're having a wow of a time and have got the shopping under control like you said you would. I may as well tell you straight off the sexy underwear will be even more welcome now! Yes, Mum, you've guessed, I can just see you bouncing up and down on some glamorous bed with excitement when I tell you the news. As of last week Bron and I are a couple. Well, we've been good friends since he arrived as you know ha ha, but now it's official. No, don't panic, we're not married and won't be till he can divorce his wife, and anyway I don't want some hole in a corner affair. I can *see* the marquee on the front lawn, the full works for Roberta and then some. It's a bore I can't give Cuisine Catering a date now, they get booked up so far ahead, but do find some ivory silk for my gown, Mum. I really mean this.

In the meantime I'm over the moon. So is Bron. The wife was just a one-night stand he says, but her father got really heavy and insisted they got married. Can you imagine, in this day and age! I mean she wasn't even pregnant or anything. I said why didn't he just clear off, but apparently she's the clinging type and he said he couldn't live with himself if he didn't give it a go, and anyway there was Dad coming on strong in all directions. He takes a bit of getting to know (Bron I mean). Well not for me he didn't, but you know what I mean. But when you do, WOW!

Love from your happy, happy, whacky, slap happy daughter,

Bobby.

REMEMBER, IVORY SILK.

Molly handed the letter to Hamish. He read it and handed it back.

'She could do a lot worse. Very sound, Bronson.'

'He's left his wife. Doesn't that matter?'

'So what are you going to do about it? Shotgun him back? You can't play God, Mol.'

'I am not "playing God",' said Molly. 'That's one of the stupidest phrases I know. Just when people have almost forgotten about Him we're all suddenly accused of playing Him. I am concerned for the man's wife, yes, but I'm far more concerned for the welfare of your daughter.'

Hamish did not answer. He knew it would be unwise either now or later to mention his real reason for confidence in her future. Bobby would inherit the farm. This fact would be obvious to anyone.

Hamish loved his daughter dearly and was proud of her. He did not mean, not for a moment, that Foster was attracted to her solely because of the farm, but he did realise that it was a strong safeguard against any man, let alone a land-hungry slogger like Foster, letting her down or deserting her. The farm was in Bobby's name and would remain so.

These thoughts did not disturb Hamish but he knew better than to mention them to Molly. Women were weird about land. They didn't seem to realise how deep down a man's feeling for it goes. It wasn't their fault; they just hadn't got it in them, except perhaps the Maori ladies. Besides, he liked what he had seen of Bronson. He was impressed by the man's meticulousness, hard work and initiative. And Bronson was no slouch mentally either. Look at his interest in new techniques. Computers were going to be essential, he'd told Hamish, especially if you were in the dairy industry. He had demonstrated, gesticulated with rolling movements of one hand pursuing the flattened length of the other.

'Look at it this way,' he had said to Hamish. 'At the end of the day, with the accelerating technological advances in computer science you've got one of two choices.' His hands continued rolling and flattening before Hamish's gaze. 'Either you're part of the roller or else you're part of the road. Nothing,' he said, 'is going to stop computers.'

'If he's deserted one wife,' said Molly again, 'how do you know he won't desert Bobby? Decent men don't desert women.'

'For God's sake, Mol, we don't know if he's deserted anyone. We'll talk about it later. I'll have to change soon. Give me half an hour on my back. Please.'

He closed his eyes. 'New Zealanders only tonight, isn't it?'

Molly checked the programme. 'Yes.'

'Thank God.'

'Who are they all?'

Hamish took the programme and glanced at it.

'Haven't been briefed,' he said as it fell from his fingers. 'Fred'll tell us.'

14

I'm in love, I'm in love, I'm in love, I'm in love, with a wonderful guy, sang Bobby to her newly watered mother-of-millions.

The words beat in her heart, heightened her excitement, her wonder at the joys of the night before last. Bedded, she thought, that's what. I have been bedded like some bloody virgin. Hell's delight, have I been bedded.

Nobody knew the loving she'd had. Such fierce, innovative stuff. Previous lovers, the hairy and the smooth, the smartarse and the shy, the truly loved and the why-nots, flashed before her. Not one of them ever got to first base compared to Bron Foster, sharemilker.

She murmured his name to herself. Bronson Foster, sharemilker with knobs on. You could say that again. I, sighed Bobby, have been fucked silly.

But not last night. Monday was bookwork night. Regular as clockwork, Bron slogged away down there for hours. She'd loathed not being with him but it had given her a chance to bung off the aerogramme. Bron was so *focused*. That was one of the things she admired about him. Boy could he focus.

Giggling with joy at the thought, she flung her arms wide and hugged herself. Why wait? Go down to the sheds and give him a hand now.

Leaping over cow pats, singing to the skies, Bobby ran down the hill.

Spike appeared from the back yard of the cottage, barked a welcome and pranced beside her. Bobby fell on her knees in the grass, flung her arms around the smooth mole-coloured neck and hugged him. 'Spike,' she murmured, 'oh, Spike darling.' She sat back on her heels, ducking her head in failed attempts to avoid his slobbering tongue. 'No boy, down. Why aren't you with the boss? Come on.'

Spike backed sharply, stared at her and barked again.

'Come on, y'dope, this way.'

Spike continued towards the cottage, turning his head periodically and barking again.

'All right, don't come,' said Bobby with the flick of resentment of a dog lover whose best friend won't play.

Spike turned full face to her and backed away still barking, made a few rolling high-kneed prances in the direction of the cottage, turned again and barked louder than ever.

Bobby got it. Couldn't for the life of her think why she hadn't got it before. This was classic *Lassie Come Home* stuff. Help is needed, come this way. Bron was electrocuted, dead, flat on the floor. How could she have been so thick.

'Come on,' she yelled, and ran. They turned into the

yard at full speed. An old Volkswagen sat parked beside Bron's pick-up truck.

Doctor. Oh Christ, a doctor.

The dog looked at her. He was right again. Doctors don't drive around in 1950s Volkswagen beetles, let alone rusty ones.

She walked round the corner past the old cars. A cardboard carton lay by the back door, its few remaining contents open to the sky. A yellowing blanket, an upended car seat and a de-whiskered hairbrush lay nearby. On the kitchen window sill a half-empty bottle of Diet Coke lay beside an unwashed baby's bottle, a fly-spotted paper fan and a toy orang-utan with green hair. What the hell was going on?

'Anyone home?' she called.

Silence, the scent of wisteria and something else: the sharp sickly smell of acetone. Bobby opened her mouth to call again.

Around the corner of a connecting door came a small child naked except for a nappy. Its face was streaked with jam, its smile wide. In one hand it held the limbless torso of a pink celluloid doll. The other hand held the head with its unblinking blue gaze and vapid smile. The child lifted both hands and offered them to her as Spike gambolled around him. The child grabbed the animal's neck, hugged it briefly, then shoved the hound off. 'Go way, Pike.'

Spike went.

'Busted,' said the child, dropping its padded behind on to the top step to await developments.

'Where's your mum?' said Bobby.

There was a sister somewhere, she remembered, and a nephew. Her marriage had just folded and she was stuck with the kid. Gail, that was the name. Gail.

'Busted,' said the child again. 'Dolly busted.'

Bobby took the torso and head in her hands and sat down beside the blue-eyed hairless child. 'You smell,' she said.

The child bent double, put nose to nappy, gave a long sniff and patted its padded front. 'Moist,' it agreed.

Bobby grinned, gasped with relief and joy. Obviously there had been no disaster. Spike must have wanted her to see this weird extraterrestrial-looking kid. She put the head and torso together and handed the doll back to its owner, who disappeared inside calling, 'Mum, Dolly good, Mum.'

What was it doing in nappies if it could talk?

She followed him through to the other room.

'Anyone home?' she called again.

A young woman appeared at the doorway. She was thin as a rail, pale as the sleazy silk-like fabric of her robe. That was the word, robe; you saw them in old films with Rita Hayworth falling out the front. But not this time. Not a chance. Even the legs were skin and bone. The toes of one foot were painted black, the others were untouched. The woman held the open bottle of varnish carefully in one hand and its brush in the other, flicked back her long tangled yellow hair and stared.

'What d'ya want?' she said.

Bobby stood flat footed, startled by poise. 'I'm Bobby from up the hill.'

The woman sat, balanced her behind on the brown velvet-like stuff of one of the chairs. It rolled slightly. She swore softly, centred herself, clamped the ungarnished foot against her thigh and dipped the brush in the bottle. Only then did she reply.

'Yeah?'

'I fixed your child's doll,' said Bobby idiotically.

'Tray,' yelled the woman. The child appeared chewing the doll's head. 'Some fix,' his mother grinned and continued applying the polish with the absorbed concentration of a small child learning how to tie its shoelaces. The black shiny stuff flowed like oil slick.

'Forget it,' she said after some time. 'He likes them better in bits, don't you, matey?'

Tray flung one arm around his bulbous stomach and patted his front with the other. 'Moist,' he said.

'You! You're never not moist, are you, you little toe rag.'

168

She went on with her work in silence.

Bobby sat down and stared at the cowboy. 'Nice poster,' she said.

'It's his.'

Naturally, thicko. Bobby tried again. 'So where's Bron?'

The woman was now staring at her fingernails. 'How d'ya know he's called that?'

'He works for my father, like I said. I'm Bobby Carew. And you're Bron's sister. Right?'

Silence, total silence once more, broken only by Tray's lisping chatter from the bedroom.

Finally the woman spoke. 'So what d'ya want?'

Bitch. Bobby cleared her throat, thought quickly. 'Dad's not happy with the mess in the back yard, he said. Those cars.'

The woman took her time, blew on her fingers one by one. 'What about them?'

'They're an eyesore.'

'Who says?'

'He does. Dad.'

'Not to me they're not. I think they're beautiful.'

Her task finished the woman spread her fingers wide and proud for inspection, lifted both arms to her head, dragged lank hair languidly behind each ear and changed tone. Her small black eyes flashed. She sprang to her feet, pulling the silky stuff tight around her.

'Bully!' she cried. 'Pack of sodding bullies, the lot of you. I'd have you know, all that out there's my livelihood.'

Bobby's head reeled. She felt bloodless, faint, sick as a dog. She leaned her spinning head against the back of the chair and gripped the armless sides hard.

'Yours?' she gasped. 'They're your cars?'

'Of course they're my bloody cars. Mine. Mitty's, that's whose. Whose the hell did you think they were?'

She waved her fingers, clenched and unclenched the black-tipped weapons at Bobby's stricken face.

'I'm a trained mechanic, see, that's why I use black. It's great to hide the muck. I don't like looking mucky. How d'ya think we're going to save for our own herd on what he earns? Well, I got news, I got news for you. Him and me'll be off like a rocket when we've got the dough.' Her face tightened, clenched like her fingers. 'You make me toss, you know that. I've worked for it, done my apprentice, exams, the lot, year after year of slog, and you swan in down here . . . "Dad says it's got to go",' she mimicked. 'Well we're not going till we're good and ready, and neither are the cars. Got it?

'Look at you,' she snarled. 'Sitting there, I bet you can't even use a spanner. You've gotta have the strength. Look!' Mitty pulled back a sleeve, exposed a pale arm and flexed it. A small bump the size of a table tennis ball appeared. 'And wrists. See?'

'So you're, you're his . . .' whispered Bobby. 'And the child.'

Mitty was not listening. Her head lifted, she scented the air, one black-tipped finger raised.

'Listen! He's here.'

Boots thudded on bare boards.

'Bronziebum,' she cried and flung herself at him.

Bobby clung to the television. Never, never, never had she felt like this. The pain, the sick all-engulfing weakness swamped her, stopped her breathing and drained her heart.

'Hi Bob,' said Bron over his wife's head. 'You've met Mitty then?'

She stared at him in shock. 'Yeah. And Tray too.'

'Yeah.' He dragged the back of his hand across his face. 'They came last night. Unexpected.'

Bobby sat down.

Mitty was now wrapped around her husband as though attempting to climb him. He looked down at the blonde head against his chest and sighed.

'Not even dressed yet?'

Mitty tossed her hair. 'I haven't had a chance. What with her coming, and Tray and all.' She gave a sharp intake of breath. 'You know what? She says he says I gotta get rid of the cars. How can I get rid of the cars? I can't get a job in town, not with Tray around, I can't. I've gotta do them here, stuck here like I said. What else can I do?'

Bron looked at her, his face tense, exhausted. 'How many times have I told you, Mits? Leave it to me. Don't go off at half cock, leave it to me.' He turned to Bobby, nodded. 'Me and Bobby's Dad'll work it all out. Don't do y' bun, kid, calm down.' He gave his wife a quick pat on her bottom. 'And get some clothes on.'

Mitty dragged her robe around her once more, gave a disgusted heave of her shoulders and disappeared into the bedroom.

'Bobby,' said Bronson.

A wail from the bedroom, followed by yelping rage: 'What the hell've you got now? Put it *down,* Tray. There's no knowing where it's been. Put it down, can't y'.'

Bobby stared at her lover.

'You sod. You fucking lousy sod,' she said, and walked out.

She was blinded, disoriented, terminally bewildered and in need of help. She clutched the kitchen table, felt for the support of the doorjamb, almost fell down the steps and tripped over Spike who lay beside the half-empty carton with his paws in the air. Bobby pulled herself upright and swore. She could have kicked the emaciated beast, kicked it to death and beyond. Spike rolled upright, took a step towards her and growled.

Some shred of self-preservation remained. 'Get stuffed,' snarled Bobby, and walked on.

Looking neither left nor right, head high and heart thudding, she strode past the cars and out the gate. She would go home another way, round the back past the calves, anywhere, any way that she couldn't be seen by the sod and his wife.

Rage, red hot flaming rage sustained her temporarily. The fool, the idiotic flaming fool. How could he, how could he have married that tart, that sleazy mucky no-hoper of a tart. And the kid, the stinking blinking Tray. Tray, for God's sake. It was a shotgun job, obviously. But how could he?

Rage could sustain her no more. Tears of grief, humiliation and loss poured down her cheeks as she strode onwards to the calves.

He had done everything with that woman. Everything she, Bobby, had known, had lived and died for with her naked writhing lover, Mits had known too. She was mad about him. You could see that. Crawling all over him, practically eating the man.

Bobby saw the exhausted face above the woman's head and wept again.

And that pat worried her, that married sort of pat on the bottom. Would he have done that, could he have done that, if he had hated the woman? It had been resigned, gentle even.

The repercussions of such thoughts lacerated her. Half blinded by tears she tripped in a rabbit hole, fell on her face and lay spread-eagled. Still sobbing she clutched the grass with her hands, smelled the pungent smell of fertile loam and ancient cow pats. Nearby cows lifted their heads, looked her over and munched again. Bobby closed her eyes and lay still.

'Dad,' she said, 'Dad.'

Ever since she had known Hamish he had had the same words for time-wasting, unproductive activities such as sitting in the sun doing nothing or reading useless magazines. He would stand, drawl, 'Yeah, well, this won't buy the kid a frock,' and return to work.

Bobby dragged herself up and went to check the calves.

She heard him calling from the French doors.

'Bobby, heh Bob, I got to talk to you.'

She took her time, turned off the element under the calves'

mash, took a quick check in the hall mirror and came from the kitchen with a good imitation of her usual buoyant gait. Her bright hair was combed, her lipstick coral and her mascara in place. She stood looking at him.

'You've got a nerve.'

He stepped inside. 'I owe you an explanation.'

'*Explanation.* Jeez, what a laugh. Get out.'

He stood in front of her, hands on hips and back to the light. There was a glimpse of the cottage through the crook of his right arm.

'I didn't know she was coming,' he said. 'Either of them. They arrived out of the blue, like I said. Ten o'clock last night.'

Bobby said nothing.

He tried again. 'You knew about her. So did the boss. I said, I told you.'

'You bloody didn't. Not about the kid.'

'Shit, you didn't give us a chance. I would've!'

Bronson dropped on to the sofa and stretched his legs. Bobby shut her eyes briefly and remained standing. Both hands clenched the back of Hamish's old chair.

'That's the thing, see,' he continued. 'She can't cope with anything, let alone a kid. Hasn't got a clue, I mean. Never had.'

'Get out.'

Bronson didn't give her a glance. He sat staring at the carpet with his head in his hands.

'She's all over the place,' he said. 'One minute she's all over me like a rash and the next minute she's throwing a wobbly, screaming her head off, throwing things. You wouldn't believe the rows, the bloody awful rows. Any moment soon it'll be a knife, then it'll be a domestic, cops and all. I've tried to get away before, twice now, but either she turns up like now or Tray gets crook and my Mum's sick of being dumped with him. She just takes off, know what I mean. It's not the poor little bastard's fault.'

He sat silent.

'It's Tray,' he said eventually. 'Tray.'

Bobby watched the broken figure. Her face and voice were calm, her heart a block of dripping ice.

'You never told us the cars were hers,' she said.

He stared up at her blankly. 'So what?'

She spoke slowly. 'If you weren't expecting her, why did you cart her effing cars all the way down here?'

Bronson stared up at her face, her pretty sneering face. 'I was going to. I was . . .'

'It must've cost a bomb, I bet. Getting them all down.'

He leapt to his feet, grabbed her arm and held it tight.

'I didn't know you then, did I? I was going to, I was . . .'

Bobby ducked, tore herself away and grabbed a potted white cyclamen from a nearby table.

'Get out,' she said.

His yell was anguished. 'Bob! *Listen* . . .'

Bobby hefted the thing in her hand and threw it at him, screaming for the first time.

'Get out!'

It was a near miss. Bronson leapt to the door and ran, followed by shards of terracotta, dirt and mangled leaves.

Bobby, hyperventilating and shaking all over, stared unseeing at the wreck of her favourite cyclamen. She touched the spilled potting mix and the broken shards of the pot with her shoe. Finally she dropped on her heels, picked up the upended corm and held it to her.

15

Freddy stood. '18.37,' he said glancing at his watch. 'They're due down at 18.40.'

'So?' said Violet.

'It's always better to be found standing. It creates an impression of attentiveness.'

'Which you don't have.'

'Not at all. I can be just as attentive sitting, but it doesn't look like it. The whole art of a successful Swing Around is to keep the boss happy, massage his ego. The screws are tightened for him offshore. It's good for his morale getting away from the PM but on the other hand there's no one else to sheet balls-ups home to. If he's happy, well served by attentive staff, he will be more relaxed, more efficient and all will go well. To you pleasantness comes naturally. I know the drill. The end result is achieved either way.'

'Some day someone will believe your lovable-old-cynic routine.'

'Not cynical. Just clear sighted. Kamil couldn't be a cynic if he tried and he will have been sitting on his butt out there for far longer than we have. Nevertheless he will be standing to attention when the Minister appears. Similarly, our kit (especially Kamil's) will be in perfect condition and our expressions reasonably alert.'

None of which, except alertness, applied to Violet. Even Freddy's friendly eye could see that. There is a height beyond which no one should wear droopy long frocks of flower-sprigged cotton. Her breasts, normally quite obviously two in number and well formed, were squashed and confined within the high yoke like two plum puddings in a single cloth. She looked, he thought tenderly, like a cross between a Jane Austen heroine and a guardsman in drag.

'You look wonderful,' he said.

'Liar. I discovered this in the bottom of the bag.' She held up the skirt, stared at pink and white blossom. 'Ghastly, isn't it? I should've stuck with the green.'

'Ah,' said Freddy, moving forward. 'Here they are.'

The Minister advanced with buoyant steps, followed slowly by Molly in her maroon.

'That letter for Molly from the bag, Fred,' he boomed. 'Bobby's going to marry the sharemilker, Bronson Foster. I thought you two would like to be the first to know.'

'Thank you. How exciting,' burbled Freddy. 'Very, isn't it, Violet?'

She gave him a quick harried glance.

'Yes, indeed, congratulations,' she said, embracing Molly's deflated-looking form. The maroon seemed to have sagged also, to have lost some of its robust substance. 'I hope she will be wonderfully happy.'

Molly gazed straight into her eyes. She did this quite often, but Violet found it disconcerting at the moment.

She meant every word. She would not have said it otherwise. However, the chances of continuing marital happiness for Bobby and Bronson seemed slim to her. Why? Just because the man was loaded with testosterone didn't mean he was not husband material. But there remained the famished-looking Spike. She gave an involuntary shiver. Dogs should not look like that.

Besides, what else could they do but enthuse? Molly was miserable enough without obvious lack of enthusiasm from the staff.

'Thank you,' said Molly. 'She says she wants some ivory silk.'

'Easy,' said Violet. 'They'll be knee deep in Thai silks here.'

Hamish stopped in his tracks, peered at Freddy's wrist. 'Good God, Manders, when did you get that damn fool thing?'

'In Hong Kong,' said Freddy, displaying the frenetic-looking dial of his watch. 'It's for my nephew.'

'I hope you're not going to wear it on official occasions. With our Malaysian friends, I mean.'

'As a matter of fact, Minister, I'm doing time trials. I don't want to give a present that goes dog on the child.'

'Oh. Well, keep it in your pocket or something. The term "Mickey Mouse",' said Hamish, stabbing a finger at the jigging image, 'has unfortunate connotations. I don't want it to be seen officially. Is that clear?'

'Certainly,' said Freddy, undoing the strap.

'No, no. It doesn't matter tonight. Keep the damn thing on now.'

'Thank you, Minister.'

Molly turned to Hamish. 'We mustn't keep Kamil waiting.' She headed back towards the Reception Desk. 'Such a nice man. Two little boys apparently,' she murmured.

'Every time, every time a coconut,' laughed Hamish. 'This way, Mol.'

Kamil, as predicted, was smarter than ever in his evening gear, his trousers whiter, his jacket more trim. He laughed at Molly's reaction to the steaming black night. 'Cool inside, ma'am.'

'Oh, look,' cried Molly, veering off to a nearby column. 'A lizard, how lovely. Do look.'

They looked, they agreed, they climbed in.

The darkness was drowned by light as they swung into the city, the traffic as clotted and vociferous as ever. The place was vibrating, pulsing with noise and action. A road had been closed off, the space transformed by dozens of food and drink stalls lit by kerosene flares and winking fairy lights. The city was on the move, pressing ahead, thrusting forward on bicycles, carrying children, animals dead or alive; one had a length of timber over his shoulder. Another held a squawking parrot to the window of the High Commissioner's air-conditioned cocoon as it rolled past. Indian, Malaysian and Chinese faces flashed by, glimpses of silk saris or coolies in shorts. And people, always people, surging, laughing, lost to the world or eating on the run.

I'd like to be out there, thought Violet. Dashing about with Freddy, who I have not yet seen dash, trying steamboats or peanut pancakes or tandoori or nasi lemak. Why not?

'It looks wonderful,' she whispered.

'We'll go tomorrow.'

'Good.'

Darkness enclosed them again as they drove through quiet outer suburbs. They climbed from the car into damp heat. Something screamed. And another, and another.

'What's that?' cried Molly.

'Bats,' said Freddy. 'Just little ones.'

'Oo. Do they really get in your hair?'

Hamish took his wife's arm. 'The High Commissioner is waiting.'

Molly snatched her arm from his and marched forward.

Penn McPhee, scrubbed and pink and supported by two Chinese servants, waited beside a teak table weighed down by brass urns of coral and red hibiscus.

He greeted them affably, especially Molly who lingered by the flowers. 'Beautiful,' she said. 'Datin Ahmad tells me the red hibiscus is the native flower of Malaysia, but they do drop.' She picked a fallen blossom from the table and handed it to Penn who thanked her and handed it to the senior servant who bowed and handed it to his junior who disappeared still bowing.

'The other guests, of course, have already arrived,' said Penn. 'May I introduce you? This way. Just a small party this evening, as you requested. Amanda is so sorry she is unable to be here. She asked me to give you her apologies, Mrs Carew.'

'Ah yes,' said Molly, 'something to do with boarding schools, I understand.'

Penn's laugh was hesitant but friendly. 'I hope not,' he said. 'Now Minister, I don't think you've met our Deputy Head of Mission, Mrs Banstead.'

Mrs Banstead, a small, serene-looking woman, put out her hand. 'How nice to meet you, Minister.'

Hamish was equally delighted. Molly smiled. She had put aside her concern about Bobby and her crossness at Hamish's bland reaction and was now in official mode. Polite, friendly, even chatty, she had slipped into overdrive and would cruise through the evening with apparent ease but little attention to detail.

She listened as the new Trade Commissioner, Mr Barney Kinsella, and his dinner partner Miss Ruby Tan, were introduced. Bowed, smiled and had lost both names by the time the Defence Attaché, Colonel Lance Beaucott, and his wife Susie appeared. She paid particular care with Susie Beaucott, who was shy and wordless, factors which made her especially unmemorable and thus deserving of more effort. She would remember Susie longer than the cuff-shooting, time-checking young Army officer who fidgeted beside her. A challenge makes you try harder, she had noticed. She had never forgotten the name of a neighbour who had introduced himself saying, 'A difficult name to remember, Kwiatkowski, is it not?'

Hamish and Molly mingled from group to group, going through the rituals of social converse, backing and advancing, instigating topics of general interest and tactful inquiry. Hamish was telling Lance and Susie Beaucott stories of his war. 'I well remember Churchill's visit to the Division in Tripoli. After Alamein it was. He called Freyberg "the Salamander of the British Empire". One of the chaps beside me said, "What the hell's a salamander?" and his mate said, "He called him a bloody lizard." Great men, both of them.' Hamish gave a brisk laugh. 'Churchill and Freyberg I mean. Great men. Yes.'

Lance Beaucott pranced from foot to foot with excitement; Susie made no comment, no movement, nothing. Even her eyebrows were muted.

Hamish was on to artillery. It was time to move on.

Molly turned to Mrs Banstead who was ordering a drink from the Chinese waiter. 'Fresh lime,' she murmured.

Fresh lime, thought Molly. It will appear in a moment, freshly squeezed, iced and dewy. How cool, how restorative, how wise of Mrs Banstead. From now on I will stick to fresh limes.

One appeared immediately. 'The working girl's best friend,' said Mrs Banstead.

The comment was not only unanswerable but slightly deflatory. No one would describe a minister of the Crown's wife as a working girl. Molly knew that. Not that Mrs Banstead would have meant it like that, goodness me no.

However, something must be said. But what.

'Tell me about Mr Banstead,' said Molly in desperation.

'There is no Mr Banstead,' said Mrs Banstead.

A servant appeared and murmured in her ear.

'Will you excuse me a moment, Mrs Carew? Some minor problem . . .' Still smiling, she moved away.

Oh Lord. No Mr Banstead at all. It serves you right. Not you, Mrs Banstead, my question was idiotic and your answer well phrased. Nevertheless, the fate of Mr Banstead interests me. Someone must know.

Freddy appeared. 'Hullo, Mrs Carew.'

A nice man and so much happier-looking. 'I was wondering what happened to Mr Banstead,' she said.

'I don't know, ma'am,' he said, 'but I'll find out. American Army cadets are taught to answer a senior officer's queries like that if they don't know the answer.'

'But what else would they do?'

'Pretend they did know.'

'How very odd. But don't bother about Mr Banstead.' She looked up. His eyes were beautiful, shaped like miniature flounders, with brown pupils and long dark lashes banging against his spectacles. 'I'm worried about Bobby, you see.'

'Oh,' said Freddy, unsurprised by the leap in conversation. In his opinion she had every reason to be. 'I think . . .' he began, but was interrupted.

'Have you seen Bridget since we've been here?' she said.

He had seen this attribute in her before, a tendency probably incurable and decidedly unattractive. Just when you were most aware of her vulnerability and anxious to help, she would cut you off at the knees, would flatten you with the dead weight of her gaucheness.

'I thought I had made it clear, Mrs Carew. My wife and I have separated. She is now based in Paris and I . . .'

Violet was at his shoulder. Freddy looked at her, felt his arms rise in greeting. 'Hullo,' he said.

'You look like a shepherdess, dear,' said Molly. 'Doesn't she, Freddy?'

'Yes,' he said. 'She looks wonderful.'

Her unconvinced grin met his. 'Thank you. I've brought the new Trade Commissioner Mr Kinsella and his friend Miss Tan to talk to you again, Mrs Carew. Mr Kinsella has recently arrived from a posting in Paris, haven't you, Barney?'

Barney Kinsella confirmed this. He told them of the wonders of Paris. He explained how it is only when you have lived there for some time that you really begin to appreciate the culture, the lifestyle, the – well, perhaps he could say the *ambience* of life in Paris. And of course one had to have the language, be sufficiently fluent to have a proper conversation. Survival French got you nowhere with any of the interesting people in Paris. He had first become aware of this when a young French woman had asked him about race relations in New Zealand. He had been able to tell her that they were excellent, except perhaps for a few isolated incidents – Bastion Point, say, and a few Land Marches. However, being intelligent as well as beautiful, his friend had not wanted to leave it at that. Was it like Tahiti, for example, she had asked, where there were none of those problems at all because the French colonisers had been so much more civilised than the British in their attitudes to native peoples? How shocked she had been on a recent visit to see, when filling in landing papers for arrival in Auckland, that one had to state one's race. She went on to say that that would never happen in Tahiti. Just 'Nationality – FRANCAIS'. Barney tossed his palms to indicate the complexity.

'I don't mind telling you I was treading water for a few minutes, though of course I'd more or less just arrived in Paris at that time.'

Sparrow-boned and smiling, the exquisite Miss Tan stood beside him in silence, holding her wine glass before her as though it were a chalice.

'Have you been to Paris, Miss Tan?' asked Molly.

'Of course.' Miss Tan smiled, sketching a hand across her non-existent stomach. 'Twice a year I go for the openings. I am an economist.'

'How nice,' said Molly.

Barney Kinsella patted his friend's shoulder. 'She gets around, our Ruby. Don't you?'

Miss Tan's lips tightened.

Barney Kinsella continued to entertain them, a process which gave Freddy the satisfaction of discovering that his instinctive reaction to the man had been correct. Penn had described him as a bit of a shit. Manders would not put him that high. A man enamoured with himself for no visible reason, waffling on as though Paris had been created expressly for him. Paris of all places. How the flaming hell had Kinsella got to Paris when he hadn't? Not that it mattered now. It didn't matter at all.

He glanced at Violet who had appeared at his shoulder. Desire, lust, all the good ones rushed to his aid. 'Violet,' he murmured.

'I was saying that Barney once had the same office as you, Freddy,' she said. 'In CLAT.'

'Yes, some time ago now.' Kinsella laughed, making it clear that small dark offices, if they ever had featured in his life, had done so only briefly and in another country. He put his arm round Violet's shoulders and squeezed. 'Vi and I are very good friends, aren't we, petal?'

Petal.

'And I'm also a great friend of your ex-wife, Fred. Bridget and I had some wild nights together in Paris. Great girl, Bridgie. You know she's here at the moment?'

'Yes.'

Miss Tan gave Kinsella a long look, turned on her three-inch heels and swayed her way towards Hamish and Penn.

'Shall we join them, Violet,' said Molly.

Good thinking, lady. Good thinking.

Kinsella watched them go. 'Yeah,' he said, 'it's a funny old world, no doubt about that.'

'Why did you tear up your daughter's photograph?' said Freddy.

'What?'

'The pieces were still in the desk.'

'That grotty desk still there? Huh. Who said it was my kid?'

'Me.'

'Get stuffed,' said Kinsella, and headed for the Beaucotts who stood twinned on the edge of a large Chinese rug, she silent and still, he continuing to check his watch as the party revolved around them.

Freddy watched Kinsella go, noted the fat bum, the odd hair.

To hell with his looks. There were worse things to consider. First, he, Manders, would be seeing this man each day for considerable periods, would be working closely with him, taking down every word the creep uttered, being deferential to his greater knowledge and attentive to his every word. There was not even the comfort of knowing that Kinsella's job here was a downgrade from the one in Paris. He would never have been Trade Commissioner there. KL was a step up.

These points, he knew and admitted to himself with an inward snarl, were not the true reason for his abhorrence. This man, this man was a 'very good friend', complete with accompanying leers, of both his ex-wife and Violet.

He looked at Violet with longing. So tall, so straight in her maidenly clanger of a dress. He would deal with that later. The macho adolescent thought went to his knees like kava. And to his crotch. He turned away, heard Hamish, still in reminiscent mode, booming away at Miss Tan: 'Yes, my dear, as our Colonel used to say about the ladies. "They'll drag you further than gunpowder will blow you."'

Miss Tan smiled, clasped her glass tightly.

Penn McPhee tapped a glass with a knife handed him by a silent servant. 'May I have your attention for a moment, ladies and gentlemen? As we all know, this evening is an informal occasion, there will be no speeches, so these words are more in the nature of an in-house welcome.

'But I do want to say how delighted we all are in KL to greet the Minister of Cultural Links and Trade and Mrs Carew, and to wish them both a profitable and enjoyable stay in this country.'

Huffs, nods, small keen smiles flickered around the room.

'Also I would like to take this opportunity, if I may, to run through the programme while we're *en famille* so to speak. I realise this may be rather an irregular time to do this but I have found' – he gave a quick nod to Mrs Banstead – 'haven't we, Joyce, that it is always a good idea to check visitors' programmes constantly. We have found sometimes, in the past, that things tend to be changed without liaison.

'You have copies of the latest programme, I assume, Fred?'

'Yes.'

'Then may I suggest, Minister, that instead of Fred and Mrs Banstead checking them in private, Joyce reads both programmes to us now and we can pick up any inconsistencies which may have occurred.'

Hamish bent his head.

'Good,' said Penn. 'Then we'll all know where we are. Joyce?'

Mrs Banstead, looking faintly amused, put down her fresh lime and moved forward. The professionals, especially Colonel Beaucott, listened attentively and consulted their own programmes. Molly, who was pleased to hear that the programme could be altered, stood watching as Miss Tan yawned, revealing for a moment the inside of a mouth as pink and neat as a kitten's before hiding it behind her hand in a pretty little flutter of apology. Fascinating, thought Molly. They can make even the effects of boredom look captivating.

'Ready Freddy?' cooed Mrs Banstead.

Freddy beamed at her. He loved po-faced old Joyce Banstead. How could he not.

He had discomfited B. Kinsella. More than that, Violet was nigh and smiling at him.

'I'll be very brief,' Mrs Banstead said. 'The Minister's programme first, then Mrs Carew's. No ETAs or ETDs. Fred and I will check them later with the escorts. If there is anything important either of you would like changed please tell me when we come to it. Obviously tomorrow is Day Two.'

A nod of agreement from Fred.

Mrs Banstead read:

MINISTER'S PROGRAMME

Day Two.

A.M., talks with Minister Dato Ahmad Kamarul Ridza and staff.

Noon, lunch in honour of Minister Carew hosted by Prince Peter at the Royal Selangor Golf Club.

'Does anyone know Prince Peter?' asked Mrs Banstead. 'No one? A cousin of Datin Ahmad. A good friend of New Zealand. Two children at university there. Cheerful and hospitable.

P.M., talks.

Evening, cocktail party hosted by Mr Kinsella at his residence in honour of the Minister and Mrs Carew. Followed by early informal dinner hosted by Minister Dato Ahmad and Datin Ahmad at the Yangtze Chinese Restaurant. Followed by Official Party's attendance at the Glen Campbell Show.

A.M., talks.

Noon, working lunch at Hibiscus Restaurant hosted by
Mr Carew for Minister Dato Ahmad and his staff.

P.M., Mr Carew and party visit the Milk Powder
Reconstitution Plant.

Evening, official dinner in honour of Dato and Datin
Ahmad hosted by Minister Carew and Mrs Carew at
the Tower of London Room, Kuala Lumpur Hotel.

Day Four.

A.M., talks.

P.M., Minister Carew plays golf with Prince Peter, the
Minister and Mr Kinsella.

Evening, cocktail party at New Zealand High
Commission in honour of Minister Carew and Mrs
Carew. Followed by official farewell dinner hosted
by Minister Dato Ahmad and Datin Ahmad in the
Banquet Room, Kuala Lumpur.

Day Five.

Depart.

'Correct?' asked Mrs Banstead.

'Yes,' replied Freddy.

'Have you any queries, Minister?' continued Mrs Banstead.
'Anything you would like us to change' – her thin smile
widened – 'or perhaps I should say try to change at this late
stage? Any comments?'

'No comment,' said Hamish.

'And now Mrs Carew's programme. Are you ready, Miss
Redpath?'

'Yes.'

MRS CAREW'S PROGRAMME

Day Two.

A.M., drive to Genting Highlands escorted by Datin Ahmad.

Lunch at hotel. Tour of the hotel complex and Genting Casino.

P.M., return journey. At leisure.

Evening, same as Minister. Cocktail party, informal meal, Glen Campbell Show.

Day Three.

A.M., visit to Campbell Island to a palm oil plantation managed by Mr George Harman, followed by a visit to the Orang Asli people. Mr Manders will accompany.

Lunch, hosted by Mr and Mrs Harman at their home.

P.M., return journey.

Evening, same as Minister.

'Correct?' asked Mrs Banstead.

Violet agreed.

Day Four.

A.M., short visit to a diamond factory and a batik factory followed by a visit to the National Museum with Datin Ahmad.

P.M., visit to an exhibition of needlework by wives of the armed forces in celebration of the fiftieth anniversary of the founding of the Malaysian Army.

Evening, same as the Minister.

Day Five.

Depart.

———

'Correct?'

'Yes.'

'Mrs Carew,' said Mrs Banstead, 'have you any queries or suggestions?'

'Yes,' said Molly. 'I would like someone to find out where my friend Bridget Cox is staying. She is with the delegation called Humanitaire from Paris and I would like her to accompany our party on our visit to the Orang Asli people if she can. I'm sure she would be immensely interested to meet the original people of Malaysia.'

Fuck, thought Freddy. Damn and blast the manipulating old bat. Can nothing stop the woman.

Violet was staring at him in horror.

'Certainly,' said Penn McPhee. 'I suggest you get on to it straight away, Colonel Beaucott.'

'Yes, sir,' said Lance.

His wife, her small face pink with pride, watched him stride away on his mission.

'Another thing,' said Molly, taking the programme from Violet, 'I'll need some time for shopping. Please may we cancel the visits to the diamond factory and the batik factory?'

Penn McPhee, surprised at these statements from a woman who tied herself in knots to avoid being a nuisance, said that the post had understood from Wellington that Mrs Carew disliked shopping.

'Hear, hear,' said Hamish.

'However,' continued Penn, 'we'll certainly see if these changes can be implemented. I'll get someone on to it forthwith.'

Mrs Banstead said, 'Now?'

'No, tomorrow morning will do,' said Molly, 'and yes, I did ask for limited shopping time. However, we have just received word that our daughter is about to be married. She has asked me to shop for bridal materials.' She paused, looked at them bleakly. 'I imagine that might take a considerable amount of time.'

Penn McPhee clapped his hands together, 'Congratulations,' he cried. 'Congratulations from all of us at KL.
Where's the champagne? Ah, there it is. Mrs Carew, may I
offer you a glass? Champagne all round, Sun Ming.'

'Thank you,' said Molly, 'but not for me. I would prefer a
fresh lime. I believe it is sometimes called the working girl's
best friend. Ah, thank you.'

'Perhaps, Mrs Carew,' said Penn, who had a faint feeling
that the delicate balance of his party had been disturbed by
this maroon cushion of a woman, 'you might like to look at
the seating plan. Over here.'

Molly followed him like a lamb. The little slotted wooden
trays with name cards were designed to help, but Molly did
not take to them. Like a bad navigator realigning a map she
needed to turn them into an I-am-here position before they
made sense. Molly had limited patience with wives who
claimed never to read the programme, thereby indicating both
their fragility and need to be cherished, but placement boards
were silly little things, not worth the intellectual effort.

'Thank you,' she said, waiting for motioning gestures from
someone to head her in the right direction.

The seating plan, to Freddy's mind, was not a good one.
Not so much from his point of view. On one side of him Miss
Tan was becoming more serene by the minute, and on the
other was Joyce Banstead, a good trencherman and a sensible
woman. He would not to have to work hard at conversation,
and the prawns were excellent. But look at poor Violet. With
Beaucott on one side and Kinsella on the other, she would be
caught between fidget and leer.

Lance was engaged in cautioning Mrs Carew, telling her of
the inadvisability of stirring in the tropics without Wet Ones.
He whipped a packet of them from his pocket, demonstrated
their damp revitalising qualities, asked Mrs Carew to touch one.
Molly put out a tentative finger, agreed this tissue was damp but
declined to take one. Undeterred, Lance mopped his air-

conditioned forehead. 'Wonderful,' he sighed. 'Wonderful.'

Molly chewed a prawn and turned to her host. 'Do you have many orchids in your garden, Mr McPhee?'

He did and was prepared to tell her about them. The number of different species, the flowers per spike, the wonder of the different forms, the ingenious arrangements of the sexual organs were given in detail.

Barney Kinsella was demonstrating his ability to keep two ladies in play. Throughout the entrée he had given Susie Beaucott and Violet a rundown on some of the highlights of his career. Dubai, for example, his first overseas posting (one never forgets one's first overseas posting) and the sight of the pickers shinning up the date palms in the garden. He'd never thought to wonder how such things were organised. He knew the locals whizzed up the trees of course, but the thought of having to hire a man, making an appointment for one to call, as one did with a chimney sweep, for example, had appealed to his sense of humour. As for Paris, nothing could touch it. Had he mentioned . . .

By the time the servants had replaced the chilli prawns with Boeuf Wellington, he had moved on to finance.

'My advice,' he confided to them, 'would be to put your expendable income into rands. They have always been a good bet, though God knows how long that will last with all the mess in that part of the world. Now is definitely the moment. No one wants an unbalanced portfolio but I'm certainly going to put my neck out this time.' He leaned back in his chair, placed emphatic hands flat on the table. 'I can't say fairer than that, can I?'

'No,' said Susie Beaucott.

Violet gave him a long slow look. 'Oh, Barney,' she drawled. 'Who's kidding whom?'

Susie Beaucott threw back her head and laughed, a high trilling sound as unexpected as the burst of song from a small drab grey warbler.

All eyes turned to the source of such delight. Susie hiccupped, blushed and hiccupped again.

Finally Penn tapped another glass and rose to his feet. 'As I said before this is not a formal dinner, so I hope,' he said with a nod to Molly, 'that the ladies will forgive me if I suggest we have our coffee separately. The last thing we want to do is to lose your company but we do need just a few moments' discussion together. Don't we, Minister?'

More nods.

'Perhaps ladies, you might prefer to have your coffee served in the other room?'

Violet caught Mrs Banstead's eye. Was she a lady or an honorary man?

Mrs Banstead rose to her feet. 'This way, ladies.'

Violet stood to join Molly and Susie Beaucott. Miss Tan showed no tendency to leave. Mrs Banstead's herding gestures firmed. 'Miss Tan?' she said. Miss Tan stood.

The men leapt or shuffled to their feet, to stand attentive or smiling or not smiling until the door shut.

'Now,' said Penn. 'Has everyone coffee? That will be all, thank you, Sun Ming. I suggest we gather around the Minister. Fred will have told you, sir, the gist of Colonel Beaucott's brief?'

'Yes,' said Hamish.

'Just check the door would you, Fred? Thanks.'

Colonel Beaucott was well prepared, concise and articulate. Freddy watched him with professional interest. The cuff-shooting, compulsive watch-checking, the jumpiness had disappeared. He had something important to tell his senior officers and now was the moment.

Hamish listened in silence and made an occasional note in a small black notebook.

'Yes,' he said finally. 'Thank you, Colonel. Interesting information and a well-presented brief. I agree, your concern about the possible spread of Lightning Storm is warranted. I think the information should be sent, encoded of course, straight to the PM.'

'I entirely agree with you, Minister,' said Kinsella. 'In my opinion we, as a nation, have never taken the threat of terrorism seriously enough, either at home or abroad. I have always taken this stance and still do.'

The Minister looked at him but made no comment.

'The Prime Minister?' said Penn.

'Yes. Definitely. And at once,' said Hamish, picking a piece of lint from the sleeve of his jacket.

Lightning Storm would be his discovery. He would warn his superior officer, the Prime Minister, immediately. He would speak well and be heard where it mattered.

Training, thought Freddy, watching the cool authority of briefed and briefer, is all.

16

Hamish pressed the lift button. 'A worthwhile evening,' he said. 'Interesting, didn't you think, Fred?'

Manders dragged his eyes from Violet. He had watched her throughout the meal, had rushed towards her after coffee to shield her from Kinsella, had loitered beside her, stalked her through deserts of smalltalk in a turmoil of desire, excitement and sheer bloody hope.

'Fred?'

'Yes Minister?'

'Interesting evening, I said.'

'Definitely, sir. And the prawns.'

Hamish, engaged in the supervision of getting the ladies from the lift in one piece, let it pass. He scrutinised the guard at the end of the corridor with increased interest. The ladies must be alerted. Violet anyway. Perhaps not Molly, or not yet. Security for them must also be increased.

'Come in, both of you,' he said. 'I feel like a beer.'

Freddy groaned inwardly, head, heart and crotch. A beer, dear God, a beer and then another beer, and a rerun of memories.

Hamish was crouched in front of another mini fridge.

'Heineken, Violet?'

'Thank you, Minister.'

'And you, Molly?'

Molly's party face had disappeared. 'No. I couldn't face it. I'm going to bed. Goodnight.'

They stood. 'Goodnight, goodnight, goodnight.'

Freddy and Violet watched her wistfully. Bed, they sobbed. Bed.

She put out a hand to him behind Hamish's squatting haunches.

It was all right. She wanted him. He could tell. You can always tell but he had rather forgotten. Had cut himself off from life like a bloody hermit. Relief, certainty, swirled in his head, stiffened his purpose. Jesus.

Something was itching the back of his eyeballs. Frustration probably. He dragged a handkerchief from his pocket and polished his glasses.

Violet watched the long eyelashes, the desirable touch-me-not look of his unguarded eyes. He looked neither vacant nor blank, just uncluttered. Spectacles take up room in a face.

He put them on again, winked at her as she swam into view.

Violet stared into her unwanted beer as though searching for something.

Hospitality extended, Hamish leaned back and drank deep. 'Just as well my wife's gone to bed,' he said. 'I think Violet should be aware of our discussion tonight, Fred. She and Molly are the weak link in the chain, the most vulnerable, as it were, to attack.'

'Attack,' said Violet.

'I think there's no need to alarm Molly at this stage. She tends to become unnecessarily alarmed. However, that doesn't alter the fact that I think you must have an armed guard in attendance when Fred and I are working and you're out enjoying yourselves.'

'Armed guard,' said Violet.

The story of Lightning Storm was retold.'As you will know from your briefing at home, Violet, it's not always the most important member of a group who is kidnapped. One hostage is as good as another – well, more or less – as regards ransom money. Similarly, envoys from a small nation are just as likely to be at risk as those from larger ones. Especially as we understand that Lightning Storm is more a gang of thugs than an organised group of politically motivated terrorists like the Munich lot or any of that ilk.' Hamish paused, looked Violet in the eye which was not obscured by hair. 'We have no intention of allowing my wife and her right-hand man to be in any danger whatsoever, have we, Fred?'

'No Minister. Certainly not.'

'Right. So get on to the Malaysian Trade Minister's staff early tomorrow as regards the armed guard.'

'Yes Minister. However, if I may make a suggestion, would it not be a better plan to see if Lance Beaucott could be seconded to this task. Keep it in the family, so to speak. No language problems, things of that nature.'

'Good thinking,' said Hamish. 'Good thinking.'

Manders took her hand as they walked down the corridor.

'I do like "Good thinking",' she said.

'Yes, but it needs "Carstairs" or "Carruthers" or somesuch to set it off.'

'I have no objection to Manders,' she said.

He gripped her wrist to the bone, pulled her to him and kissed her. Leisurely and fierce by turns their mouths and tongues explored, broke for breath and kissed again.

A horrified Malay couple scuttled by.

'Close proximity between the sexes in public,' gasped Freddy. 'It's a sin here. Begins with K.'

Violet turned and unlocked her door. 'Have you got one?' she said.

'Yes.'

'Good. Come in.'

Sex is good and good sex is better and true sex is the wonder of the world. What a giver she was, how generous in her loving. And the shape of her, those angles and dips and valleys. Skinny bodies are more interesting to explore, he had always known that. But then look at her breasts. Ample was the word. Ample.

He sat up beside her sleeping body to check, to feel, to kiss. Perfect. To find such generosity in such a form was like discovering a pearl in a Bluff oyster.

He lay down and took her in his arms, stroked the long recumbent length of her.

'Darling,' she murmured.

Manders jolted upright, switched on the bedside light and groped for his glasses to peer at the digital clock. 03.00 and all was not well. Anything but. Something was badly wrong with his gut. He leapt from the bed, rushed to the glass–tiled bathroom and flung himself on the lavatory. He sat there for some time, rocked backwards and forwards in despair.

Tonight, tonight of all nights in the whole fucking universe to be struck down with one of the most humiliating conditions known to man. He hadn't even had time to shut the door. He could see the bed, the shape of her sleeping body. She was dead to the world, and just as well. He stretched out a leg and pushed the door shut. Clunk. First things first.

Eventually he stood, pressed the button and cursed again. What if it was of those loud thundering blast-offs? No. He was blessed with a sibilant, barely audible flush. He swallowed, filled the basin with hot water and scrubbed his hands long and hard with the doll-sized nailbrush, intent as a green-masked surgeon preparing to go in. Then he sat on the lavatory to think. He had been trained to think. Aim, assessment, alternative actions.

Aim was blindingly obvious. To lie beside her for ever, to sleep with her, to love.

Which he couldn't.

He would have to go to his own room. Now. He would have to grope around, God knows where, for his clothes, climb into his suit and depart.

The lid was glacial, a bad design fault amid such luxury. He grabbed the bath mat, slipped it under his frozen bum and continued thinking.

He would not wake beside her in the morning. He would have had to leave at some time, but he had programmed himself to wake at five and knew he would. That would have given time to meet and greet and hold each other before parting. Their first time too.

Get on with it then. Write a note. No explanations. Do that later when it will be a joke to be shared not a ludicrous let-down, some thwarted dance of the seven sodding veils. He felt his gut rumble. You're not safe. Get out of here.

Stumbling about in the half-dark he put on his clothes, stuffed his socks and tie into a pocket and stood looking at her. As he knew from the farm visit, she was good at sleeping. She lay on her side, the movement of her pale shoulders almost imperceptible. Some so-called experts say Othello and Desdemona's marriage was never consummated. Balls.

Bare footed, shoulders hunched and hands moving in front of him, he searched for paper. Good hotels always have a ton of paper; it is one of the signals. He pulled out drawer after drawer. Nothing. Extended his range, searched all the horizontal surfaces, the brochures, even the bloody closets. Still nothing. He considered alternatives. To go to his room (there must be some scrap of paper in his bag), write a note then creep back here again.

But the whole object was to get sole use of a bathroom. And soon.

All right, he sneered at nothing and no one. He went back to the bathroom with a biro, pulled out a few sheets of the yellowish-looking paper from its container, and began writing his letter on the top of the mock-marble bench.

The biro went straight through the first sheet, leaving a smeared blue D on the mottled gold slab. He tried again. *'Darling, I had to . . .'* Had to what? He screwed it up, shoved it in the pocket with his socks. Finally he scrawled, *'Good morning darling. I love you. Freddy.'*

Hopeless. But what the hell could he say? He would have to explain later.

He resisted the temptation to kiss her cheek, pulled on his shoes, took a final look and crept out.

The guard, ah yes, the guard. The man sprinted down the corridor and stood beside him with a gun in his hand. Manders glanced at his name tag and produced his security card.

'Good evening, Lieutenant.'

'Good evening, sir. Was not expecting. Sorry, sir.'

'That's quite all right,' said Freddy airily and headed for his room.

He had picked up the bug at dinner, presumably. The prawns. But everyone had had prawns. Violet seemed all right. Probably he had swallowed the rogue one. One of those quick violent tropical bugs, with any luck. It was certainly violent. He glanced at his watch. 03.00 and counting. He was going to vomit.

04.00, 05.00, 06.20: the night crawled on.

He had his second shower sometime in the middle, convinced as always that somehow something must make him feel better.

He rootled in his tartan spongebag for medical aid at intervals throughout the night, but it was not until 6.30 that he tipped the thing upside down on the sheets and shook it. Nail clippers, deodorant, a Band Aid or two, a toothbrush and a few dusty cotton buds: all the unattractive detritus of aids to personal hygiene lay staring back at him. He banged the bottom of the bag and one, no two, greyish capsules of Lomotil dislodged themselves from the seams and joined the mess. Stunned with relief, he swore gently and picked them up, could have kissed them.

These would see him right. Or rather put him on track until he could get in touch with Penn and get some more. How many should he take. One or two? Two, for God's sake, what the hell. He swallowed the rubbed chalky-looking things, had yet another shower, and fell back on the bed to ring Lance Beaucott and Penn.

Lance was disappointed at having to leave the Minister's entourage. As he said, he liked to be at the sharp end, where the action was. Surely his first job was to ensure the Minister's safety?

Freddy laid his aching head on the pillows to explain Hamish's instructions. The very best, most reliable, intelligent man must be seconded to guard the ladies. This was an order. And a very sensible one. The Minister and his party had the whole of the Malaysian Army to ensure their visit passed without incident.

'Very good sir,' quacked the phone. 'I'll come straight over.'

Penn was concerned for his colleague but not enough. He was quite all right, not a twinge. Furthermore Amanda had a standing rule that the staff could polish off any leftover shellfish if they wanted to. Never a good idea to put them back in the fridge in this climate. No ill effects there. Happy as larks. 'Poor old Manders,' he laughed. 'Came the raw prawn at you, did we? All right, calm down. I'll get on to the Lomotil. We've got a ton of it here. Kamil will hand them over when he picks you up to collect the CBs. But why's it all so hush-hush? Why so coy about a crook gut? If you've got it you've got it. Why don't you go down to the chemist in the hotel?'

'Thanks,' snarled Manders and put down the receiver.

Violet woke. Remembered, smiled and remembered again. She put out a hand to feel him and found nothing. Rolled over to verify and sat up. No Freddy. She looked at her watch: 5.30. Well, yes, possibly. It was understandable to have departed by now, but overly cautious surely. And without waking her. Things had happened at such speed last night, such delirious ecstatic speed, and then she had gone to sleep bang, instantly, as she always did. There had been little time for chat, the tender exploratory postcoital mumbles that women enjoy more than men. The where, when and whys of love. When did you first realise? Where? And best of all. Why?

She lay back, heard their phantom voices murmuring catechisms.

'But why?'

'Because you are so beautiful.'

'No, really. Tell me why?'

'Because I do.'

'Nutter. And why were you so bloody rude?'

'I'd gone off women. Gone dog on them. All women. All women but you.'

'Balls.'

'It's true.'

'Say it again.'

This, all this should have happened, and more. They might have drifted on to Bridget eventually.

Violet lay on her back feeling oddly deflated. Sad. Saddish. Not the postcoital tristesse of fable, she had never had that, but . . . something. Still staring at the ceiling she put out a hand to his side of the bed and met paper, shot upwards to grab the message, the first love letter: *Good morning darling. I love you. Freddy.*

Well. Yes. I love you too. I adore you. But the paper. Oh Freddy.

Hamish slept as soundly as one who has received an interesting briefing and responded swiftly and with authority should.

Molly lay rolling around beside him. Like all normally good sleepers she was alarmed by insomnia, felt cheated as she counted hours, half hours and the lead minutes between. Never had she felt more muddled, more worried and less in control. At 3.20, clutching her little blue torch for travelling to avoid any chance of disturbing Hamish, she crept into the next room. Bare feet sinking into carpet and her mouth dry as a bone, she stared below. Except for a slight slackening of traffic, there seemed little sign that the city had bedded down for the night. The food and drink stalls continued to do business, people still streamed in all directions or ate at noodle bars and outdoor restaurants.

Molly opened the fridge in search of bottled water. Not a drop. In desperation she opened a bottle of Coke. A mistake: the sweetness was cloying, not quenching. Why am I behaving like this, she thought. Sitting here worrying about my obviously happy daughter. Because I am worried.

Then find out how she is. Stop being such a . . . such a goop.

She picked up the telephone. 'This is Room 1304. I want to make a toll call to New Zealand. The number is . . . No. I don't mind what time it is there. Thank you.'

The ringing tone at the farm continued. She put the receiver back on its cradle and watched it for some time. It occurred to

202

her that she had not the slightest idea how the thing worked. This seemed to her careless, another lack. The thought stiffened her resolve. Of course she would ring the cottage. Now.

After some time a man's voice shouted, 'It's 11.30. What the hell do you want?'

'To speak to Bobby.'

'Why the fuck would Bobby be here?'

'Don't speak to me like that, Bronson. Where is she?'

'How the fucking hell would I know!'

'Tell me!'

The receiver slammed down.

I knew. I knew. I knew.

She returned to bed and lay beside Hamish. He lay on his back, his mouth slack jawed as a soul in torment. She noted the spittle, the gurgling snore and the occasional rumbling grunt. It was 3.30 a.m. There was nothing she could do. Not until the morning. She would go to sleep, try counting sheep although she was unsure of the procedure. Did they get counted as they ambled through the gate or did they have to jump it? She tried both methods. Definitely they had to jump. It was hard to differentiate if they just ambled.

At 5.30 she tried the sharemilker's cottage again. There was no answer.

She rang Room Service and asked for some bottled water.

'The bottled water is in the refrigerator, madam.'

'No, there is none. That is why I am ringing.'

'None at all, Madam?'

'None at all.'

'Ah. Then I suggest you ring the Receptionist and ask for Mini-bar Replacements. Except they shut at 4 a.m. unfortunately. Room Service has no water, Madam. Have a nice night, Madam.'

Her mouth was becoming more parched every moment. She would drink the tap water. Torch in hand, she headed for the bathroom, drank deep and spat it out.

Soundlessly as possible she washed at the basin and put on another crimplene. How could they have told her the stuff breathed? Not only did it not breathe, in air conditioning it clung to her legs, impeding progress like a frightened child.

Molly and Violet met at the end of the corridor. The guard sprang to attention, checked their passes. Had they permission, he asked. Permission for what? To leave the bedrooms without the escort of the Minister or Mr Manders.

'Yes,' said Molly. 'We have permission, don't we, Miss Redpath?'

'Yes.'

Nodding gravely, they moved on, studied each other uneasily in the neon lighting of the lift. Their teeth looked blue, their eyes bruised.

'I am going to get some drinking water,' said Molly.

'Ah,' said Violet.

Molly smiled. 'You are the only person I know who would have the sense not to tell me there must be some in the fridge. And you?'

'I thought I'd go for a walk.'

'What a good idea. I'll come too.'

Violet stalled. 'Let's discuss it while we have our drink.'

They sat in the foyer with their bottles and glasses. 'You can't swig as well from a glass,' said Molly, 'but never mind. Another bottle? Good. Now, shall we go?'

'No, Mrs Carew,' said Violet. 'I'm afraid we can't. We can leave our bedrooms without escort but we cannot leave the hotel.'

'But you were going!'

'Alone, yes. But I am ...' She could scarcely say expendable. 'Let's just say,' she continued, 'you are the wife of a VIP and it has been decided that you should have a New Zealand military escort whenever you leave the hotel without the Minister. I know the Minister plans to tell you as soon as he wakes up.'

'Oh.' Molly looked suspicious. 'Not the man with the Wet Ones?'

'Did he have some with him last night?'

'Oh yes, he was very excited about them.'

'Oh dear.'

They sat in silence watching the hotel come to life. Luggage passed them, pushed on trolleys, pulled on racks, carried by immaculately dressed porters and guarded by bell hops. There was an air of discreet and well-oiled bustle. A tight-run unit, Hamish would call it.

Molly came to suddenly. 'How stupid of me, Violet. You must have your walk.'

'No. I couldn't get back to sleep, that was all.'

'You didn't sleep well?'

'Oh, a . . . not bad.'

Molly put out her hand. 'I can't tell you how glad I am to have you on this trip, Violet.'

'Thank you. I'm very happy to be here.'

And will be more so once I see Freddy again. She clenched at the thought.

'What are you smiling at Violet?'

'I like it here,' she said and continued to stare dreamily through revolving circular doors and striding suits, past mountains of luggage and the buzz of tour leaders shepherding their flocks.

Finally she turned to Molly. 'Perhaps we'd better . . .' she said, and stopped short. Molly was weeping, crying in a way Violet had never seen before. Without sound or visible emotion, tears rolled down her cheeks and dropped on to damp synthetic. Violet, startled by a sight which had obviously been going on for some time, fell on her knees in instinctive apology. 'Mrs Carew. Please, what is it?'

'Oh Violet, I'm so worried about Bobby.'

'But . . .'

'Yes I know. I know she said she was engaged and in love and all that. But where is she?'

The story, bowdlerised, poured forth. Finally Molly mopped her eyes and stood. 'I must go and tell Hamish. He will be so concerned.'

'But Mrs Carew, what is there to be concerned about? Bobby's not at the cottage or at the house, but surely that doesn't mean anything bad has happened.'

'But he swore at me, you see. Why did he swear at me?'

'Oh.'

'Yes.' She paused, mopped her eyes.

'Freddy!' cried Violet.

'Violet!' He swung round. 'And Mrs Carew. Whatever are you doing here?'

'Getting some water,' said Molly, waving the second bottle. 'You look terrible. What's the matter?'

Freddy tried a light laugh. He was on his way to pick up the classified papers. Yes, yes, it was early. He was going for a walk first. No, he didn't feel like breakfast. Maybe he might find something on the street.

The thought filled him with nausea. He could scarcely look at Violet, so fresh, so clean, so *unsullied*. Why didn't he tell her, tell them both now: I've got diarrhoea, the trots, gut-rot, take your pick. He would and he should, but Molly and her frog-green garment cancelled any remnant of sense. She would go on so. She would go on and on and on.

'See you later.' He waved. 'Bye.'

'I keep telling you I'm worried,' said Molly.

'And I keep telling you there's nothing to worry about.'

'Hamish, he swore at me.'

'What dairy farmer wouldn't at that hour of night. The poor bugger would be milking cows a few hours later.'

Molly shook her head. 'No,' she said. 'No. It wasn't that.' She sat silent and thoughtful for some time, then reached for the telephone. 'I must ring Bridget about the trip to Campbell Island.'

'Why on earth do you fuss about that woman?'

'She's Freddy's wife, or ex-wife. There's some little rift between them and they're both such dears.'

'If Fred wants to see her he can make arrangements to do so. You're meddling, Mol. Playing God again.'

'But it would be so lovely for them if . . .' said Molly and dialled Reception.

'That's all settled. She would love to see the Orang Asli. Humanitaire are having a rest day.'

'Does Fred know you've asked her?'

'Oh, yes they all do,' said Molly. 'You remember. Last night.'

There was a hotel envelope under Violet's door. She seized it, ripped it open and fell on the bed.

Violet,
With solace and gladness
All good and no badness
So joyously
So maidenly
So womanly
I adore you,
Freddy.

She fell back, crushed the sheet of paper to her and flung her legs in the air.

'Oh Freddy. Freddy. Freddy.'

17

Sunhatted, dark-glassed and ready for anything, Molly and Violet stood in the hotel forecourt beside Dato Ahmad Kamarul Ridza's personal limousine, waiting while things were sorted out between Datin Ahmad and their escort.

'But why are you coming?' Datin Ahmad demanded, pointing a long finger at the wooden-faced Colonel Beaucott. 'It is ridiculous to have a foreigner to guard me. Who gave this order?'

'Your husband, Datin Ahmad,' replied the Colonel, sweating slightly. 'I was given to understand, ma'am, that he had discussed the matter with you.'

Datin Ahmad made no reply. She stood motionless, breathing slowly and deeply through her nose. The effect of a proud animal exhibiting stoicism under pressure was disturbing.

The silent Miss Raya, in attendance once more and as beautiful as ever, looked nervous, almost tearful.

Not so the guests. Molly stood gazing at her hostess with her usual calm attention. Violet watched her charge with affection and fellow feeling. Watching someone in a seething rage for which you are in no way responsible can be strangely soothing. She hoped Lance would not produce a Wet One.

'At least we have a jolly decent car,' said Datin Ahmad eventually.

The Malay driver sprang and opened the door.

'I prefer the right-hand side,' said the Datin, climbing in. 'It is safer.'

Molly, assisted by the saluting Lance, scrambled into the off side followed by Violet and the still shaken Miss Raya.

Motorbikes roared into action, their sirens slicing a way through the traffic and the limousine purring in their wake. Molly watched as people scuttled for safety. One man somersaulted from his bicycle, lifted it above his head and ran.

Nothing was said until the cavalcade slowed at the outskirts of the city and the escort peeled off. The six motorbikes turned in a slow arc around the almost stationary limousine, the riders saluting as they headed back to town in silence. Datin Ahmad sat straight and solemn, waving with upward palm until the last pair were out of sight.

They passed abandoned rubber estates of graceful trees half throttled by undergrowth and choking vines. Violet watched with awe. You could feel the struggle, sense the inevitable outcome. 'Rampant growth' took on another meaning in this place. These plants were predators, ruthless as pythons and programmed to fight for light.

The road led through several kampongs which were little more than clusters of wooden shacks with corrugated-iron roofs. A few bougainvillea struggled for existence in tins. Goats, chickens, and one or two bright exotic cockerels, roamed free. Young girls carried siblings on their non-existent hips.

'These eyesores will soon go,' said Datin Ahmad. 'Our rehousing programme is immense and very efficient.'

'So I have heard,' said Molly.

'Very. The figures tell you.' Datin Ahmad questioned Miss Raya in Malay. 'My secretary does not know the figures,' she said, shrugging her shoulders to her ears and dropping them with a sniff. There was a further exchange in Malay between employer and employee. 'She says she will look them up and let you know.'

'Thank you,' said Molly. 'How kind.'

'Fish farms,' snapped the Datin, pointing at patches of water, squares of blue from the reflecting sky. 'And rice.'

'Where?' said Molly. 'Oh, how interesting.'

She craned her head, fascinated as ever by difference. Fish farms to them must be like sheep to us. When she pointed out sheep at home Asian ladies scrambled to see. She opened her mouth to ask more but the Datin was on to transport.

'This road,' she said, 'was built by the Americans for army trucks after the war. That is why it is so big. American.'

'Ah.'

Violet sat thinking of Freddy. Extraordinary. Quite extraordinary. One minute you're minding your own business and the next minute you're another being, excited, twitchy, physically and mentally more alert. She found herself walking carefully, sitting gently.

Freddy, I adore you, hook, line and sinker. Loved the poem. See you soon. She sighed.

'Are you feeling sick, Violet?' said Molly.

'No thank you. Not at all. Look, there's a tree fern in the forest. Tropical rainforest looks like ours at first, doesn't it, dense, green, going for miles. But even from here I find it very different.' She glanced at the Datin, who was lying back

210

with closed eyes. 'Oppressive,' she murmured.

'Do you feel that too?' said Molly.

'Yes. Definitely.'

Molly agreed. 'Merciless.'

'Only to fools and foreigners,' said the Datin. 'One never hears of Malays going mad in the jungle.'

'Does anyone, Datin Ahmad?' asked Violet.

'Goodness yes.' A hand waved. 'Hundreds. Planters. Colonials. That sort of thing. Only Malays can understand the forest. White men,' she shrugged, 'simply cannot cope. It is not their country. It scares them. Let alone the tigers and forest bulls and snakes.'

Violet, who understood that *amok* was the Malaysian equivalent for bush crazy, opened her mouth and shut it again.

They stared at the jungle, so green, so silent and so solid. There was nothing else to see and nothing more to say.

Molly tried. 'Tell me, Datin,' she said. 'Is there anywhere nearby where we could see bats in the wild?'

The Datin gave a genteel shriek. 'You cannot wish to see bats. Bats are foul. They live in caves. They stink . . . No one could wish to see bats.'

Miss Raya murmured something.

'Oh yes, yes,' said the Datin. 'Of course, there are places. Yes, yes. The Batu caves have them, but fortunately they are in the other direction. There is a Hindu shrine in the major cave and they have a festival, yuck. But yes, there are bats.' She turned to Molly and smiled. 'My assistant could take you and Miss —' Her hands sprang apart in apology at the loss of Violet's name. 'Tomorrow morning, why not?'

Molly smiled at Miss Raya. 'Thank you, but no, we are busy tomorrow.'

'Ah,' said the Datin.

The road continued to climb in black sweeping curves.

Violet attempted clothes. 'I understand, Datin Ahmad,' she said, 'that it is possible to buy imitation Lacoste shirts very reasonably at the night market in Jalan Petaling.'

'That rubbish,' shrugged the Princess. 'Any fool can tell they are imitations.'

'Oh. I understood they are virtually indistinguishable.'

'Nonsense. The crocodiles go the wrong way. Ah, we must be nearly there. Good.'

The Genting Highlands were a surprise to Molly. She knew the important role the hill stations had played in the life of colonials, their coolness, the beauty of the surroundings. She had read about the Cameron Highlands. The very name sounded cool, healthy, perhaps a little misty. Mention had been made of jungle tracks and wild flowers, of waterfalls and tea plantations and flower nurseries and vegetable farms. There was a hotel which served Devonshire teas. It all sounded very pleasant.

Not so the Genting Highlands. They looked neither cosy nor invigorating.

The place looked like a smaller version of Kuala Lumpur but without the charm, a place of skyscrapers and construction and reconstruction. The same orange plastic netting surrounded similar clamorous earthworks beside similar whirling traffic.

'None of this existed ten years ago,' said the Datin, dusting her immaculate pink jacket. 'The casino exists for rich Chinese to gamble. Huh.'

The car entered Genting Park, drove past a cable car.

'That goes up the mountain, does it?' said Molly.

'I haven't the slightest idea.'

Miss Raya murmured.

'Ah. My assistant says it goes to the golf course.'

'Ah.'

Miss Raya murmured again.

'She says,' sighed the Datin, 'that the lake over there is four hectares in size and artificial. That it is encircled by a miniature railway for children and their amahs. She is unable to tell us the size of the park but the hotel is eighteen storeys high, has six hundred and thirty-five rooms and is very expensive indeed. She is unable to tell you the figure.'

Miss Raya lowered her head. The car drew to a halt.

'Here we are at last,' said her employer. 'It seems longer than an hour.'

Lance Beaucott turned from the front seat. 'Excuse me, Datin,' he said.

Diamonds flashed, hands flew to her breast. 'Good God, I had forgotten you existed.'

Not a flicker crossed his face. 'Can I have your assurance, ma'am,' he continued, 'that your driver will not leave the limousine unattended while we are at the hotel?'

'Of course he won't.' The Datin asked a question. The driver replied, laughing heartily and shaking his head. 'He says he would die rather.'

'I understand, ma'am, that we may be away for several hours.'

'So? Ah, thank you.'

Doors flung open, uniformed staff lined the route to the hotel entrance. A small Malay man came forward, bowing and bowing again as Datin Ahmad swept past him. She turned, '*You* are the manager?'

Yes, yes indeed he was, and the honour of meeting the Datin and her party was almost too much for Mr Redzuan. He strode before them, guiding the way, then swung back bowing encouragement. His excitement was catching. Violet and Molly found themselves bowing in return, tossing wild smiles around.

First, explained Mr Redzuan, there would be lunch, then the tour of the casino. All, all would be seen.

The small mobile face, the bright and glinting eye of Mr Redzuan seemed familiar. Of course, thought Violet, Jerry of *Tom and Jerry*: the same air of irrepressible optimism, a can-do-kinda-guy designed to oblige the noble, the wealthy and the obsessed till they could pay no more. He must also be very tough.

The hotel was the most interesting one yet experienced. They gazed in silence at enormous pillars, mile-high ceilings and dimpled putti. Roman urns and small delicate chairs shimmered in rooms lit by shafts from stained-glass windows. Even the towering spikes of orchids were artificial. The room into which Mr Redzuan led them for lunch had a dark rough-hewn oak table and equally rugged-looking chairs. Fishing nets, supported at intervals by lifebelts, fell across pseudo oak panelling and casement windows. Child-sized suits of armour stood at the ready.

'Ah,' said Molly. 'And what is the name of this room, Mr Redzuan?'

'This is the Tudor Room, ma'am.'

'Yes, of course,' said Molly. 'How silly of me.'

I do like her, thought Violet. She is a truly good person. Never to hurt anyone, even unintentionally: that is her essence. She should be a Buddhist. I must tell Freddy.

'I will collect you later, ma'am,' continued Mr Redzuan. 'For coffee in the Ladies' Lounge if that still pleases, Datin Ahmad?'

The Datin gave a nod.

Mr Redzuan bowed himself out backwards.

'I will sit here,' said Datin Ahmad. 'As my guest, Mrs Carew, you may sit on my right hand. You three' – she shrugged – 'sit where you like.'

White-robed young men pulled back chairs. Violet sat warily. Chair pushers never make any distinction in the leg length of the pushed. She had learned to clutch the chair seat to avoid cracked knees.

Molly remarked on the small size of the suits of armour.

'English,' sniffed the Datin. She made a half-hearted attempt to swallow a yawn and lapsed into silence.

'I understand, Datin Ahmad, that we visit the National Museum on Friday?' tried Violet.

Miss Raya smiled and nodded. The Datin said, 'Yes.'

'How interesting,' said Molly. 'And what is your favourite exhibit?'

'The circumcision of the King's son.'

Even Miss Raya looked startled.

The . . . circumcision?'

'They don't *do* it,' said the Datin. 'There is a life-sized model of the newly circumcised royal prince being carried around in a curtained litter to show him to the people.'

'Oh.'

'Yes. He is a young boy. We are a proud race. We learn courage at an early age. Ah, here is the food. I have taken particular care with the menu today. I have ordered genuine Malay food. Rich and spicy. No pork of course, and as you see no alcoholic drink. What are we eating, Miss Raya?'

Miss Raya spoke for some time.

Datin Ahmad translated. '*Kari laksa kerang* is a spicy noodle soup with cockles, she says. *Solong kangkong*, rich red sauce with squid. *Poh pia*, she says, is impossible to describe and I have no idea how it is made, nor indeed any of them. *Sambal rarang* is a hot spicy peanut dish, and of course satay. And to finish we have our famous pudding, *gula melaka*, sago, palm sugar served with rich thick coconut milk. Very good.'

Everything was very good. Spicy treat followed subtle treat, young men slipped silent and attentive about the room with a wary eye on Datin Ahmad. The *gula melaka* was much praised.

It was all very interesting, thought Violet, and coffee in the Ladies' Lounge sounded promising. Lance Beaucott had not blinked an eye. Would he stand guard at the door or lounge with the ladies?

The Ladies' Lounge was aptly named. Low raised platforms or divans piled with cushions lined the stone walls around the largest Persian carpet Violet had ever seen.

'Wouldn't mind the rug,' murmured Lance.

She glanced at his dead-pan face. 'Where would you put it?'

Lance closed one eye. 'We've got a double garage at home. Drive-on access.'

Unexpected jokes, like gifts, have more value. Violet came out of her Freddy-induced daze and grinned at him.

The only furniture other than the divans were small intricately carved tables and large leather pouffes. On the divans lay pallets covered with more Oriental rugs – exotic glowing things, all blues and purples and ruby reds – piled with Thai silk cushions. Small plump bolsters and puffed-up monsters in sharp greens, hot pinks and yellows sang together in opulent harmony. More, more, more cried the colours and the columns and the tables and pouffes. Let us rejoice, wallow, drown in such luxurious recumbency.

This was no place to sit upright. It seemed absurd amidst such comfort and excess. This was a place, or rather a pretence of a place, where women would recline, be indolent and await their fate.

Or was it, thought Violet, sinking back with the rest of the party. The place was a Ladies' Lounge, where Ladies could lounge in comfort. It probably has no harem connotations at all. She smiled at Lance Beaucott, who was standing at ease by the door staring straight ahead. A little lounge might do Lance the world of good.

The Datin reclined with languid grace, Miss Raya hardly at all. Molly fell backwards as though collapsing into a hammock. Violet was making decisions about her legs, whether to fold them decorously beside her or let them spill over the edge.

Mr Redzuan, seated on a leather pouffe, made a sign. Two beautiful young Malay men in turbans, silk trousers and embroidered waistcoats slipped into the room bearing engraved brass coffeepots with long curving spouts and handles. Underlings dressed in white offered tiny cups to the ladies: the young men bowed low, dropped to their knees and, holding a pot in one hand and pushing themselves along with the other, slid their way towards the guests' knees, poured their coffee and pushed themselves backwards to disappear behind a nearby screen. The process was repeated with the same young men bearing silver trays of sweetmeats: little slabs of pink nougat, sugared almonds and Turkish Delight. The youth serving the Datin was practically on his stomach. She made her choice. He shoved himself back with downcast eyes.

Posters, chocolate boxes and silent films featuring concubines, seraglios and eunuchs swam before Molly's eyes. The place was mind blowing, as Bobby would say, quite mind blowing, and goodness me how interesting. She wondered who she could tell about it at home. The only person who would be interested and understand, she thought sadly, would be Arthur. And he could tell Lollipop. She made a small unhappy sound, somewhere between a hiccup and a sob. The one person she could never attempt to tell was Bobby. 'What are you on about, Mum,' she'd say. 'The place sounds a hoot.'

Where is she? Where?

Eventually, replete and slightly drowsy, Molly heaved herself upwards and turned to the Datin. 'And when do we see the Casino itself, Datin Ahmad?'

The Datin popped a Turkish Delight between carmine lips and puffed icing sugar at her. 'Now,' she said. 'Where is the man? Ah, there. My assistant and I,' she murmured, sinking against silk once more, 'will wait for you here. Au revoir.'

The Casino was to scale with the rest of the building, both in size and opulence. It consisted of one room so large that its further reaches were out of focus to Molly. Baccarat, Black Jack, roulette, all the Western games of chance and Eastern favourites such as keno and tai sai, explained Mr Redzuan, were played on all tables all day and all night for every day of the year. 'Twenty-one thousand people passed through last Sunday, ma'am,' he continued. 'We have everything organised, also for children. Parents tell me they never see the children from the moment they arrive. They spend all day, nights at the tables.

Yes, ma'am, sometimes they do forget them but that is no problem. There are care centres, big care centres with many toys and friendly staff. The parents have a rest from their cares and everyone is happy. A high standard is set, ma'am. Patrons must be twenty-one years of age and wear ties at all times.

'Yes, ma'am there is indeed a sign denying Muslims entrance. Gambling is against our religion, as is alcohol and bad behaviour.'

'But how is it you can be the manager, Mr Redzuan?'

'Ah that is a happy thing, ma'am. It is the nationalisation programme for Malays, OK? For years Malays have been oppressed in their own country, you see. Also I am very efficient.'

'I'm sure you are, Mr Redzuan,' said Molly. 'And I suppose a proportion of the takings from the Casino go to charity, do they not?'

Mr Redzuan took a step back. 'Oh no, ma'am,' he gasped. 'Not a ringitt. Not a sou. No, no, no ma'am. Not at all.'

'May I, Datin? said Lance Beaucott, stepping forward as the driver leapt to open the right-hand door of the limousine. Datin Ahmad, assuming that the young man wanted the honour for himself, stepped back.

'Can you give me your word,' said Lance to the driver, 'that you have not left the car while the party has been indoors?'

'Yes indeed, sir.'

'You will swear to that?'

The driver, in a torrent of Malay, appealed to the Datin.

'How dare you insult my employee,' she cried. 'How long have you been in this country, you little pip. Six months! I am a member of a most esteemed family. If this man left his post when told not to, it would be prison, worse than prison, would it not?'

The driver, with wide expressive gestures, agreed vehemently.

'And you, you pip squeak, ask him to swear on Almighty Allah. I shall report you, sir. Yes, I shall. Definitely and straight away.'

Lance stood his ground. 'I accept that your driver is a truthful man, Datin. I had to check in case there was any chance someone could have tampered with the car.'

'Tampered with Dato Ahmad's personal limousine?'

Molly looked at the driver, then at Lance. 'Both young men have done their duty, have they not, Datin? Shall we get into the car?'

Datin Ahmad climbed into the car and closed her eyes.

Molly, unsure whether she had made things better or worse, but pleased by the Datin's example, closed hers.

Violet looked at Miss Raya in her tight-fitting jacket and long batik skirt. As always she sat demure and silent. This woman had been with them for days on end and still they had no idea who she was or what she did (apart from being the Datin's assistant which could well be a full-time job). Eighty percent of communication, Freddy had told her, is achieved by body language. She and Molly had both tried their best to communicate in every way they could. The hell with it. She leaned back.

A group of young men in shorts and T-shirts appeared from the forest and jogged across the road in front of them.

'Hash House Harriers,' said Miss Raya, sitting bolt upright.

'Really?' cried Violet, overreacting. 'How exciting. They follow a paper trail, don't they?'

But Miss Raya was lost to her once more.

The sky had been getting darker by the minute. A crack of thunder, followed almost immediately by a long strike of pink forked lightning, lit the sky. The car rocked like a dinghy in rough seas; the jungle turned black.

'Storm,' laughed the driver as the car shuddered onwards. Coin-sized drops hit the windscreen as the cloud burst. 'Big storm,' he said.

Lance turned. 'Don't be concerned, Mrs Carew,' he said. 'This happens all the time here.'

'I presume the tyres are made of rubber,' said Molly. 'I find it exciting – when I am inside of course.'

Miss Raya shook her head. 'Poor Hash House Harriers. My boyfriend. Army.'

'Where?' squeaked Violet. 'Did you see him?'

'Not today, not today.'

'Tomorrow perhaps?'

Miss Raya smiled.

Datin Ahmad opened her eyes, grunted and closed them again. She awoke refreshed and smiling and with no trace of displeasure, exuded magnanimity and friendliness for the remainder the voyage, left them with despatch at the hotel and departed waving merrily.

'Well,' said Molly.

Violet slumped her shoulders in agreement. 'I'll get the room keys.'

She swung around at the scream. Molly, crimplene clinging to her legs and her arms wide open, was embracing a figure in flared jeans and a backpack. The head was hidden but the boots looked familiar.

It was Bobby. Good God. Bobby, tousled, bedraggled, all buoyancy gone, was sobbing her heart out on her mother's shoulder.

Violet picked up Molly's discarded handbag and held it tight. Hell's fangs, she thought. Hell's fangs and goodness me. Poor Bobby.

'What's happened to the calves, darling?' asked Molly in their room an hour later.

'That's typical of you, Mum,' sobbed Bobby. 'Typical, y'know that. The one thing you're fussed about is the damn calves. I should've known.'

'I just wondered.'

'As if I'd leave them. I'll tell you what's happened to the calves. Mac next door is feeding them. He's had his eye on them ever since I started breeding. He knows he'll get first choice if I sell.'

'Sell?'

When you've built up such a good line? No don't say that. But what could she say? She had listened to the whole disastrous saga twice through with all the love and sympathy she had to give. Had kept her mouth shut as to where the money for the flight had come from, even about what assurance Bobby had had that Bronson would stay with the cows. But no, she shouldn't think that. He would never desert them. No dairy farmer would, and he loved cows. Think of those New Zealand soldiers hopping over fences in France to milk cows bellowing in agony.

What am I doing, what am I thinking? Cows, calves, Kiwi soldiers. Concentrate, she told herself.

She turned to her daughter and took her in her arms again. 'Don't worry, darling. It will be all right.'

'Don't keep saying that,' sniffed Bobby. 'When will Dad be back?'

Hamish was shocked, outraged, totally flummoxed. He never would have thought it, never in a thousand years would he have thought that any man, let alone a sensible straightforward sort of cove like Bronson, could do such a thing to his daughter. The man was a swine, absolute swine, no doubt about that.

'Leave him to me, Bob, leave him to me,' he said. 'He won't know his arse from his elbow by the time I've finished with him.

'No, no,' he said, mopping her face with his handkerchief as he had done when she was a baby, 'no more tears. Listen, now listen, this is what you do. He's gone, right? Exited, vamoosed, scrammed. He's deader than a dead duck to you. Right?'

'No, no, no.'

'Listen, listen. What difference does it make to him if you go on weeping and wailing and crying your eyes out? First, he probably won't know. He won't dare show his face in the district once I get home, believe me. And second he'd probably love it if he did find out how miserable you are. The man's got enough tickets on himself already. I could see that straight off. Nothing wrong with that. I like a man with confidence. But I won't have my little girl being a feather in any bastard's cap, let alone a cocky swine like Foster's.

'Look, Bob. You're free as a bird. OK, you don't want to go back to the farm at the moment. I can understand that. To be quite frank I didn't know why you wanted to go back there in the first place. Sure I was pleased when you decided, but look at you. Look at your talents. The world's your oyster. This place, for example. It's jumping, that's what. Jumping. Not that I suggest you stay here, God no, but there are opportunities, no doubt about that. Ask Kinsella about it – Barney Kinsella, our Trade man here. He'll have it at his fingertips. This part of the world is about to take off. Opportunities galore for a sharp go-ahead young woman like you.

'What time's the cocktail party at Kinsella's, Mol? We'll take you along, why not? No, no, I'm not suggesting she comes to the dinner with the Minister and his wife, or the Glen Campbell Show. Don't be such a wet blanket, Mol.'

'But I'd love to hear Glen Campbell,' wailed Bobby.

'Not tonight, love. Not tonight. I'll get Penn McPhee's team on to it. See if he can jack up a ticket for tomorrow. He's very big here, I gather. Campbell, I mean.'

18

Barney Kinsella would be delighted. 'Yes indeed, Minister. Please do bring your daughter. Delighted. Delighted.'

Bathed, shampooed and changed in her room along the corridor, Bobby felt like a different animal, a rational woman with her head screwed on. Dad was right, she could see that. Sure, sure she had been crazy about the guy. How could she not, so damn sexy, so lean and tough. But he had ditched her; lied like a flatfish and crawled back to that tramp and the smelly kid. That was the bottom line.

No wonder she'd been flattened. Livid. In shock. Anyone would have been. But think about it. That poor sod will be trapped for ever. What had she been doing, bawling her head off for days? Look at *him*. Gutted. Sunk without trace.

The scalding rage of being tossed aside like some dumb bimbo was softened for Bobby by sense. Dad was right. She was still furious. But it had happened. He was gone, dead. Leg-roped to a nutter he couldn't leave.

And look at you, mate, look at this room, this place. Violet had fixed it up in a tick and Dad had come to the party. You couldn't ask fairer than that. And like he said, she was as free as the air.

Her eyes matched her newly pressed A-line; her bright hair gleamed as she strode around the pastel decor, then swung back to the mirror to clench her fists and shake them at herself.

Go for it, Bob. Have a ball. Some day she might be sorry for the poor shit. But not yet. Not by a long chalk.

She picked up the receiver and dialled.

'Hi, Mum,' she cried. 'Tell me about this Kinsella guy. What's he do here? Trade? Oh really? Tell me more.'

Molly was surprised at her daughter's change of tone but not astounded. Practical, down-to-earth Bobby's emotions were mercurial. She had always had this ability to swing from glad to sad and back again within hours. Childhood tantrums had never lasted. She had never been a grizzler, a sulky child.

'And what's his wife like, Dad?' Bobby said as Kamil edged the car out into the traffic.

'I understand he's divorced, isn't he, Mol?'

'I believe so,' said Molly with her eyes on her transfigured daughter.

'What about Ruby Tan?' asked Hamish.

'I think she was just his partner.'

'What sort of partner?' said Bobby.

'Well, dinner-party partner. A friend.'

'Oh.'

'But of course I don't know.'

———

'Mnn,' said Bobby. 'Nice house.'

Barney Kinsella reiterated his pleasure. He couldn't be more pleased. He clasped Bobby's hand in both of his and shook it warmly. 'And you came all this way for my party. What marvellous timing, Bobby.'

Bobby, having seen no evidence of Ruby whatsit, responded in kind. 'Be worth it, I bet.'

Hamish took her elbow. 'Come on, Bob,' he said. 'I want you to meet the team.'

'But I've met them.'

'No, no. I mean the High Commissioner, the people at the post. Come along.'

Bobby gave an apologetic pout and followed in her father's wake. Molly, in her silk which did breathe, followed, relaxed by the apparent speed of her daughter's recovery. 'It just goes to show,' she thought, a phrase which had served as her mother's reaction to any form of human behaviour from the devious to the unexpected, the praiseworthy to the farcical. All just went to show. A meaningless phrase but useful as a reply, an acceptance of mysterious forces, even a source of consolation. And it saved thought.

Molly and her fresh lime moved over to Violet and Freddy.

'What a pretty frock,' she said, touching the loose floating blues falling from Violet's shoulders.

'Guess where I found it?'

'From the night market with the wrong-way crocodiles?'

'Right first time. Jalan Petaling, when we got back.'

'Oh look, there's Bridget with Barney,' said Molly, heading off in their direction.

Violet watched them. Bridget and Barney did not appear to be having their usual wild time. Bridget spoke seriously, listened with care. A beautiful woman with *gravitas*. Which is like style. You can be beautiful without style and serious without *gravitas*. However, if you have both attributes together it shows you have worked at it, are more earnest about the matter in hand.

Thank God for light-heartedness. How else would you survive? How else could you love?'

She turned to Freddy, expecting the besotted smile of a few moments ago. It had gone. He stood glaring at Molly's lilac rear.

'Why does the woman keep on about Bridget. Why should she go to the Orang Asli tomorrow?'

'It's a bind, yes. But you'll be there, I'll be there. The two of us in a speech balloon saying *Shove Off*. Her smile widened. 'And she won't be with us later tonight.'

He seized her hand. 'There's something I must tell you. Two things, (a) We can't, not tonight, and (b) . . .'

'Why?' she gasped.

'Darling, I can't tell you here.'

'Why not? There's no one around.' She flicked a dismissive hand at a hundred or more shouting guests. '*Why*? And incidentally, why loo paper?'

'What?'

'Loo paper, that crackly stuff. For your note, the first one.'

'That's part of it.'

'Whaat!'

'I mean . . . oh Christ.'

'Tell me. And why did you clear off so early? *Tell* me.'

'Because I've got diarrhoea, gut rot, the shits.'

'I don't see what that's got to do with the paper you chose.'

'The wha . . . oh fuck the paper.'

A mistake. A definite mistake. He looked at her, his gut rumbling as the temperature dropped.

'Sweetheart, we can't have a row about bumph. I'll explain it all, I promise. And I can't give you this bug. It's a killer. It's better already. It'll be gone tomorrow. There's tomorrow and . . .'

'Can't we just lie there, hold each other?'

'Don't be ridiculous,' he snapped.

'Oh Freddy, poor Freddy.' She bit her lip to hide the smile, a cheek pleated with the effort. 'Of course you're right. It's just that it's rather a let-down.'

'What? Having it or not doing it?'

'Both.'

'Yes,' he said, suddenly aware that a group of almost silent guests had formed a loose circle around them. 'Disappointing.'

'*Disappointing*. You sound as though you're giving a verdict on a new brand of fish fingers.'

Bridget appeared at her side. 'Why are we talking about fish fingers? Hello, Violet, nice to see you. Freddy, I've come over to make sure you don't mind if I join the party tomorrow? I'd really like to meet the Orang Asli, but do say if you'd rather I didn't. I realise it's a bit of a . . .'

'I don't give a damn,' he said. 'I won't be there.'

Violet gaped. 'Why on earth not?'

'Wet One's going instead. To guard you.'

'But why not you?'

'Presumably he's licensed to kill or something.'

Violet's voice was cooler than ever, her head high. 'Why didn't you tell me?'

'I've only just heard. Penn told me. Wet One and I have been swapped. Visit to Campbell Island for dried milk and vice versa.'

'You still could have told me.'

He looked into her eyes. They appeared to be snapping at him. 'Violet,' he said, moving his head from side to side in slow emphasis. 'Honey, I haven't had time to tell you anything.' He looked around the large room. 'Where's the toilet? Thanks. Excuse me.'

Honey. The word echoed, hung in the air as they watched him go. The space around them closed as faces, torsos, hips and thighs slipped back to fill the gap.

'Are you wearing high heels?' asked Bridget.

'Me, why?'

'Nothing. I'd just forgotten how tall you were.'

'Are.'

'Yes, of course. Are.'

Bobby was enjoying herself. She had been going to official parliamentary parties for yonks but had given them up some time ago. They had never been anything to write home about, not much in the way of talent, and little fun. Most of the older men present were shufflers and huffers in crappy suits with little pot bellies, even the thin ones. And so thrilled with themselves, flirting away with young women like frisky zombies. Who did they think they were, with their 'What's a pretty girl like you?' routine and their busy hands. They were worse, on the whole, than the younger ones.

But this was different. This was a real party with duty-free booze in decent surroundings and a decent host and beautiful people. The locals particularly looked more interesting, and much better dressed. That group over there – she hadn't seen clothes like that since Princess Anne hit town. Not the colours or the style, hell no, but the way they were made. These garments had been designed for them. And they looked so *clean*. Their clothes would have been pressed and laid out for them. No scrabbled head-down bottom-up in wardrobes hunting for the missing shoe. And their *rings*. And their men. Handsome, well dressed and obviously charming. One of them, with a socking great ring on his middle finger, seemed to be holding court.

Even the pale faces looked better than usual. Maybe it's the air conditioning, the servants, the life in general. I like it here, thought Bobby.

She looked around for Barney. He was talking to some woman who moved towards her and held out her hand.

'Hullo, how nice to meet you. I'm Bridget Cox, Freddy Manders' wife.'

'Hi,' said Bobby. 'He didn't say he was married.'

'Barney will explain,' said Bridget and drifted away.

'Explain,' said Bobby.

Barney gave a slight cough. 'I suppose I could say she's Fred's ex-wife.'

'But she's going to talk to him.'

'Yes, it's rather a long story, but seeing she's asked me to fill you in . . .' Barney glanced around the room. The party was going smoothly, but no, this was not the moment to peel off to the patio with the Minister's daughter.

An ancient song somewhere. Something about sitting in the water with the Lord Mayor's daughter on a sunny Sunday afternoon. Good idea, but no.

Barney opened resigned palms. 'I must look after my guests. I don't suppose . . .' He snapped his fingers. 'I know! Are you by any chance free after this? Or are you going on with the Minister?'

'I'm not going anywhere.'

'Excellent. What a bit of luck. Let's have a meal somewhere in town.' He gave a short bark of laughter. 'I did have an engagement but the lady stood me up.'

Ruby Tan, I bet. 'Oh, I'm sorry,' lied Bobby.

'I'm not. Anything but. Can you stick it out to the end of this shindig then we'll organise something?'

'Yes.'

'Excellent, excellent. Couldn't be better. Now, if you'll excuse me, I'll have to do my stuff. Who would you like to meet?'

Bobby did not hesitate. 'That group over there.'

More laughter and a gentle pressure on her elbow. 'You're a good picker, Bobby. That's Prince Peter and his friends. Charming man, absolute character.'

The party was over. Bobby and her host sat beside one another on one those white sofas you see in *House and Garden*, usually in pairs with a few African masks around and a lot of marble.

The stuffing must be swan's-down; they sank into it for miles and the heavy white fabric puffed up round them like nests as they raised their glasses to each other. There was no mess to clear up, not a nut or a lemon rind, a loaded ashtray or an unplumped cushion in sight. Silent men and women had slipped in and out, and that was that.

Bobby felt so at ease she had to restrain herself from discussing the guests, which she always found fun. Liked him, couldn't stand her, that sort of thing. She felt as if she were one of a couple. Married with servants.

'So you enjoyed Prince Peter and his mates?' asked Barney.

'Oh yes, especially him. I thought he was lovely. He told me he loves parties, and so do I – well, good ones. Not like Mum. She was hopeless at parties. Slaving away for days, you know how they do, then all jitters and exhaustion when the bell rang. At least she's given that up. Dad said no one would shoot her if she stopped and they didn't.'

They turned to each other, smiled. He wasn't bad-looking either.

'What's your preference as regards food,' he said. 'Malay, Chinese or Indian? I'm no expert, I haven't been here long enough, but from what I've heard it's damn good. They say you get better Indian food here than in India. Better Chinese too. Something to do with the proportions, I understand. The minorities are large enough to support their own social as well as religious practices. Fascinating place. I can see I'm going to be very happy in this post. Paris will always be my spiritual home, of course, but I can see there's a lot to be said for life here.'

'Yes, so can I. And I've only been here half a day. Half a day. It seems incredible.'

'A lot can happen in half a day,' he said earnestly.

Bobby took a chance, giggled and was rewarded by a slow smile.

'Now,' he said. 'Food. State your preference.'

She played safe. 'Chinese please.'

'Chinese it is.' He stood, walked to the door. 'Kam Sung? What's a good Chinese restaurant?'

'Boss place?' asked Kam Sung.

'Of course.'

'The Inn of Happiness, sir. Very good place, sir.'

'Oh, we can't go there,' cried Bobby. 'That's where the oldies are going.'

Barney gave a solemn nod. 'I take your point. We'll try elsewhere, and on the way I'll tell you about Manders and his wife. I'd forgotten all about them.'

They were dealt with en route. Bobby thought the whole thing was weird. Barney agreed, and the subject was dropped.

He drove fast and well, seemingly unfazed by the traffic, then slipped into a park not far from the restaurant.

'I always find a park. Anywhere. Even here. I send up a quick prayer to Hughie and he takes over. Never fails.'

'Hughie,' giggled Bobby. 'What a hoot.'

'The egg fou yung's very good here, I believe,' said Barney, handing his menu back to the waiter with that quick flip of despatch of the seasoned diner-out. 'But I don't think it would marry well with the chilli crab which is big news here. Messy but delicious. We'll leave the old egg fou till next time.' He leaned forward, folded his hands near hers. 'How long are you staying?'

That's a thought. How long was she staying? Bobby moved a hand an inch nearer his. 'I haven't decided yet. It rather depends.'

'On what?'

'I left in rather a rush. I was being hassled out of my life by a mad sharemilker Dad hired a few months ago. He started off all right, efficient and that, but the last few weeks he's been a pain in the neck. Worse than that, he wouldn't take no for an answer. Don't get me wrong, I can look after myself, but all of a sudden I thought, I don't *need* this, and I rang the airways and bingo here I am. Dad's going to fire the creep tonight

231

when he gets back to the hotel. I wanted out, a real change, know what I mean.'

'Yes, I do. What a bloody nerve.' Barney pulled out a packet of cigarettes, offered her one.

'I don't usually,' she giggled, 'but what the hell.'

Barney leaned forward again. 'What the hell indeed. And what do you think of KL so far?'

'Fantastic! And I haven't set foot in a shop yet.'

'That shouldn't be too much of a problem.'

'I know,' said Bobby, wriggling with excitement. 'I adore shopping. I find it therapeutic.'

The time has come, she thought as they laughed together, pleased with themselves and each other and the paper dragons breathing fire at mirrored walls and the three-sized pagodas and the monster lantern thingies of the Ming Sun Pavilion. The place was busy, successful, full of well-dressed people enjoying themselves. Bobby liked it like that. Restaurants should be full. And theatres: there was nothing worse than empty seats and bored-looking waiters standing about. She liked places to throb, and not having to clap too hard.

Maybe it might be better to wait till after the chilli crab if it was messy eating. But what the hell.

'This kerfuffle with Bron's got me thinking,' she said as the soup bowls were swept away. 'Maybe I've made a mistake holing up in Waikato.'

His eyes were all attention.

'I got sick of the city after a few years, and I like the country and animals and that, but I feel like I'm vegetating just with the calves. Jerseys. I breed them. Nice little money-earner, but I'm not using my business skills. There's not much customer orientation with stud breeding. They sell themselves, calves from a good line.

'I've done retail and I'm good at it and it teaches you a lot. Customer satisfaction is the thing, and if you don't learn that you'll never get to first base. It's just a case of going that extra mile. I've been there, done that, got it under my belt. What I want to move on to is, well, like, more . . . management. I've got all my commercial qualifications, excellent sales experience and know-how. I'm into quality management, outputs, the lot. I've got a good head for figures, an excellent CV and a thousand tons of energy. All I need is an opening.'

Barney dragged hard. Watched the smoke drift across her crisp tawny hair. A greeting card flashed to his mind. *You're all woman, And that's the best sort.* He'd sent it to Glenda years ago when they were newly engaged – and look what happened to that one.

That prick Manders thinking he'd give a damn about Gemma's photo. Got the wrong guy there, fuckwit.

Barney extinguished his cigarette with force. 'What sort of an opening?' he asked.

'Well, I was thinking. A place like this, say. What I'd like to do is stay here for a few months and suss things out, find the right product. Something that's dirt cheap here and you can't get at home, or if you can it costs the earth. I'd start in a very small way at first, maybe just friends, word of mouth. And of course it would depend on shipping costs, import restrictions, stuff like that.'

She was getting excited. Calm down, she told herself. The last thing she wanted was for Dad's trade representative in Malaysia to think she was picking his brains.

Barney leaned across, took the cigarette from her fingers and inhaled deeply. 'You're not enjoying it, are you?'

Bobby felt herself blushing. She never blushed, but the gesture had seemed so . . . so intimate. She thought of Bron, almost giggled. Bron was sinking in his own juice half a world away.

'No,' she said.

He took another drag or two and squashed the lipstick-tipped butt beside his. 'You know life is extraordinary, quite extraordinary.'

'Oh?'

'I've been here just two months and the same thought had occurred to me.'

Oh, bum. 'To do it yourself, you mean?' she said.

'No. I couldn't do that. Not for a minute. Conflict of interest and all that. I'd be out on my ear, and quite right too. But that doesn't mean I don't see the opportunities. This place is ripe for it . . .' He stopped. Exploitation was not the word of choice. 'Expansion of trade in small quality lines,' he said, 'which as you say are virtually unobtainable in Australasia.'

'Australasia?' gasped Bobby.

'Why not?'

'Nnnn. But what?'

He felt like a croupier who had dealt a good hand. 'Pots,' he said. 'All sizes from . . .'

'*Pots*?'

'Garden pots. Pottery. Magnificent things.' Barney cupped his fingers together, then spread his arms. 'Every size from eggcups to Ali Baba's hideout. All colours, shapes. Dragon pots. Can you get them at home now? The big ones? You certainly couldn't when I left, and that's only what, four years, five.'

'No,' said Bobby. 'I adore pots, I've got them all over at home. But we can't get the big ones.'

'Wait till you see the ones here. All the girls love them. The wives go home laden. Rings and pots. Mad if you don't.'

She could feel her heart beating. 'But Barney, I can't just take your advice and make money out of it.'

'Why not?' He smiled. 'Everyone else does.'

He patted her hand, croupier turned generous uncle. 'Not to worry, Bobs. We'll work something out.'

Bobs. No one had called her Bobs before. Bobs. She liked it.

Pots of Fun (Bobs Carew). She could just see it.

234

19

Dato Ahmad Kamarul Ridza snapped his fingers at the waiter and bent his handsome head towards his guest.

'Another fresh lime perhaps, Mrs Carew?'

The disadvantage of this excellent drink, Molly had realised, is exclusion. After a while you realise you are missing out on something, some agent of change which transforms civility to warmth and warmth to jollity. The time had come.

'No thank you, Minister,' she said, 'I would like a gin and tonic, thank you.'

'A good idea,' said Dato Ahmad, lifting his glass of ginger ale. 'Let us drink to that.'

And so they did, and dined and talked and laughed, and talked again around a circular table with a central 'lazy Susan' on which the specialities of The Inn of Happiness followed each other in endless cycles. Like the Swing Around, thought Molly, which seemed to be getting more cyclical by the day.

She woke each morning to luxury, drifted about, or rather was drifted about having an agreeable time meeting interesting people and visiting exotic places and eating too much delicious food, then met more interesting people of varying customs and cultures, then went to bed to prepare for the next round.

And all the time the men were working for their country. Molly was ashamed of her lack of enthusiasm for the visit. Malaysia was a wonderful place and tonight she was enjoying her favourite pastime, finding out. And Dato Ahmad was so devoted to his country, so tolerant of differences, so wise. Molly was tempted to tell him about her confusion about the Ladies' Lounge in the Genting Highlands. She was not sure what she wanted to say about it but felt he might understand.

She glanced across the table, hoped Hamish was having as entertaining a time. He was seated beside Datin Ahmad, who was wearing a diamond and jade ring the size of a thrush's egg. Both seemed happy. Freddy, on the other hand, looked peaky and was almost silent. Violet was talking to Colonel Beaucott; there was no sign of Mrs Beaucott. Presumably the Colonel was guarding them. It was high time Molly found out more about what or who they were being guarded from. She seemed to have missed a briefing somewhere. The flow between briefings and busy doings had been disturbed by Bobby's sudden arrival, as had her peace of mind.

Bronson had disturbed Molly. He loved cows, certainly, but there was something unnerving about those dazzling blue eyes. Bobby was well rid of him. But now there was this sudden leap from damp dishevelled waif to lively party girl. Bobby's emotions had always taken both time and understanding.

Datin Ahmad was telling Hamish about the Paris Fashion

Shows and how much she enjoyed them. As Hamish no doubt knew, those freak garments one saw on the catwalk were just a form of publicity stunt. No woman, or no woman she had ever known, would be seen in them for love or money. The thing to do, she explained, was to find a designer whose style suited one and stick to him. Hamish listened, nodding gravely, then told her about his government's plans for the construction of a new hydro-electric plant in the South Island near Cromwell, in Otago. She told him how much she enjoyed New York. He asked her whether she had heard of his government's Think Big programme. She shook her head. They seemed at ease with each other as they waited their turn.

Molly turned back to Dato Ahmad. 'I must tell you again how much I am looking forward to hearing my hero *live*,' she said. 'As I said before, it's a wonderful treat.'

Dato Ahmad smiled at her. 'And I continue to be happy to hear such good news.'

The auditorium was packed, the buzz of excitement continuous. Datin Ahmad leaned over her husband to talk to Molly.

'Do you know whether he's making a new series of his TV programme?'

'I didn't know he had one,' said Molly.

'Oh Lord yes. *The Good Time Hour*. Marvellous.'

'We don't have it at home,' said Molly, determined not to sound apologetic and wishing they had.

'Did you see him in *True Grit*?'

'No.'

Datin Ahmad gave up. 'Huh,' she said.

Her husband and his opera glasses had remained immobile during the exchange. He continued to scan the audience.

'Excuse me,' said Molly, ducking below his line of vision to talk to her hostess. 'I had heard,' she said, lowering her voice, 'that he has been having problems.'

'Problems! What problems?'

'Alcohol, I understand. And drugs. I saw it in a magazine at my hairdresser's. A "tumultuous affair", it said. With Tarya someone. I do hope it's not true.'

'Americans are always having tumultuous affairs,' said the Datin. 'It is their thing.'

'No, I mean, you know, *drugs*,' Molly whispered.

'Nonsense. If that were true he would not be here.'

'I do hope you're right.'

'Of course I am right. It is illegal. Look, here comes the group.'

Molly forgot the Datin's abruptness, the twinge from her hiatus hernia; even the worry of Bobby's confusing behaviour disappeared in her excitement. Shimmering with expertise, and true professionals to the core, the group was superb. From time to time a small self-contained man with a goatee beard put down his trombone and moved from one player to the next, bowed solemnly as an ushering verger, then took over his colleague's trombone, sax or horn, played a few riffs, bowed once more and moved on. His final burst of glory came from a small electric-blue violin.

Then came Glen, in person. Glen dancing about, strutting, striding, loving them all. The audience went mad, but discreetly so. They clapped and waved, screamed and uttered shrieks of joy but there were no surging masses, no hysteria and definitely nothing like thrown panties. They were orderly fans, albeit ecstatic.

Half buried by the continuous applause, people shouted for their favourites. 'Where's the Playground, Susie', cried the Datin; 'Gentle on my Mind', begged Molly; 'By the Time I Get to Phoenix', roared Dato Ahmad. The large theatre was bathed in joy and praise and worship. Molly had tears in her eyes. It was wonderful, wonderful.

Hamish yawned behind his programme. Lance Beaucott's watchful eyes never left his charges.

Lance, thought Freddy somewhere inside his aching head, was also professional. He reached for Violet's hand and held it. His head was getting worse.

'Knows what he's doing, Glen, doesn't he?' murmured Violet.

'I'm a snob. I prefer New Country.'

'"Feeling good was easy . . ."?'

He nodded. His head nearly fell off, his eyeballs bulged.

'Are you all right?' she whispered.

'Fine. Fine.'

'Will you last out?'

'For God's sake, woman.'

She gave a sympathetic snort and mouthed a kiss.

The group played on and Glen was generous, his voice strong, his pelvis pulsing. Freddy shut his eyes.

Her bed was turned down on one side only. He hadn't noticed that last night. Or the heart-shaped chocolate on a card saying *Sleep Well.*

'I'm practically better,' he said.

'You look green. You have done, all night.'

'I've got a headache.'

She stifled a laugh, pulled him back on to the bed. 'Oh Freddy, not so soon. Not after one night.'

'I think I should tell you,' he said, heaving himself on to one elbow and falling back again, 'I have severe sense of humour loss when I'm crook.'

He felt the cool hand on his forehead. 'Men do,' she said, and gave him aspirin, took off his shoes and held him in her arms.

'Lie still,' she said. 'Lie still.'

He woke with his head buried on her breast, wondered idly how he had managed to breathe. But what a way to go. My sweet love. 'Nice,' he said, 'Very.'

She kissed his forehead. 'I've been thinking. This is a good chance to talk about Bridget.'

'Are you mad?'

'Have you still got a headache?'

'Not quite.'

'Guts ache?'

'No.'

'Well then. Don't you see we have to talk about her? I'm going to be stuck with her all day tomorrow.'

'Yes, but I don't see why we have to talk about her tonight. I can see it's a bind for you, but remember, Bridget left me for higher things. I met you, I fell for you. Think how difficult it would have been if Bridget had still been around. All that angst.'

Violet sat up. 'Would you have left her for me?'

'Oh God, yes.'

'Then why were you such a mess when she left?'

He sat up beside her, stroked her foot and thought hard. 'I honestly don't know,' he said finally. 'Bitchiness? Wounded pride? It seems ridiculous now. I suppose I didn't like playing second fiddle to disaster areas.'

'Don't be so glib.'

'I am glib. Superficial. Haven't you noticed?'

'No,' said Violet, nibbling his left ear. 'You have beautiful ears. What time do you pick up the CBs from Penn tomorrow?'

'Usual time.'

'If you still refuse to sleep with me,' she murmured between nips, 'you'd better shove off.'

'Not yet.'

'I hope Kamil is not ill,' said Molly to the young Indian driver standing by the car.

'No, no, ma'am,' he replied. 'Kamil is the driver of the number one car. Today he is driving the VIP gentlemen.'

'Oh yes, of course.'

'My name is Muthu, ma'am. I am a temporary arrangement for the ladies. Only for today.'

'Ah well, Muthu, I'm sure you'll do splendidly.'

Muthu, looking slightly puzzled, opened the door.

I wish she wouldn't go overboard being pleasant, thought Violet. Her desire to make the whole world happy can end up sounding slightly bizarre. Can mask her common sense.

'And we go north again today, Muthu?' continued Molly.

'No ma'am, south.'

'Ah south. And how long does the journey take?'

'An hour and half each way, ma'am.'

'Goodness, as long as that.'

Lance Beaucott glanced at his watch. 'Perhaps we should be on our way. Our ETA at the plantation with Mr Harman is 10.30.'

'Yes, of course,' said Molly. 'Bridget, you're our guest today. Where would you like to sit? We'll be rather crowded, I'm afraid, but never mind.'

Bridget, lettuce-crisp in linen, took charge. 'Mrs Carew, if you sit on the right-hand back . . .'

'The safest. How kind.'

'I'll sit in the middle and Violet can sit on my left. How about that?'

'No, no. We can't have you squashed in the middle. Violet wouldn't mind, I'm sure, would you?'

Irritation was nagging at Violet. What did I mean about her good sense. Let's just get *in*. Then I can continue with my reminiscences.

'No, of course not,' she said.

'But where will she put her legs,' laughed Bridget. 'She'll have to wrap them round her neck.'

Violet's smile was radiant. Not mine, kiddo, just your estranged husband's. 'Thank you so much, how thoughtful of you,' she murmured.

Lance leaned from the front seat, offered her a Wet One.

'10.30,' he read as they set off. 'Meet Mr Harman, manager of the palm oil plantation now owned by the firm of McAllister and Saxby, Edinburgh. 11.00. Visit to the local Orang Asli settlement. Headman of village to meet and escort Mrs Carew and party on tour of the village. 12.15 for 12.30. Lunch with Mr and Mrs Harman. 14.30. ETD.'

'Thank you, Colonel,' said Molly. 'Now Bridget, this would be a good time to tell Violet about Humanitaire and the work they do and about your training in Paris.'

'But Mrs Carew, I've told you everything already. You surely couldn't stand a second time,' said Bridget.

'I certainly could, and Violet would love to hear all about it, wouldn't you, Violet.'

'Yes indeed,' said Violet who was thinking how beautiful life is, how interesting it was to be sitting cheek to cheek with Freddy's estranged wife, squashed as tightly against her as she, Violet, had been beside him on the Peak Tram.

There were other similarities. Bridget sat staring straight ahead as Freddy had done; Violet looked out a different window at a different world and remembered Bridget's startled face when Freddy had called her 'Honey' last night. 'Hon' would have been even better, worn down by tumbling like a polished stone. But 'Honey' would do, beautifully.

This close encounter of past and present rumps must have occurred before, she realised, but there was something so outwardly cosy, so day-out-with-the-girls about the present situation that she was in danger of sniggering.

She turned to Bridget. 'Please do tell me,' she said. 'I would be most interested.'

Bridget presented her facts as if giving a briefing. She spoke clearly and concisely, with some detail but not too much. It was an interesting and impressive story, but Bridget's motive for applying to join Humanitaire remained inexplicable to Violet. To do this noble, interesting, sometimes boring and often horrifying work, this woman had left Freddy Manders.

Who can explain it, who can tell you why? The banal phrase swam into her mind, annoyed her with its accurate expression of reality. She was in awe of this woman.

'How wonderful,' she said. 'And how wonderful to have found your vocation.'

Bridget's voice was crisp. 'Vocation had nothing to do with it.'

'But the call doesn't have to come from on high, does it? You can have a vocation for teaching. Or not, as the case may be.'

A slight frown appeared beneath the gold hair. She doesn't like being worsted, this good woman, thought Violet, even in semantics. I have worsted the secular saint. Good.

Shamed at such pettiness, she tried harder. 'And of course your bilingual French must be a help too.'

'I'm not bilingual,' snapped Bridget. 'It's ridiculous the way people fling that word about. Who told you that?'

Violet paused, shoved her hair back with one hand and looked into Bridget's toffee-coloured eyes. 'Freddy,' she said.

Bridget gave a snort. 'Freddy! I suppose it might seem good to him. His French isn't nearly as good as he likes to think. In fact it's hopeless.' She gave a little wriggle, felt by Violet in her right buttock now stiffened by rage. 'I remember once he wanted to buy me one of those bras, you know, one of those *vraiment français* ones with holes for the nipples.'

'Oh,' cried Violet, 'we saw one of those the other day, didn't we Mrs Carew? At the Lan Lan Emporium. Remember?'

Molly was sitting forwards on the seat, her eyes moving from one to the other. 'No,' she said.

'Do you know what he asked for?' crowed Bridget.

'No.'

Bridget chuckled. '*A brassière ouverte.* He couldn't even get the *soutien gorge.* Hopeless.'

Hopeless my foot. Violet leaned forward. 'Seeing we're playing girls' talk, did you wear it?'

Molly spoke into the silence. 'Do we know the name of the headman of the Orang Asli, Colonel?'

Violet was unabashed. I'll bet she didn't. I'll ask him tonight.

'I'm afraid not ma'am,' said the Colonel.

The car turned off the main road. 'How lovely to be out of the traffic,' murmured Molly. 'I do so prefer the country, the simple life. Time has stopped here, has it not?' She indicated a toiling figure behind a hand plough. 'And look, a water buffalo. Beautiful.' She waved at the lugubrious beast and his master. The man lifted his stick in salute, the buffalo lifted one enormous black rubber lip and sneered.

'Dear beasts of burden,' said Molly.

Freddy is right, thought Violet. Sometimes childlike innocence can be hard to take. 'You mean *Honest labour bears a lovely face,*' she said.

'I know you are joking Violet,' said Molly, 'but have you ever wondered why butchers are so cheerful? They have to work so hard, you see. Fishmongers are quite different. Ah, look, a ferry. Just like the one at Opua only smaller.'

'10.30 exactly,' said the Colonel. 'Well done, Muthu.'

The only ferry passengers other than themselves were two small boys holding a bamboo pole from which hung a large and spiky fish. Followed by her entourage, Molly climbed from the car to inspect the haul.

'What is its name?' asked Molly.

'Fish,' they replied. 'All same – fish.'

Mr Harman, the manager, greeted them on the other side of the river. He was of medium height, bald, bearded and enthusiastic.

'Shall I give you a quick rundown on the island?' he asked.

'Yes please.'

'Yes, well. The original Mr Campbell drained the mangrove swamp in 1905.'

'In this heat. Goodness!' said Molly.

'Indented labour of course,' continued Mr Harman. 'Campbell originally planted rubber trees but they didn't thrive, just sort of sat there. You know, neither thrived nor died. One of the most difficult horticultural situations to deal with, I always think. One has to cut one's losses eventually and take the poor doers out and start again, but it's an expensive decision. However, definitely the answer in this case.' He waved an arm at acres of luxuriant palms behind him. 'Eventually McAllister and Saxby changed to palm oil. Tropical botany was in its infancy when Campbell started, of course. The main menace here is acidity, sourness of the soil, so we have to maintain the water levels by irrigation and other means I won't bore you with. "Control the water table", that's the secret.'

'So you are a botanist by trade,' said Bridget.

'Originally, yes. I specialised in tropical botany at Edinburgh.' Mr Harman replaced his white hunter's wide-brimmed hat and tugged at the lip of an impressive-looking boot, a beautiful object. It was a field boot, he explained, like an anti-snake jungle boot but lower cut.

They stood gazing at this courteous well-kitted-out man.

'You are a long way from home,' tried Molly.

'No, no, this is home now.' Mr Harman laughed. 'Wonderful place. Wonderful. Ask my wife at lunch time.'

'It's very kind of you to invite us,' said Molly, who was thinking rubber trees would have been more interesting, lovely feathery-looking things with those dear little clay pots to collect the sap.

'Not at all. Not at all,' said Mr Harman. 'Margaret will be delighted to meet you. Now if you'll excuse me, I must get on with the job.'

'Aren't you coming with us to visit the Orang Asli?' said Molly.

'No, no. Never set eyes on them as a matter fact. *Au revoir* then. *Au revoir.*'

The Orang Asli people were pleased to see them and vice versa. Bridget took charge, signalling her intentions to Lance Beaucott with a quick smile. Lance, still irritated at being seconded from the sharp end where the action was, looked annoyed but said nothing. Concerned by the prospect of inappropriate offerings of Wet Ones, Violet felt disloyal to their protector but relieved. Bridget would undoubtedly know what to do and do it well.

Which she demonstrated as she introduced Mrs Carew to the headman, a small beaming man in shorts, less than five feet in height with tight grey curls and skin the colour of burnished teak.

His name remained unknown. Visitor and visited stood looking at each other, returning the gaze with civility as they shook hands in the forest clearing, surrounded by ancient trees and the sharp cries of unseen birds.

The headman called other men forward to meet the foreigners while the women, smaller and more shy, stood behind their men, clutching wide-eyed toddlers or naked comatose babies. Bridget asked pertinent questions. How did the settlement of sixty or so survive? What were their main health problems? Did they receive medical attention?

'This is ridiculous,' she said to Lance. 'Why do we not have an interpreter? How can we find out anything?'

The headman, bewildered by too many questions and too many difficult words, looked from one face to the other and smiled.

'School,' he said motioning the party to follow him. 'Orang Asling this way.'

'I thought they were called Orang Asli?' whispered Molly.

'They are,' replied Lance. 'Orang Asli means original people. We are Orang Asling, "Foreigners".'

'Ah,' said Molly. She dragged herself away from the ladies and their young. 'It's just like the New Forest, isn't it? The clearing, I mean. Lovely.'

School was a one-roomed hut. Language instruction to twenty or so children of varying sizes continued after much bowing and smiling and attempted conversation with the young teacher. With pride and enormous concentration the children lined up to sing their song. 'Three languages, OK?' said the young woman, demonstrating with slim upswept fingers. 'Our own language, then Malay and English last, OK?'

'Three,' exclaimed their guests. 'Goodness.'

The tune was familiar. After two indecipherable renditions the children stood straighter, smiled more widely and burst into English.

Mary had a little lamb, little lamb, little lamb,
Mary had a little lamb
Its fleece was white as snow.
And everywhere that Mary went, Mary went, Mary went,
Everywhere that Mary went
That lamb was sure to go.

Their audience clapped till their hands hurt. They were honoured, delighted. Molly, surrounded by performers, seemed overwhelmed with joy. Violet, usually calm in the presence of children, was grinning wildly. Lance squatted on his heels, shaking the hands of small boys.

Bridget retired to the back of the hut with the young teacher. They talked; Bridget took notes, asked to see more work. What equipment, what salary did she get? How long did the children stay? Was there perhaps a measuring tape anywhere? No? Oh.

They walked on through the clearing, past well-worn huts and primitive shelters, admired glossy-leaved coffee trees laden with green beans, inspected the small area of food crops, were offered coconuts and drank with relish, still smiling, still enquiring, still nodding their heads.

Freddy is right again, thought Violet smugly. Eighty percent of communication is achieved by body language.

Finally the headman introduced them to the male wood carvers, five men, obviously of high standing in the community,

247

who spent their days chipping and shaping mythical creatures from large blocks of red-brown wood. There were baboon men, serpents with grinning heads, an orang-utan suckling a human child. They were powerful images, as inexplicable and foreign as pre-Colombian artifacts.

Carvings were bought and stowed away. Molly, red faced and overcome with embarrassment, handed the headman a cheque on behalf of the government and people of New Zealand. Lance Beaucott took photographs.

'I think,' said Molly as they drove away, 'that was one of the happiest visits of my life.'

'One must remember,' said Bridget, 'the Orang Asli are still by far the most economically disadvantaged group, even though they are entitled to the same economic advantages as the indigenous Malaysians, the *bumiputra,* literally "sons of the soil".'

'But they *are* indigenous Malaysians,' said Violet. 'The *bumiputra* before the *bumiputra*. What do you mean by "even"?'

Bridget ignored her. 'Did you know,' she continued, 'that the majority of the Orang Asli have resisted conversion to the Muslim faith from their original animistic religion?'

'No,' said Molly, 'I didn't know that. Tell me more.'

Mr Harman had changed for their arrival. Neither his wide white hat nor his beautiful boots were in evidence. He and his wife greeted them outside the front door of their 1920s colonial baronial mansion, a large two-storeyed stucco building surrounded by parched lawns and even more parched flowers. Zinnias died slow deaths in would-be herbaceous borders backed by wilting chrysanthemums and edged by ragged catmint. Climbing roses struggled to meet over the arch of an aluminium pergola beside an asphalt tennis court. The only things visible which were either flourishing or green were the native trees of the shelter belt. The water supply, water table or no, obviously had little left over for non-essentials.

Mrs Harman, as friendly as her husband, confirmed this during lunch.

'People tell me I'm silly,' she said, 'not to grow natives, plants that like it here. But I couldn't live without my English friends. I had a lovely garden in Wimbledon. Lovely.'

'And how long have you been here?' asked Molly.

'The younger one was two when we came, wasn't he, Edward? That's twelve years ago now.'

'And you enjoy the life?'

'Oh yes,' said Mrs Harman, signalling to the white-robed Malay servant to remove the plates. 'And Edward and the boys love it, don't you darling? They're both at boarding school at home now. Yes, ever since they were seven. No, I'm wrong. Christopher was eight, wasn't he dear? But we see them every holiday now. It's much better than it used be. Such seasoned travellers, you wouldn't believe. They can never wait to get back here.

'Keep busy? Me? Well, let me see. There's the house and garden and looking after the servants, of course. And quite a good social life at the club if you like that sort of thing. There's a swimming pool there which the boys adore. And bridge, of course. And tennis. Edward likes a game after work, don't you dear? And my tapestries. They're my main hobby I suppose.' Mrs Harman laughed. 'As you can probably guess.'

Her guests nodded, smiling at the framed tapestries which lined the walls of the dining room and continued through the arch to the walls of the sitting room. There were no other paintings or prints on the walls, no photographs of the boys. These were crowded on to polished tables about the house, studio photographs of every age and stage from nappies and sunhats to school uniforms with and without caps. Snapshots of small crop-haired boys laughed from tricycles, bicycles, aircraft gangways and the wide backs of water buffaloes.

The dining-room tapestries all depicted hunting scenes. Pink- and black-coated men and women on large horses leapt high fences or dashed across fields featuring naked trees with church spires in the distance. Hunting terms were embroidered at the base: *View Hallo*, *Gone Away*, *Gone to Earth*. The foxes looked very small.

'Are you a keen huntswoman, Mrs Harman?' asked Molly.

'Goodness me no,' said their hostess. 'But the figures are fairly blocky, if you know what I mean. Not too difficult to do. Needle in, needle out, I can almost do them in my sleep. And Edward likes them, don't you dear?'

'Yes,' said Mr Harman.

'No incidents, I trust, Mutha?' said Lance Beaucott as they climbed into the car.

'None, sir.'

'Good, good. And they brought you some lunch?'

'Yes sir. Curry, sir, very nice.'

They drove for some time.

'Zinnias,' said Molly. 'Zinnias. And how kind of them to invite us. Delightful. And as for the Orang Asli. Do tell us more about them, Bridget?'

'I wouldn't want to make generalisations or facile comments about any race,' said Bridget. 'Especially as we didn't have an interpreter.'

'I don't think I would know how to do that,' said Molly. 'But I'm sure they would discuss us. Read us over our shoulders, as it were. That's what makes life so interesting.'

20

Lance Beaucott, checking occasionally to ensure the three sleeping women were still present, noticed the different attitudes assumed: Molly squat as a bun loaf behind the driver, Bridget centred tidily and Violet all over the place on the left.

Dry-mouthed and torpid, Molly awoke with a thought. Perhaps there might be some bottled water on board. On the other hand, what a fuss if she asked and there was none. The Colonel, already attentive to excess, would insist on stopping the car, despite her protestations that her query had been nothing more than a passing whim. He, or rather Muthu, would have to find a park, find the product, buy the bottles and trot back to the waiting car. It could take hours in this traffic. And think of the kerfuffle.

What she needed was a pebble to suck, an anti-thirst trick she had learned forty years ago when tramping in the Kaimanawas with her friend Betty de Castro. Betty was engaged to be married, with a small diamond flashing, a three-tiered wedding cake, and a strong determination to walk down the aisle as a size fourteen not sixteen. She and Molly had lost touch years ago. She could scarcely ask for a pebble.

Suggestions had been made that Bobby might like to join them, that perhaps it would be possible to arrange a bigger car. Bobby had declined. More than declined. Had laughed the idea to scorn.

'Not likely thanks,' she'd said. 'Barney Kinsella's going to lend me one of the girls from his office, a switched-on young Malay called Milly who knows everything, and she's going to take me shopping for the whole day. Normally, he said, he'd meet us for lunch at a cute little Malay place he knows, but apparently Dad's hosting some lunch thingy today, so I'm into personal shopping. All the way with Milly Malay.

'And I haven't told you the most amazing thing,' she continued, bouncing on Molly and Hamish's bed. 'Barney'n' I have had the most fantastic idea. He's going to show me the pot industry himself, when he has a chance. Take me round the more up-market places where they're made – shops, outlets, factories. Like he says, we're only interested in the quality stuff. "Every defect a treasure", you know what I mean. He wants me to see what I think about it all. Whether I have a *feel* for pots. Well, as you know, I'm mad about them and I told him about all mine but he says they're different here and I have to make sure it's the right product for me, something that gives me a blast. So many import people, cottage importers, he calls us, they start off on something but they're not committed, he says. You've got to be really keen, live and breathe the business and have all the energy in the world. And of course there's all the stuff like shipping costs, import restrictions, I'll have to do a ton of research.'

'Bobby . . .'

Bobby pulled the sheet up to her chin. 'Now don't go all wet blanket, Mum. And before you start, Dad thinks it sounds a great idea. In principle, he says. We're going to talk about it in depth later, he says.' She stroked the crumpled sheet. 'He sounded mad keen actually. He'll soon be chatting on as if the whole thing was his idea. So I don't want to hear a word, OK?' She pulled the sheet over her head, a teasing child hiding for laughs.

Molly paused. Sitting in front of the mirror with a blob of Flawless Finish Ginger 5 mousse on her finger and her behind rooted firmly on the padded stool, she had felt once more that sensation which seemed to accompany what she thought of as important moments with Bobby. A lack of equilibrium, balance, a sense that things were slipping out of control and she was unable to right them. Her voice sounded old, croaky.

'When did you speak to Dad?' she asked.

The face reappeared. 'I rang him when you were in the shower. I didn't want him getting it second hand from you.'

'Why on earth not?'

'Because you're so *negative*,' said Bobby and disappeared again.

Hamish and Penn McPhee were waiting in the foyer of the hotel. They came to meet them, side by side and step by step, their faces solemn.

'I have something extremely unpleasant to tell you, I'm afraid, ladies,' said Hamish. 'Fred Manders and Kamil have disappeared. This morning.'

Violet put a hand to a pillar, made a small odd sound. 'Nnn.'

'But why didn't you ring me?' cried Bridget.

'I've had someone on to it all morning,' said Penn. 'We

couldn't get through to the Harmans. The car's disappeared too, which is a bit . . . Everyone got on to things straight away of course – police, army, special forces – but I thought I should tell you immediately, Mrs Manders.'

'Thank you,' said Bridget.

'Come upstairs, everyone,' said Hamish. 'We'll tell you all we know, Mrs Manders. A debriefing, if you like, before we take you back to the hotel.' He took her hand. 'Don't worry, my dear. I'm sure everything will be all right. Nasty shock, though, I do see that.'

'Bridget,' said Molly, taking her in to her arms. 'Oh Bridget.'

Lance Beaucott knocked on Violet's door half an hour later. He was furious, distracted, kept jumping from his chair to straighten a venetian blind or pick up a sandal and stow it beside its mate, then flop back again.

'I knew it,' he said. 'I knew it was mad. I should have *been* here. It's the car. The car's the thing. They've obviously been watching, monitoring its movements.'

'Sit down and tell me what they said.'

'You should have been there. Why didn't you come up to his room with the rest of us?'

'Because Freddy is my lover and I couldn't face everyone oozing sympathy over his ex-wife?'

'Oh.'

'Shameful, I know . . .'

Lance stopped fidgeting. His voice deepened, became tolerant, a man of the world at ease with the irregular. 'It's nothing to do with me,' he said.

'Good heavens, I don't mean I'm ashamed of sleeping with him. Anyhow, Bridget knows, or I think she does. I'm ashamed of myself for peeling off, not being upstairs, especially as it looks as though I'm not going to get any sense out of you. Sit down and *tell me*.'

'What a bugger, Vi,' he said. 'For you too, I mean.'

'If you start being nice to me,' she snarled, 'I'll scream the place down.'

He nodded. 'Yes. Apparently at 09.00 Fred was picked up by Kamil as usual. No one saw the car arrive at the office. At 09.40 Penn McPhee rang the hotel to see where he was, what had happened. No one here had noticed anything untoward. They hadn't arrived at the hotel and nothing had been seen of the car. It just disappeared into thin air too.' He glanced at her eyes, looked away quickly.

'So what did they do? Tell me.'

'No one noticed at first. Fred hasn't been down for breakfast since we arrived here, and the talks this morning weren't due to start till 10.00.' His voice sharpened. 'Did you see him any time this morning, Vi? Were you together, er . . .'

'No.'

'No, no. Just had to check, of course.'

'Of course.'

Her eyes were darker than ever, black pee holes in the snow. 'Is it Lightning Storm?'

Lance rearranged his buttocks. 'Oh no no no,' he said. 'Not necessarily, not at all. One of the things against that is they got the wrong guy, if you see what I mean. Not very professional. Yeah, well. Nobody noticed, like I said, until Fred hadn't appeared back in the foyer at 09.30. Very unlike him, apparently. Someone tried his room. No dice there, and the corridor guards hadn't seen him come back. The daytime Malaysian security officer had expected to meet him in the foyer. Those were his orders. Twenty-four-hour protection for the Minister and Mrs Carew. But he wasn't required until they were outside the hotel because of the corridor guys.'

'Then what?' she whispered.

'As I say, the flap didn't start till Penn rang, and then all hell let loose. I wasn't here of course, but I can well imagine. So can you. Think of Mrs Carew's snafu and treble it. Everyone rushing round in small circles.'

'And nothing?'

'Nothing. No. But hell,' he said quickly, 'it's not eight hours yet.'

Violet said nothing. She had noticed when people disappeared at home and TV reporters shoved fluffy mikes at distraught parents or anguished lovers and asked them how they felt now their ten-year-old had been lost in the Tararuas for three days or their partner not seen for four months, how so many of the stricken faces had stared back at the cameras and said, 'It's the not knowing that's the worst.' Why was that the worst?

She sat very still, willing herself to be calm, positive and completely in control. *Nothing hideous has happened to Freddy.* She repeated the thought over and over, beating the words into the nerve cells, dendrites, the little jumps between. Nothing hideous. Nothing hideous. Nothing.

'And then what?' she said eventually. 'Did the Minister cancel the talks?'

'Oh no, he couldn't do that.'

'Why not?'

'No, no, of course not. He rang to apologise for the delay. Dato Ahmad was right on the ball, came round immediately, got on to their Minister of Defence, saw the Chief of Police himself, and when everything was up and running in that direction the Minister and Kinsella and their armed bloody guard drove to the KL Ministry. At about 11.00 I gather.'

'In the number three car?'

Lance gave her a wary look. 'What? Perhaps. I don't really know. The High Commission produced a secretary from somewhere, I gather.'

Her eyes were boring into his skull. 'And then straight on to the milk powder reconstruction plant, I suppose?'

'After lunch, er, yes.'

'And the dinner tonight?'

'The official one? That's on hold. My guess is it will be postponed.

'Certainly if Mrs Carew has anything to do with it. She's terribly upset.'

'Balls to Mrs Carew!' cried Violet and burst into tears.

Lance put a hand on her heaving shoulder, 'It'll be all right, Vi. I promise you that.'

He dug in his pocket, was offering her something. Dear God, not a Wet One.

She peered over sodden tissues at a clean white handkerchief. 'Thanks,' she bawled.

Molly wanted to explain things herself. Could Violet slip up in about a quarter of an hour?

She opened the door, took Violet's hand in hers. 'This is a terrible business. Unbelievable. Bridget is being wonderful but . . .'

She sat on a small overstuffed sofa and turned to Violet. 'Freddy of all people,' she said, her pale blue eyes puzzled. 'I know it seems an odd thing to say and please don't misunderstand me, but it's such an *unlikely* thing to happen to Freddy somehow. Do you know what I mean?'

'No, I don't, Mrs Carew,' said Violet. 'I can't imagine what you mean. And I think I should tell you, Freddy and I are having an affair.'

She sat up straight, her mind racing as she towered over Molly who sat shrunk in the opposite corner with her mouth open. And if you're not careful, lady, I will tell you more, a great deal more which I don't doubt you would be interested to hear because you are a people person and people persons love to know everything about other people which is why they are called people persons, and why not? I also am a people person, Mrs Carew, but I call it gossip because I'm so fucken honest. She took a deep breath. Calm down. Calm down.

Her voice continued. 'Bridget and Freddy are separated, and have been for six months or more. She left him to join Humanitaire.'

257

'But that was a wonderful thing to do.'

'I agree. I'm all for it.'

'But. I had no idea . . . Won't she go back to him after her training?'

Violet leaned back, picked up a small cushion and slapped its perfect form into shape. 'I don't think he would want her. In fact I know he doesn't.'

'Oh,' said Molly, memories crowding through her worried mind. 'I think I may have . . .'

'Please, don't apologise. What did you want to see me about?'

'Yes, of course. As you may know, the Minister's Official Dinner for Dato and Datin Ahmad has been cancelled. Hamish and I are to dine with them at their residence. The only other New Zealander there will be Colonel Beaucott, for security reasons apparently. It's very kind of the Minister and Datin Ahmad. Such short notice. I think everyone hopes that by tomorrow all will be well and . . .'

Enough is enough. Violet was on her feet and heading for the door which shot open as Bobby appeared, her arms deep with shopping bags. Large shiny bags of distinction and style jostled smaller ones; a cinnamon one labelled *Rembrandt* in black was overlaid by a burnt-orange *Poppy* in scarlet. An ivory bandbox slashed with gold letters said *Cindy's*.

'Hi,' she cried, dropping the slithering pile as she fell back in a chair and kicked off her shoes. 'Wow, have I had a ball.'

Violet sidestepped the pile. 'Excuse me,' she said, and headed for the door once more.

Bobby's eyes opened. 'Don't go because of me. I just had to show Mum the loot and . . .'

'Bobby dear,' said Molly, 'something terrible has happened. Freddy and the driver, Kamil. They've disappeared.'

'Jeez,' said Bobby, suddenly wide awake. 'So Barney was right. He was telling me last night. Some kidnapping gang. Lightning Something. He was saying how hopeless we are at security. Us, I mean. Kiwis.' She shook her head slowly. 'Whew. He's right on the button, that one.'

'Violet, please come and sit down,' said Molly miserably. 'Nobody knows what's happened, Bobby, we're all very worried. Do be . . .'

'Well, I'll put my money on Barney,' said Bobby. 'Poor old Fred. I guess he was just in the wrong place at the wrong time.' She turned to Violet. 'You were quite keen on him, weren't you?'

This too will end. 'Yes,' replied Violet, 'and still am. Now if you'll excuse me . . .'

'Please Violet,' cried Molly, putting out her hand. 'Would you do me a favour?'

'Yes,' said Violet, still standing.

'Now there you are, Mum,' interrupted Bobby. '*That's* how you want to be. Like her. Positive. Did you hear what she said? "Yes, and still am."' She nudged the disordered pile with a bare foot for a second and looked up. 'Good on you, Vi. Good on you.'

Violet sat down abruptly. Molly, after an anxious glance, spoke quickly. 'Now Hamish's official dinner has been changed to a private one, you two girls will be on your own tonight. I wondered if I could suggest that you have a meal together in the hotel. I do know how you're feeling, Violet, really I do, but I don't think either of you should go into the city, and I thought . . .'

Molly broke off, her eyes on Violet's face. Her mind scrambled. She must help Violet, but what about Bobby, who was quite likely to charge off anywhere all by herself. All this talk from Hamish about how level-headed his daughter was, how she could look after herself. Look at the mess she had got herself into in Hamilton. Thirty kilometres *out* of Hamilton, for heaven's sake. And look at him now. She could have guessed he'd be enthusiastic about this hare-brained pot scheme. It might be a good idea, but on the other hand it might be a disaster. Bobby was so this way, that way, up and down. Damp heap to kamikaze shopper in a matter of hours.

But Hamish would refuse to see that. Men don't. It's what they do. They refuse to see anything they don't want to, and you're left picking up the pieces. A self-pitying old bat with nothing better to do than pick up pieces and be negative. Look at the realities of the proposal! Bobby's total lack of business expertise for a start.

Bobby had always been highly strung (words Molly preferred to temperamental). Had swung from one enthusiasm to another. Think of the succession of discarded Wellington jobs. The typing pool had been the answer; Kirkcaldies had a good training scheme, she would become a buyer in Ladies Casuals, would open her own boutique. She would get into meteorology or open a cafe with *really* good coffee. All, all projects had fizzled. Sometimes Molly wondered whether it was not the same with her men friends. At the beginning they had fantastic senses of humour, they jogged regularly to keep in shape, they adored her, made her scream with laughter and had their heads screwed on. Then they melted away. Or she ditched them.

Hamish and Molly had both been pleased when their daughter returned to the farm. The ties, as Hamish had said, went deep. Bobby was a country girl like her mother, and it would be nice if she married a farmer.

But look at her now. Was she not perhaps a little self-centred, opening her mouth at the most inappropriate moment she could have chosen when Violet was screaming inside, you could see she was. How could one see that face and describe its owner as being 'positive'? Molly's eyes were hot with anger.

'There's something I want to say to you, Bobby,' she said. 'I realise it's not the right moment, but then it never is. It's like cuttings. If someone offers you a cutting of a plant you should take it then and there, there might never be another chance, and that's how I feel now. Everything is so awful and

– what I'm saying, Bobby, is that I think you're being a little too concerned with your own affairs. Violet is having a very anxious time and I think it would be nice if you and she had a meal together tonight in the hotel.'

Bobby scratched her neck in thought. 'Yeah, I realise that, Ma,' she said, 'but not tonight. Sorry about that, Vi, but Barney Kinsella's wangled tickets for Glen Campbell from some guy and we're going to The Inn of Happiness first because I like Chinese.' She bent over, sorted her shopping bags into order and squeezed her swollen feet into shoes. 'And,' she said at the door, 'he's going to start taking me round the pot places tomorrow afternoon when Dad's playing golf.'

'Dad will not be playing golf tomorrow afternoon. Talks yes, but not golf,' said Molly, becoming more distraught by the minute.

'Then he can come with Barney and me,' said Bobby, and opened the door.

Her head reappeared. 'By the way, Mum, what happened when Dad rang Bronson last night?'

'He didn't.'

'Why on earth not?'

'You said you wanted to be here, and he waited but he wouldn't ring after twelve and you still weren't back. He said Bronson would be milking, or he hoped he would be.'

'That's right, blame it on me.' Bobby rolled her eyes and departed.

The two women looked at each other. 'I'm sorry,' said Molly, 'I'm deeply sorry.'

Violet stood for the final time. 'Forget it, please.'

'So what will you do tonight?'

'Jump in the river. No, no, I'm joking. Doff would kill me. Bad joke. No-joke joke. If I'm starving I'll dial Room Service.' She gave a sick grin. 'I used to think Room Service sounded so romantic when I was a kid. Like in the movies.'

21

He had rung her as soon as he woke.

'Hi,' she said. 'How's the gut?'

'Excellent. Seized up completely. Probably never function again.'

'Fantastic. And the headache?'

'Oh, you fixed that. You fixed everything.'

'Good,' she said. 'What time do you leave?'

'Nine. Tell me what you have on.'

'Nothing. I'm still in bed.'

He groaned. 'I'll come and wave you goodbye.'

'But Kamil picks you up then.'

'Christ, so he does. I've just said so, haven't I. I'd better not keep him waiting. He tends to panic after thirty seconds. Give me a kiss.'

She smacked her lips into the mouthpiece.

'Disgusting. Tap your fingernails on it.'

'Nutter,' she said, and did so.

'Good. You really are there. I love you. See you later.'

'Yes please.'

He bounded, literally bounded from the bed and headed for the shower, found himself singing, singing for Christ's sake, belting it out from sheer bloody cheerfulness. '*A big yellow taxi,*' he bawled, '*took away MY old man.*'

'Morning Kamil.'

'Morning sir.'

'Nice morning.'

'Always a nice morning in KL, sir.'

'Yes. I can believe that.' He could believe anything. He leaned forward. 'Sometime, Kamil, you must tell me the story of the cobra in the kampong.'

Kamil's white teeth flashed in the mirror. 'Oh, that is a long story, sir. Would take longer time.'

'But we leave the day after tomorrow.'

'I promise sometime, sir.'

'Excellent.' Manders leaned back, humming 'Big Yellow Taxi'. He had always liked Joni Mitchell. It was just that he had forgotten about her, had forgotten about every damn thing that made life worth living. Sourness had been creeping up on him before Bridget left. He had shut himself away like a cave-dwelling anchorite, one sunk into self-pity and rancour rather than piety. What a fool. What an unmitigated bloody fool.

Whereas now?

Unbelievable. Quite unbelievable. This must be how Born Again Christians feel. *A land transfigured. A new creation.* A being with an aim in life. This must be what Bridget had found, a compelling reason for existence.

And here was the Chancery and the New Zealand flag glimpsed through a gap in the trees. How impressive your own flag looks in another country. He peered out the window for another look but it had disappeared.

As a child he had been relieved to find New Zealand's four red stars floating on their sea of blue in his grandfather's *Flags of the British Empire* cigarette cards.

'But why wouldn't we be there, Fred?' said his grandfather. 'We're the best bit.'

Freddy's apprehension, his fear of not being present, was hard to explain at the age of six, and he hadn't tried. Australia had one more star. Another cause for concern.

He felt the slight jolt as the car crossed the culvert on to the drive, followed immediately by a wild yell from Kamil as he slammed on the brakes. The engine stalled. Kamil leapt out cursing.

Two men, disguised by black balaclavas and armed with short sticks, slid from the van and ran to meet him. One lifted his stick and tapped Kamil on his forehead. He fell like a sack, collapsing into the smaller man's arms. Manders yelled, jumped from the car and ran towards them, one hand lifted in an attempt to shield his lenses from the blazing sun. Half blinded, he sensed rather than saw the man lunge.

The ground heaved about him, the sky dazzled and shook as he threw a wild punch. Another stick, another tap and he fell, his knees folding beneath him as he sank forward with a sigh.

Kava, he thought as he opened his eyes. That was the feeling as his legs had gone beneath him. Kava goes to the knees before it hits the head.

His was splitting, cracking apart, a split pumpkin. He closed his eyes. Lie still. Don't think. Can't think. He was on his back, swaying about on the deck of the van as it hurtled along.

Nausea rose in his throat. He dragged himself up, leaned against the unlined panelling and breathed deeply.

On the other side of the van Kamil was rolled in a ball with his head on his knees. He rocked himself back and forth, presumably praying. Manders put out his shoe, touched the stained white trouser leg.

'Kamil? Are you all right?'

The eyes snapped open. 'No, I am not all right. How can I be all right? Look at me, look at my head, where are we going? I have a wife, two sons, two beautiful boys. What will they do, my boys?' He lifted his bloodied head and scowled at Manders. 'It is all right for you, you have no wife, no boys . . .'

'No it is not all right for me. Stop this crap. Can you tell where we are, which way we're going, which direction?'

'No I cannot. Are you going to vomit?'

Manders swallowed. 'No,' he said.

'Well, don't.'

Kamil put his head down and rolled into his other world. His chant continued. The sound was eerie as well as excluding, an elemental wail to Allah, the one true God. There is no god but God.

Manders leaned his head back, closed his eyes and tried to ignore the closeness of the sound. He put his hands over his ears and felt worse than ever.

'Kamil,' he murmured after some time, 'could you try praying a bit more quietly?' He put a hand to his forehead to demonstrate pain.

No response and no lowering in tone.

Manders examined his sticky fingers, attempted to wipe them on the filthy deck.

He must look for clues, remember things. But there was little to remember. There were no windows in the back, but there seemed nothing distinctive with the van itself, no special features. Oil stains, patches of grease, a few hanks of straw and what looked like powdered earth plus the ingrained dirt of years covered the metal deck. There must be thousands of dirty vans like this rattling about the country. Delivery vans, builders' pick-up trucks, anything.

The smell, however, was distinctive. Freddy tried to analyse it, keeping his battered head upright. Sump oil, grease, dirt and something else: a faint odour of decaying vegetation, although there was not a leaf in sight.

The lurching, brake-slamming progress of travel through traffic continued, jarring his head at every jolt. But he knew if he lay down he'd toss. His neck was about to snap.

The van was very hot. People died in the backs of vans, didn't they, in windowless vans like this one? Panel vans are not designed to transport people. Strictly delivery at home. Ghostly garments swaying from steel rods in drycleaners' vans, that one glimpsed outside the Opera House, with gilded cherubs waving plump legs in the air. But never people. Not in the back.

The jolting eased, the traffic noise lessened. They must be getting to the outskirts of the city. Wherever they were, it was obviously not central.

He glanced at his Mickey Mouse watch. 10.40. He should have looked at it the moment he came to, but he could not have been out cold for long.

Kamil had finished his prayers. He now leaned against the opposite side of the van, his uniform dishevelled and his head flung back, his eyes staring straight through Manders.

He would not think about Violet. Not yet. The first thing was to rid himself of the idiotic sensation that this had not happened. That was his main feeling: not panic, not even fear, or not at the moment. Just sheer gut-based disbelief. This was not happening.

The disbelief of something that so obviously *has* happened could give you some faint inkling as to how people could fall apart, be unable to accept the sudden death of a child, a lover, a ninety-year-old spouse. How you could hear a laugh and swing around, put out two mugs instead of one, a hand in a dark bed and find nothing. Shock, he supposed. Chopped nerves give phantom pain. You would get used to it presumably. After a while.

'Kamil,' he said.

'Yes,' said Kamil, still staring through him.

'Have you any idea who these thugs might be?'

Kamil spat. A quick forceful strike to the left. 'Chinese,' he said. 'Coolies.'

'How do you know?'

'They smell.'

Every man likes the smell of his own farts: Inuit proverb. Manders had found this statement during a library period in a book called *Wise Sayings of the World*. The rest of the fourth form had also been pleased. Quite a coup at the time.

And what about the bucket. There is always a bucket. Thank God for Lomotil. He did not want to share a bucket with Kamil. Nothing personal. He did not want to share a bucket with the Pope of Rome.

Thank God also that it had happened before he picked up the Confidential Books. He thought about this, was interested to find how relieved he was, how enraged he would have been if the sods had got hold of New Zealand Eyes Only.

He tried again. 'You could tell me the story of the cobra in the kampong, Kamil,' he said.

Kamil's limpid dark eyes looked at him with loathing. 'Shut up,' he said. 'Tell your own filthy stories. My boys, my boys.'

'Yes,' said Manders. 'Your boys.'

Her solace and gladness / All good and no badness.

The van stopped with a jolt. Manders and Kamil fell over, rolled together, sat up quickly, exchanged horrified glances.

The door flung open and two wiry-looking men in balaclavas stood pointing automatics at them. Guns are different. They can kill with a slight squeeze. Kamil was praying harder than ever. Manders was in a cold sweat. One man covered the prisoners as his colleague leapt on to the deck to blindfold them. 'Shut up, Kiwi,' he barked into the silence. He pulled Kamil to him. 'Kiwi,' he joked, slamming the length of black cloth around Kamil's head and tying it tightly. He turned to Freddy who found himself staring at thick lenses through the eyeholes of the balaclava. Hope flickered. If the bugger needed lenses like that he might let him keep his specs. Would know that without them you scarcely exist.

The man put out a hand and wrenched off the glasses. Manders flung out his hands, a blind beggar begging.

'Please, please, I can't see.'

'Wanker,' spat the man, giving the blindfold an extra tug. Bent and reeling, Manders felt hands dragging him from the deck of the van, accompanied by kicks and unknown obscenities. 'Down,' shouted the same voice, pressing Manders' head with a hand. He bent to avoid decapitation, tripped on the sill and fell spreadeagled on to hard earth or something that tasted like it. There seemed little point in attempting to get up. He lay winded until heaved upright.

'I'm going to toss,' he cried, and did so, violently.

The fury increased. Most foreign languages sound angry if spoken fast enough but these enraged sounds were accompanied by blows and worse, the muzzle of a gun pinning his sodden shirt to his back. Someone shoved a putrid towel at his face. He seized it and passed out again.

His eyes flickered and stayed open. Automatically he flung out his right hand in search of his glasses. Nothing. He tried the left. Nothing but beaten earth. Christ.

He levered himself gingerly on to his elbows, groaned and fell back. He tried to take shallow breaths; deep ones hurt more. After some time he sat up more warily and felt around. Nothing – or nothing but a lumpy mattress on the dirt floor.

The worst thing so far was no glasses. He pinched the bridge of his nose, fingered an absent rim. They had taken his thinking processes as well as his eyes. He could not even hear without specs.

His shoulders slumped. How could he explore the room, search for anything useful – a loose brick if there were bricks, a hidden nail, a sliver of glass – when all he could see was a blur of whitish walls, the fact that the mattress had once been green and that there was a source of light high up on the right-hand back corner.

The space was hot and humid, and again there was little air. He couldn't even read his watch. He fingered the cheap metal, heard its loud tick. They would have taken a good one immediately. Lucky, that. He rolled on to his knees and crawled upwards, slapped his trouser pockets in what he already knew was a futile gesture. His wallet had gone.

He groped his way towards the right-hand wall.

'Kamil,' he shouted, 'are you there?'

No reply, only the sound of a tap dripping and something that sounded like the chatter of quick indecipherable voices coming from the direction of the window. He must listen. He stumbled his way over and peered out.

The voices became more distant; there was a single sharp cry, an answering one and then silence except for the still dripping tap. Where the hell was he?

Was there a table? There is sometimes a table. A table, a chair and the fucking bucket. Where were they?

He was thirsty too, bloody thirsty.

The walls were whitewashed concrete, not brick. After a while he stood straighter and began pacing out the space, then checked the height of the stud, feeling the space above his head with a flattened hand. The ceiling was not much more

269

than two metres in height and the area no more than three metres either way. No wonder it was hot and airless. He felt the ceiling again. It was practically sitting on his head. Nasty. The small window was one of those barred gaps in the wall you often see in the tropics – or did; they are less common now.

Manders gave a long sniff. Once again the predominant smell seemed to be of vegetable, old stored vegetation rather than active decay. He sniffed harder and hurt his bruised chest.

Keys jangled in the door and a blurred shape entered. A shape not seen before, taller, bigger and more solid, strode up to Manders, who peered back at another balaclava with holes.

'G'day cowboy,' said the man in a strong Aussie accent. 'How's it coming?'

Manders took a step back, stared speechless at the bulk before him. They were not Lightning Storm then.

'It's not,' he said finally. He swallowed hard, dragged up the right submissive tone. 'I would be grateful,' he said, 'if I could have my spectacles returned. I can't see without them, I can't . . .'

'Whadya have to see?'

Shit. What did he have to see?

'The shit bucket,' he cried.

The man moved nearer. Nicotine and garlic blasted from the mouth hole. 'You kinky or something?'

'I'd kick it over,' babbled Manders, 'by mistake, I mean. I keep telling you, I can't see.'

'If you do that,' drawled the voice, 'I won't call you cowboy any more.'

'Look,' begged Manders, waving arms around the blurred room, 'look at that window. What could I see out of that? You're all masked, armed, the door's locked, what the fuck could I do if I *could* see, except feel human.'

'I'll think about it,' said the voice. 'Come and sit over here.'

'Where?'

'Here, fuckwit.' The man laughed, grabbed his arm, lugged him forward then dumped him. 'Sit,' he said.

Manders sat, clutching the punched wooden seat of the chair with sweating hands.

'How much money do you think you're worth to your government?' asked the man. He spoke without emphasis or anger, a man raising a rather boring topic which had to be dealt with sometime.

The trail of sweat running down Manders' backbone turned to ice. Think, man, think. If you say very little he'll think you're joking or kill you straight away. If you say too much he'll laugh that hideous laugh and still not believe you.

There was something wrong with the voice too. Not the sounds, the *eees* were there, the strangled *ows,* but there was something different about the rhythm, the cadence of the drawl.

'I don't know,' he said.

'Then we'll have to find out, won't we?' continued the man. 'There was a bit of a fuck-up. The guys thought you were the big cheese, or what passes for a big cheese on your side of the ditch.' The dark black woollen head moved sadly from side to side. A man let down by incompetent staff. 'Yes,' he said, 'you won't see them around for a while.'

The combination of the casual voice and sudden spine-chilling comment was terrifying. Sheer bloody terrifying. Manders swallowed.

'How's Kamil?' he asked. 'The driver.'

'Aw, he's around somewhere.'

'How is he?'

'He won't get off his knees long enough to find out. Not much profit there.' The blurred shoulders sagged. 'Jesus,' sighed the man, 'you wouldn't read about it.'

'Can I have some water?'

'Yeah, why not. D'y'eat rice?'

Manders nodded. 'If I don't have my glasses,' he said, lulled momentarily by calm, 'I can't see to write my signature on the . . .'

An arm solid as a log flung sideways. Manders, unseeing and off guard, fell sideways. The man stood over him and kicked him in the balls. 'Listen, smartarse, you've been here five hours and your shelf-life's short. Get it?'

The door clanged shut. Manders lay groaning, his face flat on the evil-smelling floor. He wept for the pain, the slaughter of innocents and the power of cruel men.

He heard keys jangle once more, rolled on to his back with his heart racing. The door swung open, was kicked shut and relocked. Through half-closed lids he could just make out one of the smaller masked figures with something indiscernible in his hand. The unknown voice roared, 'Kiwi,' and banged something on to the table. 'Water, Kiwi.'

Manders waited till the door was locked again, then crawled to his feet in search of the table. His searching foot banged into a bucket, a yellow bucket, a bucket with a lid which rolled and clattered after its plastic base.

He found the table and chair, sank down and patted about with his hands for the vessel containing cool, clear water. His hand met a spout, a bulbous body and a curved handle. A teapot, a large aluminium teapot. He hefted the thing up with both hands and tried to drink from the spout. Water splashed down him. Tears, of frustration this time, dimmed his sight further.

He swore bitterly, loathed their guts and damned their souls to hell, then put out both hands and patted them about. Surely the shits must have left a mug. His flattened fingers closed on polystyrene.

The water was neither cool nor clear. It tasted brackish, with hints of stale tea. But it was water.

He drank slowly at first, and carefully, sip by sip. Wasn't there something if you drink too much, too quickly. Bloat. Or was that cows? He drank deeper, stopped suddenly. How many teapots would he get per day? Should he make it last? Certainly he wouldn't risk stripping and upending the spout over his stinking body as he had thought of doing.

His thirst was slaked, satisfied. He put the mug carefully over the spout for ease of contact later, stroked the curve of the teapot. He thought of Violet. He was going to get out. No doubt about that.

Like many people, Manders had wondered occasionally how he would react in a situation like this. Would he be the one found hiding under the bed, the one who betrayed his comrades to save his own skin? How strong was his will? He knew himself to be a decent enough man by and large, but by no means a leader. A man lacking in piss and vinegar. A sceptical sod. His absolute conviction that he would get out of this dump and live with Violet for the rest of his natural life pleased him.

The problem was how was this to be achieved. They would not give him back his glasses. He must find out what he could without them.

Of course you can concentrate without glasses.

Count the steps between mattress and table, find the bucket and put it somewhere safe. (Where?) Start exercising. They all exercised, these strong incarcerated men and women. They accomplished wonders of concentration. They recited reams of Latin and other verse, they worked their ways through phantom dictionaries, they retrod well-loved walks. There was one astonishing woman, an older woman, who had translated ancient Greek poetry into her own language. He could not remember her name, her nationality or the circumstances of her confinement, but he remembered having been astounded at such disciplined courage. How could she, how could they all?

Now it seemed more like common sense. Stoic common sense requiring strength and discipline, but definitely sensible. He would work out a plan of exercise . . . well, tomorrow. It had been a long day and it was not over yet. He walked towards the light, counting his steps, peered through the bars, tried to think of poetry to recite. The day was fading; his 'little tent of blue' (the only Wilde he knew by heart) changed to the lemon-pink which floods tropical skies before the sudden dark. He could see nothing except sky and something like concrete huts on the other side of a flat space.

He could hear them again, the lilting inexplicable sounds, the ever-present 'La' at the end of sentences. Chinese then? They seemed so unconcerned, the people outside, chatty, busy, getting on with some business or other. He longed to shout for help but knew it would be a mistake.

The sky was darkening rapidly. It would be pitch black in a moment. He must get himself organised. He hadn't even found the bucket yet, let alone stowed it aft or forward or where the hell. He would need a pee soon.

Again the jangle of keys. Manders ducked from the window. Two masked figures entered, one of them pointing what he assumed was a gun at him. 'Rice,' snapped the other, dumping a bowl on the table. They exchanged a few words in their language as they stared at him. One asked a question, the other lifted his shoulders, gave a massive shrug and laughed as they backed out in silence.

He wouldn't eat it yet. He must sort things out. He measured metres again, striding about with something like confidence; centred the table and chair, put the bucket and lid in the left-hand back corner and marched back to the table.

The rice was just that, with a set of throwaway chopsticks alongside. He broke them apart and tried to use them, but poor sight made the process too erratic. He tossed the sticks away and began scooping with his hand, ate slowly, masticating each mouthful as if it were his last. Which it could be. But would not.

He searched the air, splayed fingers patting for the polystyrene mug. It was there still there, thank God. Perhaps he should hide it, but where? He concentrated on the pouring, his face inches from the action. Water must not be lost either, although from the weight of the pot it seemed to be holding well.

A quick pee and on to the mattress.

Which smelt fungoid as tree stumps sprouting toadstools. He had found a blue one once beside a track through beech forest. Blue beyond blue, unexpected as aliens. A good thing.

He must sleep, not think — but how. They come, these night thoughts, they sneak into the mind and fester. Were they Lightning Storm or not? How much ransom would they demand? Would the New Zealand government pay up? Manders had no illusions about his employers but they would have to, wouldn't they? Or would he and Kamil end up paired like a couple of unwilling martyrs.

Night terrors. Just night terrors. And pain all over. Think of Violet.

He slept.

He was woken by the door clanging open, accompanied this time by shouts and snarls. Again something was flung on the table, again its bearer was small and masked. He barked something at Manders and disappeared.

He fell on the rice, thought again and scooped the handfuls more slowly. He was hungry now. Bloody hungry.

He had found no tap; there was no water except in the teapot. He felt his stubbled chin, took a tentative sniff at an armpit and stopped quickly.

Pale light was coming from the window, and the sound of voices once more. He began his exercise routine. He had decided on thirty circuits of the area once an hour, and was irritated to discover that it was difficult to remember how many he had already done without any visual aids. More concentration required. More discipline. He glanced at Mickey Mouse waving and bouncing about on his wrist, imparting time he couldn't see. God knows what they had thought of Mickey.

Now. Mental exercise. He sat at the table. No paper, no pencil, just the teapot. Poetry first. He thought, thought harder and thought again. Every line, every phrase of his favourites seemed to have disappeared. Go further back. Try school.

Las Posena of Cluseius, he bellowed,
by the Nine Gods he swore,
That the great house of something . . .
Should suffer wrong no more
By the Nine Gods he swore it . . .

The jangle of keys, slam, bang, clang.
'If you say so, mate,' said the larger shape.
Manders was silent.
'Have you fired the morning gun?' said the voice.
'What?'
'Shat?'
'No.'
'No,' said the man affably. 'That's interesting, you know that? Mostly they're at it like it's going out of business. Nerves, I suppose. Well y'might as well empty the piss anyway.' He made a sort of half bow, was probably grinning like an ape. 'My colleagues will be here soon to escort you to the toilet. Blindfolded, I'm afraid. Any questions?'
'Can I have a wash?'
'Naa, it's just a dunny, see, and a pretty ropey one at that. See yer, Chucky.'
'Can't you tell me about . . . ?'
The door slammed, was locked and unlocked again within minutes.

The two smaller masked men manhandled Manders on to the chair, blindfolded him with what felt like the same black cloth and barked inexplicable orders at him which he ignored.

What else could he do. Eventually they shoved the bucket at him. He grabbed it, checked its lid and waited to be shoved in the right direction.

Their progress through a narrow passage was slow and shambling, impeded by the bucket which kept banging Manders' blind legs. One of the men swore violently and grabbed it from him. Ah, that was better. At the same moment the man put a hand to his chest and flung him back against the concrete wall.

'Back, Kiwi,' he yelled. 'Back.'

'I *am* fucking back.'

Disoriented and more bewildered than ever, Manders stumbled, fell forward with wide arms and found them around a body. His blindfold had risen a fraction in the upheaval. By flinging his head back he could catch a glimpse of white, and a brown face.

'Kamil,' he cried. 'How are you?'

Their four guards, seemingly panicked by this unexpected encounter, tore the prisoners apart, kicked their wounded shins and screamed their displeasure. Manders heard the bucket and lid clatter to the floor.

In the ensuing pandemonium, he heard Kamil's whisper.

'I shall pray for you, sir.'

'Thank you,' said Freddy.

A door opened; an authoritative voice shouted at the guards in their own language. Manders flung his head back once more and froze.

The man was not Asian.

He ducked his head and swung round to face the wall. They hadn't noticed the risen blindfold. They couldn't have noticed. If the boss had noticed, he was dead. Terror glued him to the wall with his arms up.

More curses, more shoving and he was back to his room. He missed the chair, fell on his knees at someone's feet. The blindfold was ripped from his head. He was staring at the

277

yellow bucket. He collapsed beside it and lay still.

'Wanker,' said a voice. 'Kiwi wanker.'

The door clanged shut and he lay still, would lie for ever.

After some time he noticed that the chattering voices had disappeared. He must go over to the window, try and work things out. Later.

He crawled to the green mattress and rolled over.

22

Few of her thoughts had any answers. Where was he. How could anyone find them unless someone squealed on the thugs, and who would. Why had there been no ransom demand. Because it was too soon. Who said. What were the police, the Malaysian Army, the New Zealand government doing?

She saw men sitting around smoking, drinking coffee perhaps, inwardly exalted as they made their plans for action at the sharp end. For the whiff of gunpowder they had been trained to follow. Lance would be in his element.

She got up, stalked around the darkened room, drank water and fell back on the bed, tugged up bedclothes and threw them off in sweating misery. A few hours later she woke beneath that dead weight of sorrow which clicks in seconds before you remember why. 'Freddy,' she said. She felt under the pillow for a handkerchief and pulled out Lance's white one, turned to snivel into the pillow and discovered it was wet. How could that be. How could you weep when asleep. Sleep is meant to be oblivion.

I will get out of this hellish bed, have a shower, go for a walk – what Doff would call a good walk – and then I will be all right. In possession of my senses and able to concentrate.

She looked at her watch: seven o'clock. Plenty of time. Wash your hair.

The telephone rang on the second rinse. She leapt from the shower, skidded on the damp floor, righted herself and raced to the phone.

'Freddy,' she screamed.

'Violet,' said the voice after a pause, 'this is Bridget. I'm sorry to ring so early but I must see you.'

A shivering pink rat topped with drowned black hair stared back at her from the long mirror.

'I'll get a towel,' she said.

Wrapped in a bath sheet and turbaned with a smaller one, she sauntered back to the telephone.

'But I don't want to see you,' she said.

'Please, I must see you. This is a nightmare.'

Yeah, you're right there. A nightmare, a mare in the night that kicks and squeals and destroys sanity.

'No,' she said.

'But you don't understand. I feel so wretched, so guilty.'

'Why would you feel guilty?'

'I should never have left the poor darling.'

'Oh, shut up,' Violet said, and replaced the receiver.

The phone rang again. Obviously, however angry, however sickened, she had to answer it. It could be something new. It could be him.

'Yes,' she barked.

'Would you do one thing for me?' said Bridget.

'Try me.'

'I'll be at meetings all day. If you hear anything, anything at all, will you ring me?'

'The Minister will ring you immediately if there's any news.'

'Please.'

'All right.'

Explanations had to be made to the guards in the corridor. Yes, she was a member of the Minister's entourage, but unlike Mr and Mrs Carew she was allowed to leave the hotel alone. She was not under twenty-four-hour protection by the Malaysian Armed Forces. She produced her card. Nor she was, they smiled, and let her go.

Looking neither to right nor left she strode along major streets, taking note of the route back. It was exercise she was seeking, nothing more. Wet hair clung to her scalp. Humidity. Nothing untoward, as Lance would say. She ignored the food stalls, the crowds and the honking traffic, except when taking her chance on pedestrian crossings. After twenty minutes she turned and swung back.

On the other side of the road near the hotel she was stopped in her tracks by a strong stench of urine. A man was hosing out the tiny cages of the occupants of his pet shop. Monkeys leapt screaming from the blast of water; kittens crouched rigid with shock; puppies squealed. The only apparently calm animal was a large snake coiled in a cage not much bigger than itself.

Her hand rushed to her mouth. 'Dear God,' she whispered, and ran. Pursued by blasting horns and irate screams she dodged across the road and fell into the hotel foyer.

Molly and Bobby Carew stood watching her with interest.

'You haven't been *out*, have you, Violet?' said Molly.

'Yes,' said Violet, her hand still at her mouth.

'It doesn't seem to have done you much good,' said Bobby. 'Come and have some breakfast.'

Déjà vu, thought Violet, drinking pressed orange juice. Except this *déjà vu* is not illusionary. I *have* been here before. I was here yesterday after the shopfest. I have heard this song before. It is an unaccompanied solo.

Yeah, the concert was fantastic, said Bobby. How Barney had jacked up the tickets she couldn't imagine. And guess what! Prince Peter was there with his push and had talked to them, so obviously they had gone on the right night! What Bobby wanted to do now, and smartly, was to get today jacked up. Barney had rung while she was in the shower and would you believe it, he was tied up this afternoon.

'He says the whole place is on red alert because of poor Fred.'

'And Kamil,' said Molly.

'Yeah, Kamil, and the whole Commission has to "stand by to stand by".' She giggled. 'That's what he said: "Stand by to stand by." So he can't come but he's sending a messenger round with the list of the most likely smaller outlets for quality pots. He says these small cottage industry-type places are often the best and of course miles cheaper, so he recommends I get on to it and do a recce today.'

Molly was angry and showed it. Her normally pink face was mottled and stained with ugly red blotches.

'Bobby,' she said, 'I think you have lost touch with reality. Here we are trying to cope with a crisis affecting a dear friend and you're still babbling on about pots. Your father has made it quite clear that after this morning's talks he will join the team at search headquarters, as will Dato Ahmad. The cocktail party at the High Commission has been cancelled, and probably Dad's official farewell dinner tonight will be also. I have asked that our visits this morning to the diamond and batik factories be cancelled and they have been.'

'Then why not pots instead?' cried Bobby.

'Please be quiet. I feel, Violet, that I should attend the exhibition of embroidery by the wives in honour of the fiftieth anniversary of the founding of the Malaysian Army this afternoon, and I will do so. Otherwise I'll stay in the hotel.'

'And what good will that do?' snapped her daughter.

'Can I go to the High Commission's office this morning, see if there's anything I can do?' said Violet.

Molly opened her mouth to answer as a bell boy appeared at the table with a large envelope on a tray. He bowed and offered it to Bobby. 'Miss Carew?'

'Fantastic,' cried Bobby, ripping it open. 'He sure is on the ball, that guy. Just look at all this info.'

Violet tipped the bell boy, watched his neat little bottom wink its way back across the crowded room. The lucky guy had a job to do.

Bobby glanced up from her haul. 'Just look at this,' she crowed.

Molly made a final attempt. 'Will you please *think*, Bobby. Of the logistics for a start. There is no car, there is no armed guard available. Security has been tightened. We cannot go.'

Bobby leapt to her feet, snatched her info to her and shook it in her mother's face. 'Who's suggesting you come? I am a fully experienced adult, a traveller from New Zealand who is interested in the pottery wares of this country. I am nothing to do with Dad's piddling little Swing Around, as he calls it. I will hire a car and a driver. I don't need a guard and I am going now. I have to make use of each moment, can't you see? You guys still don't know whether you're Arthur or Martha, when you'll be leaving, anything. I'm independent of all that.' She paused briefly. 'The only thing is, where will I stay? I don't suppose Dad'll cough up for this place for long and Penn McPhee's wife, an ice maiden Barney says, is in New Zealand, which is a bind. Apparently I can't stay there till she comes back, can you imagine! But Barney says they'll have to have me then. Minister of the Crown's daughter and all that.' She paused, glanced down at their blank watchful faces. 'Anyone know when she's coming back?'

Dazed heads shook.

'Why,' asked Violet, avoiding eye contact with Molly, 'don't you stay with Barney Kinsella?'

'Yeah,' said Bobby. 'I thought of that, but he didn't seem too shook on the idea. Jobwise he meant.'

'I'll come with you this morning,' said Violet into the silence.

Bobby's brow cleared, smiles came quickly.

'Gee, thanks,' she cried. 'Good one, Vi.'

'I'm so sorry, Lance,' said Violet as they waited in the foyer, 'I had no idea she'd drag you and the car and Muthu back. How on earth did she do it?'

'She asked Daddy.'

'I just wanted her to stop nibbling away at her mother like a piranha fish. Plus, I couldn't stand the thought of sitting in the hotel for hours.'

'Mrs Carew is coming too.'

'What?'

'I suppose she thinks she can't let you cop the full force. Ah, here they come.'

Bobby, freshly powdered and at her bubbly best, moved towards them, followed by her mother looking wan in pink.

'First of all,' said Bobby, 'we'll have to get Muthu in here to have a session with the map. Best routes and stuff. Go and get him, will you, Lance?'

'I don't think Muthu would want to come in here,' replied Lance.

'Why not?'

Lance persisted. 'Let's go out to the car. What time do you have to be back for the embroidery exhibition, Mrs Carew?'

'Three o'clock.'

'Right.' Lance glanced at his watch. 'That gives us five hours including comfort stops.'

Molly's eyes met Violet's, swung away quickly as Muthu produced his map. Barney's list was consulted. Time motion studies as regards direction (Lance) and local knowledge of traffic routes and locations (Muthu) were brought to bear.

'Twelve of them all told,' said Lance, 'and in every conceivable direction. I'm not sure we'll make all twelve today.'

'Yes, we will,' laughed Bobby. 'Keep your foot down, Muthu.'

Muthu, again puzzled, smiled politely.

As Lance said, the route was as complicated as a Hash Harriers' run with no hare to lay clues. He crouched over the map beside Muthu, navigating every inch of the way.

Violet had given up attempting to work out anything. Her eyes filled with infuriating tears.

Glimpses of village life alternated with ancient farms. They passed an area which Lance said was a wet market. Caged chickens stood inches from the entrails of their butchered kin; snakes hung from rails.

Muthu lifted a hand to the snakes and chuckled. 'Sold by the yard, ma'am,' he said to Molly.

At roadside stalls squatting owners leapt to their feet shouting, offering bright lengths of cloth, ornate teapots, lengths of bamboo.

Lance became fidgety, clock-spotting as the car turned off the main road. Violet noticed him touch what was presumably his gun holster. How good it would be when all this nonsense was over and she was squeezed beside Freddy once more. She continued the thought and went further, elaborated it in some detail.

The retail outlets of the best-quality cheap stuff varied greatly. Some were little more than huts with makeshift awnings under which a man, woman or child guarded a small collection of earthenware pots and bowls coated with slapdash slip or pastel glazes. 'Domestic,' sighed Bobby for the third time, handing back an erratically glazed bowl to a bored child in a turban.

'Look,' cried Molly, falling upon a column of small earthenware bowls glazed with yellow ochre on the inside. She picked up a cockeyed-looking one and waved it at the smiling man. 'Rubber?' she asked.

'Ya, ya, ya,' he replied.

'How much?' said Molly. 'Is that all? Lovely, I'll have six.'

'You're meant to *bargain*,' hissed Bobby on cue. 'And why on earth do you want that crappy stuff?'

'I wish you wouldn't use that word all the time,' said Molly. 'They're rough hewn certainly. They're meant to be. They collect sap. They are virile workaday pots.'

'What on earth will you do with them?'

'I'll put miniature crocuses in them. Thank you so much,' she said to the man. 'Shall we move on?'

'Honestly,' said Bobby, as the car drove on. 'I don't know who Barney got to do his research but if this is someone's idea of quality stuff they need their head read. The other guy, I mean. I think it's hardly worth stopping unless it's a reasonable-looking place. You know what I mean, Lance, a decent sized set-up with proper presentation and staff who know what they're talking about, like the one before last with the dragon kite flying. Still,' she said, suddenly cheerful again, 'I suppose I am culling out the crap so Barney and I'll have a clear run tomorrow.'

The silence in the car at the word 'tomorrow' was palpable. No one knows what will happen tomorrow, screamed Violet and Molly into the silence. Certainly there had been no mention of deferment of plans. If there had been top-level exchanges on the matter with Wellington the Minister had kept their content from his ladies. I will bail him up the moment I see him, thought Violet. This Boys' Eyes Only business is obscene. And I won't go home without him.

'You want us to stop at the larger-sized ones only then, Bobby?' said Lance.

Bobby backtracked. 'Well,' she said, 'we'll slow down at the little ones, make an educated guess. Take what the Yanks call a windshield tour. I certainly don't want to miss anything.'

Which left them where they had been before. Lance breathed deeply. 'Where would you like to have lunch, Mrs Carew?'

'Oh, we won't have time to sit down anywhere,' said Bobby. 'Muthu can buy takeaways for us somewhere. Barney says they have ace ones here.'

Molly, hating herself and her weakness and her daughter's behaviour, procrastinated. 'Let's just wait and see,' she said.

Windshield tours took place in a whirl of dust. Puzzled brown faces stared back at Bobby's searching gaze. 'On,' she said, or occasionally, 'Stop.' In either case the vendors were disappointed. The number three car drove on.

Upmarket establishments were inspected in depth. Muthu was pressed into service as an interpreter. There were legions of pots, many of them very large and beautifully glazed in what Bobby called smoochy greens, blues and russet browns. Mouth-watering stuff. She spoke to the owners, wrote careful notes on a clipboard file, asked questions as to size, prices, guaranteed availability of supply. As she told her retinue, she was not going to get set up with some fly-by-night cowboy who didn't deliver the goods. She asked for their business cards and occasionally achieved one. The possession of a decent card, she told them, was a good sign. It was more professional, showed they were on the ball and in for the long haul.

She became more and more excited.

'We've got *nothing* like this variety at home,' she cried, 'especially sizewise. Those dragon ones'll do a runner. Out the door like hot pies.'

'Yes,' said Lance. 'All the girls go for the dragon pots.'

The vendor smiled, nodded in agreement. 'Ladies love dragon pots OK.'

The rest of the party stood around while these inspections were taking place. They were pleasant places, these larger pottery outlets, well shaded by trees and bamboo shelters, the packed dirt paths swept and the range of pots interesting. There were classic flowerpots, Ali Babas, traditional urns, round bulbous shapes and tall narrow tubes. Pots sized to accommodate anything from a snowdrop to a tree. The glazes differed according to house style, were darker or more luminous, brighter or more subtle.

These glorious things were made from mud and water and the ingenuity of man. Molly wondered who worked it out first. These are things one should know. She also wondered what the local word for toilet was, and in which direction it was likely to be. She turned to ask the Colonel but Bobby was hustling them into the car: 'Come on, Mum, we haven't got all day.'

'At the next place,' she said, 'I must find a toilet.'

The next place was one of the most attractive and also one of the largest they had seen. The pottery shed was open on all sides under a corrugated iron roof. Ten or so men were at work, feet pedalling and hands busy with wet clay.

'Like flying a helicopter,' whispered Lance to Violet.

'Wow,' said Bobby, leaping from the car. 'This looks more like it.'

'What's down the other end, Lance?' said Molly.

'It looks like bamboo, ma'am, they grow it commercially here.'

'Of course they do,' muttered Violet sourly.

She felt a touch on her arm, swung round in fright. Nerves. Just nerves.

'Violet,' said Molly, looking up at her, 'my bladder is bursting.'

Violet throttled both her yelp of laughter and her instinct to snarl Whadya want me to do about it.

'We'll go and find a toilet,' she said, and informed the rest of the party of this decision.

Bobby glanced briefly over her shoulder, muttered, 'Rather you than me,' and continued her conversation with the bright-eyed vendor.

'I must come too,' said Lance.

'What?' said Violet.

He looked at Bobby, at the bustle of workmen around the stall and other customers milling about, hesitated for a moment and marched after Molly. Twenty-four-hour armed guard of the Minister's wife once she left the hotel. The brief had been quite clear.

Violet glanced at Molly's anxious face. 'This way,' she said.

Her confidence was misplaced. The wide space became narrower, turned into a passage. There was no one in sight, no friendly voice, no guiding hand. They came to a tall bamboo fence with a closed wooden door and an open padlock hanging by its shaft. Violet peered through the bamboo stakes.

'Look,' she cried. 'There's one over there, I can see it. No door but never mind. Come on.'

Molly's voice was strangled between rectitude and necessity. 'Perhaps it's private.'

'There's no such thing as a private one in a crisis,' said Violet. 'Come on!'

They surged through, Violet offering encouragement and Lance on the alert. Molly scuttled to the unattractive-looking shed. Lance and Violet turned their backs.

'You're fantastic, Vi, you know that,' said Lance. He offered his true compliment, his greatest accolade, 'Susie would love you.'

'I told you,' said Violet. 'Don't be nice to me.'

'It'll be all right. I promise.'

'Please be quiet.'

'I do apologise,' said Molly, panting slightly. 'Oh dear, I do wish I could wash my hands.'

There was a faint noise, a small tinny sound near their feet. Violet dropped to her heels, grabbed something from the ground and sprang up with it clenched in her fist.

'Wet One,' she hissed at Lance. 'Quick, for God's sake.'

'Thank you,' said Molly, putting out her hand to the Colonel.

Violet, wild-eyed but controlled, snatched it from his fingers and wrapped her treasure in damp tissue. 'Don't run,' she said quietly. 'Walk back calmly. *Very* calmly. Come on.'

Molly took another Wet One from the equally bewildered Lance and wiped her hands.

'Don't drop it,' hissed Violet.

'Really, Violet, as if I would. And I am coming on.'

They walked through the gate.

'Keep walking. I'll explain later. Keep walking.'

Led by Lance, they retraced their steps along the passage and reappeared at the outlet shop, walking casually and, in Molly's case, smiling graciously.

There was no sign of Bobby.

'Find her, Lance,' said Violet. 'We're going. Now. Don't give her the breeze up. Tell her the search headquarters want the car back immediately. Anything.'

Molly looked from one tense face to the other. 'I'll get her. At once, I promise. Wait here.'

Breathing deeply, Lance and Violet sat staring at each other across a wooden table shaded by a large green tree. A man came towards them, carrying a tin tray with three bottles of Coca Cola and three straws. 'Boss says lady's friends like Coke?' he said.

They shook their heads, waiting in edgy silence till he had disappeared.

'Tell me,' said Lance.

She clenched her fist inside her pocket, looked at him as though sleepwalking.

'Look,' she said, as she unwrapped her treasure beneath the table top.

Lance gaped at the broken Mickey Mouse watch.

'Jesus,' he said. 'Let's get out of here. Not a word in the car, right?'

'No.'

He held out his hand. 'Shall I take it now?'

Her fist tightened. 'No,' she said. 'Later.'

'Thank God,' he said, 'here they come. We'll drop them off and go on to headquarters. Remember, not a word in the car.'

Still that vacant stare.

'No,' she said.

23

Hamish was on the secure phone to the PM within seconds.

'The hostage release operation by the Malaysian Special Forces was a classic, Prime Minister. Absolute classic. The gang used the market garden and pottery set up for a front, apparently. We don't know yet the extent of the involvement. There will be a full report later, and of course I'll give you and our Defence people a detailed debriefing when I get home. Colonel Beaucott was with Molly and the ladies. (You've heard about increased security? Yes, Beaucott was with them.) His first-hand knowledge, recce of the place I suppose you could call it, was invaluable I gather from the commanding officer who went in with his troops. Beaucott behaved above and beyond in every respect. A gong coming up there if I have anything to do with it. Impeccable, I gather, absolutely impeccable. And I'll be putting up the other hostage for a mention of some sort. He did well, so Manders tells me.'

'Hh,' grunted the voice. 'Was it Lightning Storm?'

'Definitely. A tremendous coup for New Zealand, don't you agree, quite apart from dealing with the ransom business. You know that the ransom note was delivered at the High Commission this morning?'

'No.'

Hamish's voice dropped. 'Oh, that's a bad lapse. I'll get on to that straight away.'

'How much?'

'I haven't a copy of the note here but it's something like eighty thousand dollars.'

'NZ?'

'Yes.'

'Hh. Just as well they found him.'

'Yes indeed. We've already sent a flash to Singapore, Hong Kong, Australia. The phone's been running red hot ever since. The extraordinary thing, Prime Minister, is that the leader is an Australian.'

'Hh.'

'Yes, a deserter from the ranks during the Vietnam War, I understand, and he's been a mercenary ever since. A really bad lot apparently. Been on the run for years.'

'Hh.'

'One other thing I should mention, Prime Minister, is that Ms Redpath played some part in Manders' rescue.'

'Who?'

Hamish hesitated. Had he mentioned to the PM that Violet was on board instead of Spencer? Not that it mattered a cuss, but you never knew which way the man was going to jump.

He decided not to risk it.

'Ms Redpath,' he said again.

'Who the fuck's Miss Redpath?'

'I don't think I'll reorder the string quartet,' said Hamish, stirring beneath the water like a basking shark. 'They were cancelled when we thought the whole thing would be off. I can do without a string quartet while I eat, can't you?'

'Yes,' said Molly.

Hamish picked up a long-handled loofah from the edge of the bath and looked at it thoughtfully. 'I don't like the idea of these things,' he said. 'Not in a hotel. It might be all right at home. But we can't get them there, can we?'

'I haven't tried.'

Hamish replaced the loofah. 'Get me a whisky, would you, love? I feel I've earned it. The PM was practically cooing down the line.'

Molly handed him the whisky and sat on the wicker stool, face to face with the damp grey swirls of hair on his chest. He had always been a hairy man.

'It's wonderful, isn't it,' she said. 'Dear Freddy.'

'Bloody marvellous. Pity he's decided not to attend the dinner tonight but I quite understand. He certainly looked a mess.' Hamish laughed, took a sip of whisky and lay back. 'And smelt like one when we first met him again. I think he's earned an early night.'

'Is Violet coming to the dinner?'

'No, she asked to be excused. Headache, I understand. Tidier for the change in seating plan, I suppose.' He put out a hand to her. 'Lucky you insisted on her coming, Mol. She certainly did her stuff today.'

'That's nice of you, dear,' said Molly.

Hamish's contented sigh filled the misty space. He took another sip, submerged slightly. 'But then you've always been a good picker, haven't you?' he said.

———

Manders sauntered out of the bathroom and put on his glasses.

'I can't tell you what it's like being able to see again,' he said. 'I'm in another world.'

'Heavens, look at your bruises,' said Violet.

'Flesh wounds, as Lance would say, not even that.'

'Don't they hurt?'

'Only when I move.' He took her in his arms and kissed her. 'Don't worry, sweetheart. Redback spider mates are happy to die for it. She eats him afterwards.'

She kissed him back. 'Don't you want some food?'

'Later. There's always Room Service. For God's sake, why cry now?'

'Do you want to talk about it,' she said later.

'Not now. I might tell you more when it's sunk in. God knows how real hostages survive. I missed the real drama, but according to Lance the Malaysian Special Forces were magnificent. They're a specially trained counter-terrorist group. Our squad specialise in hostage release operations. Stun grenades, submachine-gun fire, smoke bombs, the lot. They burst in when the sods were eating lunch. One man was killed and they captured the boss. I'm glad about that. Yes. Very.

'I missed all that. I hadn't moved from the window since I heard you and chucked Mickey out. God knows what I was hoping to hear or not hear. So there I was sweating away at my post when there was a blast like a thunderflash. Some hero had shot the locks off Kamil's and my cells. The place was full of guys in camouflage gear with submachine-guns, shouting. I thought, Christ I'm dead. Then the air cleared, and we were outside and Kamil and I were flinging our arms around each other and suddenly we were heroes, a surprise to us both. We were shoved into a car immediately by a couple of the Malaysians and whipped back to search headquarters. I suppose someone stayed at that place for mopping-up operations, or whatever. There seemed a lot of cheerful Malaysian troops around.

'No more now, love. Lance will fill you in, give you the detail.'

He traced a line from throat to pubes. 'You know you saved my life?'

'Naa.'

'Lance said so.'

'Nice man, Lance.'

'Yeah. A darling.'

She sat up suddenly. 'Has anyone rung Bridget?'

'I've no idea. Why.'

'I promised I would. If I heard anything.' She rolled over. 'Do I have to?'

'Good God no. What if she asks where you are?'

'I'll tell her. No, seriously. She was very upset. Kept going on about what a darling you are and how guilty she felt. How desperate. I was quite pissed off, as a matter of fact. I'd better try.'

'Balls,' cried Freddy. 'Of course someone's got in touch, probably the Minister in person. And of course she was worried and guilty. I was a disaster area. A disaster area within striking distance and where was she?'

He leaned over, kissed one nipple and then the other. 'I do like the way they do that,' he said. 'Erectile.'

Violet stroked a hand down him. 'Yes, I'm all for it,' she said.

Hamish came across the dining room with his hand outstretched. He shook Freddy's hand yet again.

'My word, Fred,' he said, 'you're looking a lot better this morning. Excellent. Excellent. Yes, I thought it would be a nice idea to get together for a celebratory breakfast, seeing you both missed out on the official dinner.'

'How did it go, Minister?' said Fred.

'Oh, very well indeed. Sorry you missed it – the heroes of the hour missing, as it were. But don't worry, everyone quite understood. The Malaysian Defence chiefs were all there and Lance Beaucott kept the New Zealand end up. How's the headache today, Violet? All gone. Excellent.

'We were presented with a beautiful wooden statue of a Malay dancer and a commemorative silver tray. Inscribed, of course.' Hamish turned to Molly and smiled. 'And Mol got an extra gift, didn't you, dear, which was to have been presented to her at the exhibition of embroidery for the fiftieth anniversary of the formation of the Malaysian Army if circumstances had not intervened. What is it again, Mol?'

'A beautiful little embroidered cloth,' said Molly. 'So fine you wouldn't believe. For flower vases.'

'Our gifts went down well,' continued Hamish, 'which is always important. Sheepskins, of course, always do. I was not quite so happy about the pauashell and silver jewellery Internal Affairs punted up this time. Though my word they have some lovely stuff out now. Datin Ahmad seemed thrilled, didn't she, Mol?'

'Yes,' said Molly.

'There is one thing where we've been rather caught on the hop,' said Hamish, 'and that's the question of a gift for the Malaysian Army's Special Forces to whom we obviously owe a great debt. I don't feel a New Zealand Army shield would be appropriate. They probably have six already. Penn McPhee is going through his emergency stock: kauri bowls, signed copy of *Beautiful New Zealand*, things of that sort. Have any of you any suggestions?'

They shook their heads, were no use at all.

'When would this presentation take place, Minister?' asked Freddy.

'Good God, hasn't anyone told you, Fred? That's a bad lapse. I keep forgetting you weren't there last night.' He glanced at his watch. 'Plenty of time, though. Penn McPhee will be picking us up at 10.00 and we'll go straight on to the barracks. The Minister of Defence will be there, and Dato Ahmad, but it will be a very brief ceremony. We fly out at 12.30.'

'Will Kamil be there, Minister?' asked Freddy.

'He'll be driving us, yes.'

'At the ceremony, I meant.' Freddy paused, looked the man in the eye. 'He was very, ah, staunch, sir,' he said.

'That might be a nice touch,' said Hamish. 'Get on to it straight away, Fred. No, no, when you've finished your coffee.

'Yes,' said Hamish expansively. 'The whole evening was really rather a triumph, wasn't it, Molly.'

Molly paused, the draught of fresh orange at her lips. 'Yes,' she said.

Hamish glanced at his watch, leaned towards Freddy like a conspirator. 'You know,' he confided, 'I'll never see a watch again without thinking of that damn fool one of yours, Fred. Came right on the night, though, didn't it? I suppose you were going to change it when you got back to the hotel?'

'As a matter of fact, Minister, I had forgotten I had it on,' said Freddy.

'Oh,' said Hamish. 'Oh well, all's well that ends well.' He looked at his guest's plate. 'You don't mean to tell me you're not having the full breakfast?'

'No, thank you, Minister.'

Hamish looked around the table. 'No one but me then?' He laughed. 'What a lot of pikers we've got this morning.'

A small cloud swam across his blue-domed sky. 'Where's Bobby? She said she'd be here.'

'I don't know,' said Molly.

Bobby appeared at the entrance to the room, gave them a friendly wave and marched towards the battery of heated stainless-steel containers with the full breakfasts. She arrived with her plate high and swung herself on to the vacant chair.

'They've got the most extraordinary things back there,' she said, taking her first bite. 'God knows what some of them are. I like my fruit after my cooked stuff. I always have, haven't I Dad?' She looked straight through Molly to reveal this snippet.

'Ever since I was so high. Can't think why. Just one of those things, I guess. Wow, this is good. Nice to see you, Fred.'

Violet stopped caressing Freddy's trousered leg with her bare one for a moment to concentrate. What's she ratty at her mother about now, she wondered.

'Well,' said Bobby beaming at them both, 'anyone told you the latest?'

They shook their heads, re-entwined their legs.

'Good old Dad's come to the party again, haven't you, Dad? He's going to let me stay here for a few days till Amanda McPhee gets back.' She glanced around the crowded room, the elaborate set pieces of fruit and flowers, the food on her plate. 'Not here unfortunately, but Milly Whatsit is going to find the best three-star one and I'll slum around there till Mandy arrives on Saturday with her little girls. Barney says we should be well down the track after three weeks or so. And if not . . .' She shrugged, laughed and shrugged again. 'If not,' she chuckled, 'I'll just have to make alternative arrangements.'

Still ignoring her mother, she smiled at her friends with frank goodwill.

'Presumably,' said Violet, 'the last outlet we visited will not be any use to you now.'

'Funny you should say that,' said Bobby. 'I was talking to Barney on the phone just before I came down and he said, "Do you know, Bobs" (he calls me Bobs) "you and I must get into that place as soon as the Army's finished mopping up." If they haven't bashed the lot, he said, and he doesn't think they will have. Apparently, Fred, it was the potters you heard chatting outside your window. Did you know that?'

'Yes,' said Freddy, 'someone told me.'

'Yeah, that's why you only heard them at certain times, see. Barney says the guys think that the pottery thing was all quite kosher. Just a sort of front for Goldfinger and Co. Nevertheless, he says, it'll probably be closed down now, and there'll be good pickings for anyone with a flipper to the front.

'So.' She leaned back for a second to catch the waiter's eye. 'Coffee all round, thanks. Yes, you could say everything's coming up roses. Did I tell you we think I'm going to call the business *Pots of Fun. Bobs Carew*?'

Fred stopped stroking Violet's thigh, considered the question. 'Couldn't be better, could it, Violet?'

She moved her head slowly from side to side. 'No,' she said, and turned to Molly. 'What do you think, Mrs Carew?'

'Oh Mum's a wet blanket,' laughed Bobby. 'The original party pooper, aren't you, Ma?'

Molly smiled at her daughter, a smile as loving as ever. Nevertheless, there was a touch of farewell, of elegy about it. Bobs was now free as a bird, free to fly where she liked, to soar as high as the thermals of life would carry her.

She put her hand on her daughter's. 'Not at all, darling. I want you to lead your own life and be beautifully happy always.'

'Staunch, you say,' roared Penn into the telephone. 'Well, staunchness must be rewarded at all times. I'll get on to the barracks straight away if you think he would like to be there. We'll do something this end later, of course. Oh, by the way, there's a letter here for you. By hand from Bridget. Can't think why she didn't drop it off at the hotel. Her plane to Europe went at 09.00.'

'Damn. I was just going to ring her.'

'Didn't anyone tell you her ETD?'

'I didn't ask.'

Penn laughed. 'Lack of attention to detail.'

Manders was silent. He would have liked to speak to Bridget, would ring her when he got home, write her a long letter, a friendly letter full of good wishes. He would probably use the ready-made phrases and mean every one of them. Would wish her all the best for the future, tell her to take care; mention, perhaps, the good times. Offer the hope that they would remain friends.

Penn's voice dropped, 'Have you heard the latest? Bobby's descending on us as soon as Amanda and the children are back. No, of course it's not my fault, you dope, but try telling Amanda that. She'll eat me and spit out the pips.'

'Just do the best you can,' yawned Manders.

'That's a lot of bloody help. And I don't see what's so funny either.'

The Minister and Molly farewelled their exuberant and loving daughter at the hotel. As she told them, she would just be a spare lemon out there, official or non-official farewell, and now they knew that that sod Bron would hang on at the farm for a month there was nothing for them to fuss about. She had left the house secure, burglar alarm on and all, so they needn't feel they had to tear up there as soon as they got back.

She kissed them both, thanked her father, hugged her mother, and said goodbye graciously to Dato and Datin Ahmad who were escorting her parents to the airport. 'Actually,' she told them, 'I'll probably be seeing you around.'

Dato Ahmad bowed. The Datin did not notice, as she was engaged in snatching a large photograph album from Molly's arms. 'I haven't seen these,' she cried, turning the pages at speed. 'Where am I?'

Kamil drove Violet and Freddy. He was happy and full of chat. The ceremony this morning had been a proud moment for him, and he understood there would be photographs.

'Yes,' said Freddy, 'and you will get some.'

'Allah is good,' said Kamil.

He and Freddy exchanged a comradely handshake. Manders handed him an envelope. 'For your boys, Kamil.'

The smiling head moved from side to side. 'Thank you sir, thank you ma'am. Go with God.'

'Thank you,' they said and shook hands once more.

———

The non-official farewell took place in the correctly sized place, not the pink box where Mrs Carew and the other New Zealand lady had had the ill fortune to be escorted to on arrival.

'Where is my assistant?' cried the Datin. 'Ah there you are. Come and give the photographs back to Mrs Carew.'

Smiling gently, Miss Raya handed over the album.

'You needn't worry,' Datin Ahmad told Molly. 'She has taken note of the ones I want.'

Miss Raya, wearing a form-fitting batik more beautifully coloured and elaborate than any seen so far, waited till the Datin and Molly were talking again, and moved close to Violet.

'I have a gift for you,' she whispered. 'Come away here.'

'Oh how kind,' twittered Violet, 'I haven't . . .'

Miss Raya put a finger to her glossy lips. 'Sssh,' she whispered, and gave Violet a little Thai silk bag. 'From my boyfriend and me. He will get another one. It is for us admiring.'

'Can I look now?'

'If you hide,' said Miss Raya, and drifted back to the departing visitors and their non-official farewells.

Violet sauntered to the window and looked down at the airfield, her fingers busy with the tiny silk button on the bag. One more small metal object lay in her hand. It was a Hash Harriers' badge.

She looked across the room, lifted her closed hand to Miss Raya and held it against her heart like a President of the United States taking the oath.

An airport official appeared. 'Boarding time ten minutes, sir,' he said to Dato Ahmad.

'Well,' said the Minister, generous and cheerful to the end, 'all good things must come to an end.'

'What did Miss Raya slip you?' said Freddy.

Violet was startled. 'Did you see?'

'No, but I saw you talking together, then you going all casual at the window, then waving and damn near killing her with the farewell hug. I can't keep my eyes off you, you see.'